MURDER
IN A
HEATWAVE

MURDER
IN A
HEATWAVE

CLASSIC CRIME MYSTERIES FOR THE HOLIDAYS

Edited by Cecily Gayford

Dorothy L. Sayers · Arthur Conan Doyle
Carter Dickson · Michael Innes
Baroness Orczy · Margery Allingham
Ian Rankin · Julian Symons
Ethel Lina White · Rex Stout

P

PROFILE BOOKS

First published in Great Britain in 2023 by
PROFILE BOOKS LTD
29 Cloth Fair
London EC1A 7JQ
www.profilebooks.com

1 3 5 7 9 10 8 6 4 2

Typeset in Fournier by MacGuru Ltd
Printed and bound in Great Britain by
CPI Group (UK) Ltd, Croydon CR0 4YY

A CIP catalogue record for this book is available from the British Library.

ISBN 978 1 80081 774 6
eISBN 978 1 80081 773 9

Contents

The Vindictive Story of the Footsteps That Ran

Dorothy L. Sayers

Mr Bunter withdrew his head from beneath the focusing cloth.

'I fancy that will be quite adequate, sir,' he said deferentially, 'unless there are any further patients, if I may call them so, which you would wish put on record.'

'Not today,' replied the doctor. He took the last stricken rat gently from the table, and replaced it in its cage with an air of satisfaction. 'Perhaps on Wednesday, if Lord Peter can kindly spare your services once again—'

'What's that?' murmured his lordship, withdrawing his long nose from the investigation of a number of unattractive-looking glass jars. 'Nice old dog,' he added vaguely. 'Wags his tail when you mention his name, what? Are these monkey-glands, Hartman, or a southwest elevation of Cleopatra's duodenum?'

'You don't know anything, do you?' said the young physician, laughing. 'No use playing your bally-fool-with-an-eyeglass tricks on me, Wimsey. I'm up to them. I was saying to Bunter that I'd be no end grateful if you'd let him turn up again three days hence to register the progress of the specimens – always supposing they do progress, that is.'

'Why ask, dear old thing?' said his lordship. 'Always a pleasure to assist a fellow-sleuth, don't you know. Trackin' down murderers – all in the same way of business and all that. All finished? Good egg! By the way, if you don't have that cage mended you'll lose one of your patients – Number 5. The last wire but one is workin' loose – assisted by the intelligent occupant. Jolly little beasts, aren't they? No need of dentists – wish I was a rat – wire much better for the nerves than that fizzlin' drill.'

Dr Hartman uttered a little exclamation.

'How in the world did you notice that, Wimsey? I didn't think you'd even looked at the cage.'

'Built noticin' – improved by practice,' said Lord Peter quietly. 'Anythin' wrong leaves a kind of impression on the eye; brain trots along afterwards with the warnin'. I saw that when we came in. Only just grasped it. Can't say my mind was glued on the matter. Shows the victim's improvin', anyhow. All serene, Bunter?'

'Everything perfectly satisfactory, I trust, my lord,' replied the manservant. He had packed up his camera and plates, and was quietly restoring order in the little laboratory, whose fittings – compact as those of an ocean liner – had been disarranged for the experiment.

'Well,' said the doctor, 'I am enormously obliged to you,

Lord Peter, and to Bunter too. I am hoping for a great result from these experiments, and you cannot imagine how valuable an assistance it will be to me to have a really good series of photographs. I can't afford this sort of thing – yet,' he added, his rather haggard young face wistful as he looked at the great camera, 'and I can't do the work at the hospital. There's no time; I've got to be here. A struggling GP can't afford to let his practice go, even in Bloomsbury. There are times when even a half-crown visit makes all the difference between making both ends meet and having an ugly hiatus.'

'As Mr Micawber said,' replied Wimsey, '"Income twenty pounds, expenditure nineteen, nineteen, six – result: happiness; expenditure twenty pounds, ought, six – result: misery." Don't prostrate yourself in gratitude, old bean; nothin' Bunter loves like messin' round with pyro- and hyposulphite. Keeps his hand in. All kinds of practice welcome. Fingerprints and process plates spell seventh what-you-may-call-it of bliss, but focal-plane work on scurvy-ridden rodents (good phrase!) acceptable if no crime forthcoming. Crimes have been, rather short lately. Been eatin' our heads off, haven't we, Bunter? Don't know what's come over London. I've taken to prying into my neighbour's affairs to keep from goin' stale. Frightened the postman into a fit the other day by askin' him how his young lady at Croydon was. He's a married man, livin' in Great Ormond Street.'

'How did you know?'

'Well, I didn't really. But he lives just opposite to a friend of mine – Inspector Parker; and his wife – not Parker's, he's unmarried; the postman's, I mean – asked Parker the other day whether the flyin' shows at Croydon went on all night.

Parker, bein' flummoxed, said "No", without thinkin'. Bit of a giveaway, what? Thought I'd give the poor devil a word in season, don't you know. Uncommonly thoughtless of Parker.'

The doctor laughed. 'You'll stay to lunch, won't you?' he said. 'Only cold meat and salad, I'm afraid. My woman won't come Sundays. Have to answer my own door. Deuced unprofessional, I'm afraid, but it can't be helped.'

'Pleasure,' said Wimsey, as they emerged from the laboratory and entered the dark little flat by the back door. 'Did you build this place on?'

'No,' said Hartman; 'the last tenant did that. He was an artist. That's why I took the place. It comes in very useful, ramshackle as it is, though this glass roof is a bit sweltering on a hot day like this. Still, I had to have something on the ground floor, cheap, and it'll do till times get better.'

'Till your vitamin experiments make you famous, eh?' said Peter cheerfully. 'You're goin' to be the comin' man, you know. Feel it in my bones. Uncommonly neat little kitchen you've got, anyhow.'

'It does,' said the doctor. 'The lab makes it a bit gloomy, but the woman's only here in the daytime.'

He led the way into a narrow little dining room, where the table was laid for a cold lunch. The one window at the end farthest from the kitchen looked out into Great James Street. The room was little more than a passage, and full of doors – the kitchen door, a door in the adjacent wall leading into the entrance hall, and a third on the opposite side, through which his visitor caught a glimpse of a moderate-sized consulting room.

Lord Peter Wimsey and his host sat down to table, and the doctor expressed a hope that Mr Bunter would sit down with them. That correct person, however, deprecated any such suggestion.

'If I might venture to indicate my own preference, sir,' he said, 'it would be to wait upon you and his lordship in the usual manner.'

'It's no use,' said Wimsey. 'Bunter likes me to know my place. Terrorisin' sort of man, Bunter. Can't call my soul my own. Carry on, Bunter; we wouldn't presume for the world.'

Mr Bunter handed the salad, and poured out the water with a grave decency appropriate to a crusted old tawny port.

It was a Sunday afternoon in that halcyon summer of 1921. The sordid little street was almost empty. The ice-cream man alone seemed thriving and active. He leaned luxuriously on the green post at the corner, in the intervals of driving a busy trade. Bloomsbury's swarm of able-bodied and able-voiced infants was still; presumably within-doors, eating steamy Sunday dinners inappropriate to the tropical weather. The only disturbing sounds came from the flat above, where heavy footsteps passed rapidly to and fro.

'Who's the merry-and-bright bloke above?' enquired Lord Peter presently. 'Not an early riser, I take it. Not that anybody is on a Sunday mornin'. Why an inscrutable Providence ever inflicted such a ghastly day on people livin' in town I can't imagine. I ought to be in the country, but I've got to meet a friend at Victoria this afternoon. Such a day to choose … Who's the lady? Wife or accomplished friend? Gather she takes a properly submissive view of woman's duties in the home, either way. That's the bedroom overhead, I take it.'

Hartman looked at Lord Peter in some surprise.

''Scuse my beastly inquisitiveness, old thing,' said Wimsey. 'Bad habit. Not my business.'

'How did you——?'

'Guesswork,' said Lord Peter, with disarming frankness. 'I heard the squawk of an iron bedstead on the ceiling and a heavy fellow get out with a bump, but it may quite well be a couch or something. Anyway, he's been potterin' about in his stocking feet over these few feet of floor for the last half-hour, while the woman has been clatterin' to and fro, in and out of the kitchen and away into the sittin' room, with her high heels on, ever since we've been here. Hence deduction as to domestic habits of the first-floor tenants.'

'I thought,' said the doctor, with an aggrieved expression, 'you'd been listening to my valuable exposition of the beneficial effects of vitamin B, and Lind's treatment of scurvy with fresh lemons in 1755.'

'I was listenin',' agreed Lord Peter hastily, 'but I heard the footsteps as well. Fellow's toddled into the kitchen – only wanted the matches, though; he's gone off into the sittin' room and left her to carry on the good work. What was I sayin'? Oh, yes! You see, as I was sayin' before, one hears a thing or sees it without knowin' or thinkin' about it. Then afterwards one starts meditatin', and it all comes back, and one sorts out one's impressions. Like those plates of Bunter's. Picture's all there, l–, la–, what's the word I want, Bunter?'

'Latent, my lord.'

'That's it. My right-hand man, Bunter; couldn't do a thing without him. The picture's latent till you put the developer on. Same with the brain. No mystery. Little grey books all my respected grandmother! Little grey matter's all you want to remember things with. As a matter of curiosity, was I right about those people above?'

'Perfectly. The man's a gas company's inspector. A bit surly, but devoted (after his own fashion) to his wife. I mean, he doesn't mind hulking in bed on a Sunday morning and letting her do the chores, but he spends all the money he can spare on giving her pretty hats and fur coats and what not. They've only been married about six months. I was called in to her when she had a touch of flu in the spring, and he was almost off his head with anxiety. She's a lovely little woman, I must say – Italian. He picked her up in some eating-place in Soho, I believe. Glorious dark hair and eyes: Venus sort of figure; proper contours in all the right places; good skin – all that sort of thing. She was a bit of a draw to that restaurant while she was there, I fancy. Lively. She had an old admirer round here one day – awkward little Italian fellow, with a knife – active as a monkey. Might have been unpleasant, but I happened to be on the spot, and her husband came along. People are always laying one another out in these streets. Good for business, of course, but one gets tired of tying up broken heads and slits in the jugular. Still, I suppose the girl can't help being attractive, though I don't say she's what you might call stand-offish in her manner. She's sincerely fond of Brotherton, I think, though – that's his name.'

Wimsey nodded inattentively. 'I suppose life is a bit monotonous here,' he said.

'Professionally, yes. Births and drunks and wife-beatings are pretty common. And all the usual ailments, of course. Just at present I'm living on infant diarrhoea chiefly – bound to, this hot weather, you know. With the autumn, flu and bronchitis set in. I may get an occasional pneumonia. Legs, of course, and varicose veins – God!' cried the doctor explosively, 'if only I could get away, and do my experiments!'

'Ah!' said Peter, 'where's that eccentric old millionaire with a mysterious disease, who always figures in the novels? A lightning diagnosis – a miraculous cure – "God bless you, doctor; here are five thousand pounds" – Harley Street—'

'That sort doesn't live in Bloomsbury,' said the doctor.

'It must be fascinatin', diagnosin' things,' said Peter thoughtfully. 'How d'you do it? I mean, is there a regular set of symptoms for each disease, like callin' a club to show you want your partner to go no trumps? You don't just say: "This fellow's got a pimple on his nose, therefore he has fatty degeneration of the heart—"'

'I hope not,' said the doctor drily.

'Or is it more like gettin' a clue to a crime?' went on Peter. 'You see somethin' – a room, or a body, say, all knocked about anyhow, and there's a damn sight of symptoms of somethin' wrong, and you've got just to pick out the ones which tell the story?'

'That's more like it,' said Dr Hartman. 'Some symptoms are significant in themselves – like the condition of the gums in scurvy, let us say – others in conjunction with—'

He broke off, and both sprang to their feet as a shrill scream sounded suddenly from the flat above, followed by a heavy thud. A man's voice cried out lamentably; feet ran violently to and fro; then, as the doctor and his guests stood frozen in consternation, came the man himself – falling down the stairs in his haste, hammering at Hartman's door.

'Help! Help! Let me in! My wife! He's murdered her!'

They ran hastily to the door and let him in. He was a big, fair man, in his shirtsleeves and stockings. His hair stood up, and his face was set in bewildered misery.

'She is dead – dead. He was her lover,' he groaned. 'Come and look – take her away – Doctor! I have lost my wife! My Maddalena—' He paused, looked wildly for a moment, and then said hoarsely, 'Someone's been in – somehow – stabbed her – murdered her. I'll have the law on him, doctor. Come quickly – she was cooking the chicken for my dinner – Ah-h-h!'

He gave a long, hysterical shriek, which ended in a hiccupping laugh. The doctor took him roughly by the arm and shook him. 'Pull yourself together, Mr Brotherton,' he said sharply. 'Perhaps she is only hurt. Stand out of the way!'

'Only hurt?' said the man, sitting heavily down on the nearest chair. 'No – no – she is dead – little Maddalena – Oh, my God!'

Dr Hartman snatched a roll of bandages and a few surgical appliances from the consulting room, and he ran upstairs, followed closely by Lord Peter. Bunter remained for a few moments to combat hysterics with cold water. Then he stepped across to the dining-room window and shouted.

'Well, wot is it?' cried a voice from the street.

'Would you be so kind as to step in here a minute, officer?' said Mr Bunter. 'There's been murder done.'

When Brotherton and Bunter arrived upstairs with the constable, they found Dr Hartman and Lord Peter in the little kitchen. The doctor was kneeling beside the woman's body. At their entrance he looked up, and shook his head.

'Death instantaneous,' he said. 'Clean through the heart. Poor child. She cannot have suffered at all. Oh, constable, it is very fortunate you are here. Murder appears to have been done – though I'm afraid the man has escaped. Probably Mr Brotherton can give us some help. He was in the flat at the time.'

The man had sunk down on a chair, and was gazing at the body with a face from which all meaning seemed to have been struck out. The policeman produced a notebook.

'Now, sir,' he said, 'don't let's waste any time. Sooner we can get to work the more likely we are to catch our man. Now, you was 'ere at the time, was you?'

Brotherton stared a moment, then, making a violent effort, he answered steadily:

'I was in the sitting room, smoking and reading the paper. My – *she* – was getting the dinner ready in here. I heard her give a scream, and I rushed in and found her lying on the floor. She didn't have time to say anything. When I found she was dead, I rushed to the window, and saw the fellow scrambling away over the glass roof there. I yelled at him, but he disappeared. Then I ran down—'

''Arf a mo',' said the policeman. 'Now, see 'ere, sir, didn't you think to go after 'im at once?'

'My first thought was for her,' said the man. 'I thought maybe she wasn't dead. I tried to bring her round—' His speech ended in a groan.

'You say he came in through the window,' said the policeman.

'I beg your pardon, officer,' interrupted Lord Peter, who had been apparently making a mental inventory of the contents of the kitchen. 'Mr Brotherton suggested that the man went *out* through the window. It's better to be accurate.'

'It's the same thing,' said the doctor. 'It's the only way he could have come in. These flats are all alike. The staircase door leads into the sitting room, and Mr Brotherton was there, so the man couldn't have come that way.'

'And,' said Peter, 'he didn't get in through the bedroom window, or we should have seen him. We were in the room below. Unless, indeed, he let himself down from the roof. Was the door between the bedroom and the sitting room open?' he asked suddenly, turning to Brotherton.

The man hesitated a moment. 'Yes,' he said finally. 'Yes, I'm sure it was.'

'Could you have seen the man if he had come through the bedroom window?'

'I couldn't have helped seeing him.'

'Come, come, sir,' said the policeman, with some irritation, 'better let *me* ask the questions. Stands to reason the fellow wouldn't get in through the bedroom window in full view of the street.'

'How clever of you to think of that,' said Wimsey. 'Of course not. Never occurred to me. Then it must have been this window, as you say.'

'And what's more, here's his marks on the windowsill,' said the constable triumphantly, pointing to some blurred traces among the London soot. 'That's right. Down he goes by that drainpipe, over the glass roof down there – what's that the roof of?'

'My laboratory,' said the doctor. 'Heavens! to think that while we were there at dinner this murdering villain—'

'Quite so, sir,' agreed the constable. 'Well, he'd get away over the wall into the court be'ind. 'E'll 'ave been seen there, no fear; you needn't anticipate much trouble in layin' 'ands on 'im, sir. I'll go round there in 'arf a tick. Now then, sir' – turning to Brotherton – ''ave you any idea wot this party might have looked like?'

Brotherton lifted a wild face, and the doctor interposed. 'I think you ought to know, constable,' he said, 'that there was – well, not a murderous attack, but what might have been one, made on this woman before – about eight weeks ago – by a man named Marincetti – an Italian waiter – with a knife.'

'Ah!' The policeman licked his pencil eagerly. 'Do you know this party as 'as been mentioned?' he enquired of Brotherton.

'That's the man,' said Brotherton, with concentrated fury. 'Coming here after my wife – God curse him! I wish to God I had him dead here beside her!'

'Quite so,' said the policeman. 'Now, sir' – to the doctor – ''ave you got the weapon wot the crime was committed with?'

'No,' said Hartman, 'there was no weapon in the body when I arrived.'

'Did *you* take it out?' pursued the constable, to Brotherton.

'No,' said Brotherton, 'he took it with him.'

'Took it with 'im,' the constable entered the fact in his notes. 'Phew! Wonderful 'ot it is in 'ere, ain't it, sir?' he added, mopping his brow.

'It's the gas oven, I think,' said Peter mildly. 'Uncommon hot thing, a gas oven, in the middle of July. D'you mind if I turn it out? There's the chicken inside, but I don't suppose you want—'

Brotherton groaned, and the constable said: 'Quite right, sir. A man wouldn't 'ardly fancy 'is dinner after a thing like this. Thank you, sir. Well, now, doctor, wot kind of weapon do you take this to 'ave been?'

'It was a long, narrow weapon – something like an Italian stiletto, I imagine,' said the doctor, 'about six inches long. It was thrust in with great force under the fifth rib, and I should say it had pierced the heart centrally. As you see, there has been practically no bleeding. Such a wound would cause instant death. Was she lying just as she is now when you first saw her, Mr Brotherton?'

'On her back, just as she is,' replied the husband.

'Well, that seems clear enough,' said the policeman. 'This 'ere Marinetti, or wotever 'is name is, 'as a grudge against the poor young lady—'

'I believe he was an admirer,' put in the doctor.

'Quite so,' agreed the constable. 'Of course, these foreigners are like that – even the decentest of 'em. Stabbin' and suchlike seems to come nateral to them, as you might say. Well, this 'ere Marinetti climbs in 'ere, sees the poor young lady standin' 'ere by the table all alone, gettin' the dinner ready; 'e comes in be'ind, catches 'er round the waist, stabs 'er – easy job, you see; no corsets nor nothink – she shrieks out, 'e pulls 'is stiletty out of 'er an' makes tracks. Well, now we've got to find 'im, and by your leave, sir, I'll be gettin' along. We'll 'ave 'im by the 'eels before long, sir, don't you worry. I'll 'ave to put a man in charge 'ere, sir, to keep folks out, but that needn't worry you. Good mornin', gentlemen.'

'May we move the poor girl now?' asked the doctor.

'Certainly. Like me to 'elp you, sir?'

'No. Don't lose any time. We can manage.' Dr Hartman turned to Peter as the constable clattered downstairs. 'Will you help me, Lord Peter?'

'Bunter's better at that sort of thing,' said Wimsey, with a hard mouth.

The doctor looked at him in some surprise, but said nothing, and he and Bunter carried the still form away. Brotherton did not follow them. He sat in a grief-stricken heap, with his head buried in his hands. Lord Peter walked about the little kitchen, turning over the various knives and kitchen utensils, peering into the sink bucket, and apparently taking an inventory of the bread, butter, condiments, vegetables, and so forth which lay about in preparation for the Sunday meal. There were potatoes in the sink, half peeled, a pathetic witness to the quiet domestic life which had been so horribly interrupted. The colander was filled with green peas. Lord Peter turned these things over with an inquisitive finger, gazed into the smooth surface of a bowl of dripping as though it were a divining-crystal, ran his hands several times right through a bowl of flour – then drew his pipe from his pocket and filled it slowly.

The doctor returned, and put his hand on Brotherton's shoulder.

'Come,' he said gently, 'we have laid her in the other bedroom. She looks very peaceful. You must remember that, except for that moment of terror when she saw the knife, she suffered nothing. It is terrible for you, but you must try not to give way. The police—'

'The police can't bring her back to life,' said the man savagely. 'She's dead. Leave me alone, curse you! Leave me alone, I say!'

He stood up, with a violent gesture.

'You must not sit here,' said Hartman firmly. 'I will give you something to take, and you must try to keep calm. Then we will leave you, but if you don't control yourself—'

After some further persuasion, Brotherton allowed himself to be led away.

'Bunter,' said Lord Peter, as the kitchen door closed behind them, 'do you know why I am doubtful about the success of those rat experiments?'

'Meaning Dr Hartman's, my lord?'

'Yes. Dr Hartman has a theory. In any investigations, my Bunter, it is most damnably dangerous to have a theory.'

'I have heard you say so, my lord.'

'Confound you – you know it as well as I do! What is wrong with the doctor's theories, Bunter?'

'You wish me to reply, my lord, that he only sees the facts which fit in with the theory.'

'Thought-reader!' exclaimed Lord Peter bitterly.

'And that he supplies them to the police, my lord.'

'Hush!' said Peter, as the doctor returned.

'I have got him to lie down,' said Dr Hartman, 'and I think the best thing we can do is to leave him to himself.'

'D'you know,' said Wimsey, 'I don't cotton to that idea, somehow.'

'Why? Do you think he's likely to destroy himself?'

'That's as good a reason to give as any other, I suppose,' said Wimsey, 'when you haven't got any reason which can be put into words. But my advice is, don't leave him for a moment.'

'But why? Frequently, with a deep grief like this, the presence of other people is merely an irritant. He begged me to leave him.'

'Then for God's sake go back to him,' said Peter.

'Really, Lord Peter,' said the doctor, 'I think I ought to know what is best for my patient.'

'Doctor,' said Wimsey, 'this is not a question of your patient. A crime has been committed.'

'But there is no mystery.'

'There are twenty mysteries. For one thing, when was the window cleaner here last?'

'The window cleaner?'

'Who shall fathom the ebony-black enigma of the window cleaner?' pursued Peter lightly, putting a match to his pipe. 'You are quietly in your bath, in a state of more or less innocent nature, when an intrusive head appears at the window, like the ghost of Hamilton Tighe, and a gruff voice, suspended between earth and heaven, says "Good morning, sir." Where do window cleaners go between visits? Do they hibernate, like busy bees? Do they——?'

'Really, Lord Peter,' said the doctor, 'don't you think you're going a bit beyond the limit?'

'Sorry you feel like that,' said Peter, 'but I really want to know about the window cleaner. Look how clear these panes are.'

'He came yesterday, if you want to know,' said Dr Hartman, rather stiffly.

'He did mine at the same time.'

'I thought as much,' said Lord Peter. 'In the words of the song:

I thought as much,
It was a little – window cleaner.

'In that case,' he added, 'it is absolutely imperative that Brotherton should not be left alone for a moment. Bunter! Confound it all, where's that fellow got to?'

The door into the bedroom opened.

'My lord?' Mr Bunter unobtrusively appeared, as he had unobtrusively stolen out to keep an unobtrusive eye upon the patient.

'Good,' said Wimsey. 'Stay where you are.' His lackadaisical manner had gone, and he looked at the doctor as four years previously he might have looked at a refractory subaltern.

'Dr Hartman,' he said, 'something is wrong. Cast your mind back. We were talking about symptoms. Then came the scream. Then came the sound of feet running. *Which direction did they run in?*'

'I'm sure I don't know.'

'Don't you? Symptomatic, though, doctor. They have been troubling me all the time, subconsciously. Now I know why. They ran *from the kitchen.*'

'Well?'

'Well! And now the window cleaner—'

'What about him?'

'Could you swear that it wasn't the window cleaner who made those marks on the sill?'

'And the man Brotherton saw—?'

'Have we examined your laboratory roof for his footsteps?'

'But the weapon? Wimsey, this is madness! Someone took the weapon.'

'I know. But did you think the edge of the wound was clean enough to have been made by a smooth stiletto? It looked ragged to me.'

'Wimsey, what are you driving at?'

'There's a clue here in the flat – and I'm damned if I can remember it. I've seen it – I know I've seen it. It'll come to me presently. Meanwhile, don't let Brotherton—'

'What?'

'Do whatever it is he's going to do.'

'But what is it?'

'If I could tell you that I could show you the clue. Why couldn't he make up his mind whether the bedroom door was open or shut? Very good story, but not quite thought out. Anyhow – I say, doctor, make some excuse, and strip him, and bring me his clothes. And send Bunter to me.'

The doctor stared at him, puzzled. Then he made a gesture of acquiescence and passed into the bedroom. Lord Peter followed him, casting a ruminating glance at Brotherton as he went. Once in the sitting room, Lord Peter sat down on a red velvet armchair, fixed his eyes on a gilt-framed oleograph, and became wrapped in contemplation.

Presently Bunter came in, with his arms full of clothing.

Wimsey took it, and began to search it, methodically enough, but listlessly. Suddenly he dropped the garments, and turned to the manservant.

'No,' he said, 'this is a precaution, Bunter mine, but I'm on the wrong track. It wasn't here I saw – whatever I did see. It was in the kitchen. Now, what was it?'

'I could not say, my lord, but I entertain a conviction that I was also, in a manner of speaking, conscious – not consciously conscious, my lord, if you understand me, but still conscious of an incongruity.'

'Hurray!' said Wimsey suddenly. 'Cheer-oh! for the subconscious what's-his-name! Now let's remember the kitchen. I cleared out of it because I was gettin' obfuscated. Now then. Begin at the door. Fryin' pans and saucepans on the wall. Gas stove – oven goin' – chicken inside. Rack of wooden spoons on the wall, gas lighter, pan lifter. Stop me when I'm gettin' hot. Mantelpiece. Spice boxes and stuff. Anything wrong with them? No. Dresser. Plates. Knives and forks – all clean; flour dredger – milk jug – sieve on the wall – nutmeg grater. Three-tier steamer. Looked inside – no grisly secrets in the steamer.'

'Did you look in all the dresser drawers, my lord?'

'No. That could be done. But the point is, I *did* notice somethin'. What did I notice? That's the point. Never mind. On with the dance – let joy be unconfined! Knife board. Knife powder. Kitchen table. Did you speak?'

'No,' said Bunter, who had moved from his attitude of wooden deference.

'Table stirs a chord. Very good. On table. Choppin' board. Remains of ham and herb stuffin'. Packet of suet.

Another sieve. Several plates. Butter in a glass dish. Bowl of drippin'—'

'Ah!'

'Drippin'—! Yes, there was—'

'Something unsatisfactory, my lord—'

'About the drippin'! Oh, my head! What's that they say in *Dear Brutus*, Bunter? "Hold on to the workbox." That's right. Hold on to the drippin'. Beastly slimy stuff to hold on to – Wait!'

There was a pause.

'When I was a kid,' said Wimsey, 'I used to love to go down into the kitchen and talk to old cookie. Good old soul she was, too. I can see her now, gettin' chicken ready, with me danglin' my legs on the table. *She* used to pluck an' draw 'em herself. I revelled in it. Little beasts boys are, ain't they, Bunter? Pluck it, draw it, wash it, stuff it, tuck its little tail through its little what-you-may-call-it, truss it, grease the dish – Bunter?'

'My lord!'

'Hold on to the—'

'The bowl, my lord—'

'The bowl – visualise it – what was wrong?'

'It was full, my lord!'

'Got it – got it – *got* it! The bowl was full – smooth surface. Golly! I knew there was something queer about it. Now why shouldn't it be full? Hold on to the—'

'The bird was in the oven.'

'Without dripping!'

'Very careless cookery, my lord.'

'The bird – in the oven – no dripping. Bunter! Suppose it

was never put in till after she was dead? Thrust in hurriedly by someone who had something to hide – horrible!'

'But with what object, my lord?'

'Yes, why? That's the point. One more mental association with the bird. It's just coming. Wait a moment. Pluck, draw, wash, stuff, tuck up, truss – By God!'

'My lord?'

'Come on, Bunter. Thank Heaven we turned off the gas!'

He dashed through the bedroom, disregarding the doctor and the patient, who sat up with a smothered shriek. He flung open the oven door and snatched out the baking tin. The skin of the bird had just begun to discolour. With a little gasp of triumph, Wimsey caught the iron ring that protruded from the wing, and jerked out – the six-inch spiral skewer.

The doctor was struggling with the excited Brotherton in the doorway. Wimsey caught the man as he broke away, and shook him into the corner with a ju-jitsu twist.

'Here is the weapon,' he said.

'Prove it, blast you!' said Brotherton savagely.

'I will,' said Wimsey. 'Bunter, call in the policeman whom you will find at the door. Doctor, we shall need your microscope.'

In the laboratory the doctor bent over the microscope. A thin layer of blood from the skewer had been spread upon the slide.

'Well?' said Wimsey impatiently.

'It's all right,' said Hartman. 'The roasting didn't get anywhere near the middle. My God, Wimsey, yes, you're right

– round corpuscles, diameter 1/3621 – mammalian blood – probably human—'

'Her blood,' said Wimsey.

'It was very clever, Bunter,' said Lord Peter, as the taxi trundled along on the way to his flat in Piccadilly. 'If that fowl had gone on roasting a bit longer the blood corpuscles might easily have been destroyed beyond all hope of recognition. It all goes to show that the unpremeditated crime is usually the safest.'

'And what does your lordship take the man's motive to have been?'

'In my youth,' said Wimsey meditatively, 'they used to make me read the Bible. Trouble was, the only books I ever took to naturally were the ones they weren't over and above keen on. But I got to know the Song of Songs pretty well by heart. Look it up, Bunter; at your age it won't hurt you; it talks sense about jealousy.'

'I have perused the work in question, your lordship,' replied Mr Bunter, with a sallow blush. 'It says, if I remember rightly: *Jealousy is cruel as the grave.*'

The Adventure of the Cardboard Box

Arthur Conan Doyle

In choosing a few typical cases which illustrate the remarkable mental qualities of my friend, Sherlock Holmes, I have endeavoured, as far as possible, to select those which presented the minimum of sensationalism, while offering a fair field for his talents. It is, however, unfortunately impossible entirely to separate the sensational from the criminal, and a chronicler is left in the dilemma that he must either sacrifice details which are essential to his statement and so give a false impression of the problem, or he must use matter which chance, and not choice, has provided him with. With this short preface I shall turn to my notes of what proved to be a strange, though a peculiarly terrible, chain of events.

It was a blazing hot day in August. Baker Street was like an oven, and the glare of the sunlight upon the yellow brickwork of the house across the road was painful to the eye. It was hard to believe that these were the same walls which loomed so gloomily through the fogs of winter. Our blinds were half-drawn, and Holmes lay curled upon the sofa, reading and re-reading a letter which he had received by the morning post. For myself, my term of service in India had trained me to stand heat better than cold, and a thermometer at ninety was no hardship. But the morning paper was uninteresting. Parliament had risen. Everybody was out of town, and I yearned for the glades of the New Forest or the shingle of Southsea. A depleted bank account had caused me to postpone my holiday, and as to my companion, neither the country nor the sea presented the slightest attraction to him. He loved to lie in the very centre of five millions of people, with his filaments stretching out and running through them, responsive to every little rumour or suspicion of unsolved crime. Appreciation of nature found no place among his many gifts, and his only change was when he turned his mind from the evil-doer of the town to track down his brother of the country.

Finding that Holmes was too absorbed for conversation I had tossed aside the barren paper, and leaning back in my chair I fell into a brown study. Suddenly my companion's voice broke in upon my thoughts:

'You are right, Watson,' said he. 'It does seem a most preposterous way of settling a dispute.'

'Most preposterous!' I exclaimed, and then suddenly realising how he had echoed the inmost thought of my soul, I sat up in my chair and stared at him in blank amazement.

'What is this, Holmes?' I cried. 'This is beyond anything which I could have imagined.'

He laughed heartily at my perplexity.

'You remember,' said he, 'that some little time ago when I read you the passage in one of Poe's sketches in which a close reasoner follows the unspoken thoughts of his companion, you were inclined to treat the matter as a mere *tour de force* of the author. On my remarking that I was constantly in the habit of doing the same thing you expressed incredulity.'

'Oh, no!'

'Perhaps not with your tongue, my dear Watson, but certainly with your eyebrows. So when I saw you throw down your paper and enter upon a train of thought, I was very happy to have the opportunity of reading it off, and eventually of breaking into it, as a proof that I had been in rapport with you.'

But I was still far from satisfied. 'In the example which you read to me,' said I, 'the reasoner drew his conclusions from the actions of the man whom he observed. If I remember right, he stumbled over a heap of stones, looked up at the stars, and so on. But I have been seated quietly in my chair, and what clues can I have given you?'

'You do yourself an injustice. The features are given to man as the means by which he shall express his emotions, and yours are faithful servants.'

'Do you mean to say that you read my train of thoughts from my features?'

'Your features and especially your eyes. Perhaps you cannot yourself recall how your reverie commenced?'

'No, I cannot.'

'Then I will tell you. After throwing down your paper, which was the action which drew my attention to you, you sat for half a minute with a vacant expression. Then your eyes fixed themselves upon your newly framed picture of General Gordon, and I saw by the alteration in your face that a train of thought had been started. But it did not lead very far. Your eyes flashed across to the unframed portrait of Henry Ward Beecher which stands upon the top of your books. Then you glanced up at the wall, and of course your meaning was obvious. You were thinking that if the portrait were framed it would just cover that bare space and correspond with Gordon's picture there.'

'You have followed me wonderfully!' I exclaimed.

'So far I could hardly have gone astray. But now your thoughts went back to Beecher, and you looked hard across as if you were studying the character in his features. Then your eyes ceased to pucker, but you continued to look across, and your face was thoughtful. You were recalling the incidents of Beecher's career. I was well aware that you could not do this without thinking of the mission which he undertook on behalf of the North at the time of the Civil War, for I remember your expressing your passionate indignation at the way in which he was received by the more turbulent of our people. You felt so strongly about it that I knew you could not think of Beecher without thinking of that also. When a moment later I saw your eyes wander away from the picture, I suspected that your mind had now turned to the Civil War, and when I observed that your lips set, your eyes sparkled, and your hands clenched I was positive that you were indeed thinking of the gallantry which was shown by both sides in that desperate struggle. But then, again, your face grew sadder, you shook your head. You were dwelling upon the sadness and horror and useless waste of life. Your hand stole towards your own old wound and a smile quivered on your lips, which showed me that the ridiculous side of this method of settling international questions had forced itself upon your mind. At this point I agreed with you that it was preposterous and was glad to find that all my deductions had been correct.'

'Absolutely!' said I. 'And now that you have explained it, I confess that I am as amazed as before.'

'It was very superficial, my dear Watson, I assure you. I should not have intruded it upon your attention had you not shown some incredulity the other day. But I have in my hands here a little problem which may prove to be more difficult of solution than my small essay in thought reading. Have you observed in the paper a short paragraph referring to the remarkable contents of a packet sent through the post to Miss Cushing, of Cross Street, Croydon?'

'No, I saw nothing.'

'Ah! Then you must have overlooked it. Just toss it over to me. Here it is, under the financial column. Perhaps you would be good enough to read it aloud.'

I picked up the paper which he had thrown back to me and read the paragraph indicated. It was headed, 'A Gruesome Packet'.

'Miss Susan Cushing, living at Cross Street, Croydon, has been made the victim of what must be regarded as a peculiarly revolting practical joke unless some more sinister meaning should prove to be attached to the incident. At two o'clock yesterday afternoon a small packet, wrapped in brown paper, was handed in by the postman. A cardboard box was inside, which was filled with coarse salt. On emptying this, Miss Cushing was horrified to find two human ears, apparently quite freshly severed. The box had been sent by parcel post from Belfast upon the morning before. There is no indication as to the sender, and the matter is the more mysterious as Miss Cushing, who is a maiden lady of fifty, has led a most retired life, and has so few acquaintances or correspondents that it is a rare event for her to receive anything through the post. Some years ago, however, when she resided at Penge, she let apartments in her house to three young medical students, whom she was obliged to get rid of on account of their noisy and irregular habits. The police are of opinion that this outrage may have been perpetrated upon Miss Cushing by these youths, who owed her a grudge and who hoped to frighten her by sending her these relics of the dissecting rooms. Some probability is lent to the theory by the fact that one of these students came from the north of Ireland, and, to the best of Miss Cushing's belief, from Belfast. In the meantime, the matter is being actively investigated, Mr Lestrade, one of the very smartest of our detective officers, being in charge of the case.'

'So much for the *Daily Chronicle*,' said Holmes as I finished reading. 'Now for our friend Lestrade. I had a note from him this morning, in which he says:

'I think that this case is very much in your line. We have every hope of clearing the matter up, but we find a little difficulty in getting anything to work upon. We have, of course, wired to the Belfast post office, but a large number of parcels were handed in upon that day, and they have no means of identifying this particular one, or of remembering the sender. The box is a half-pound box of honeydew tobacco and does not help us in any way. The medical student theory still appears to me to be the most feasible, but if you should have a few hours to spare I should be very happy to see you out here. I shall be either at the house or in the police station all day.

'What say you, Watson? Can you rise superior to the heat and run down to Croydon with me on the off-chance of a case for your annals?'

'I was longing for something to do.'

'You shall have it then. Ring for our boots and tell them to order a cab. I'll be back in a moment when I have changed my dressing gown and filled my cigar case.'

A shower of rain fell while we were in the train, and the heat was far less oppressive in Croydon than in town. Holmes had sent on a wire, so that Lestrade, as wiry, as dapper, and as ferret-like as ever, was waiting for us at the station. A walk of five minutes took us to Cross Street, where Miss Cushing resided.

It was a very long street of two-storey brick houses, neat and prim, with whitened stone steps and little groups of aproned women gossiping at the doors. Halfway down, Lestrade stopped and tapped at a door, which was opened by a small servant girl. Miss Cushing was sitting in the front room, into which we were ushered. She was a placid-faced woman, with large, gentle eyes, and grizzled hair curving down over her temples on each side. A worked antimacassar lay upon her lap and a basket of coloured silks stood upon a stool beside her.

'They are in the outhouse, those dreadful things,' said she

as Lestrade entered. 'I wish that you would take them away altogether.'

'So I shall, Miss Cushing. I only kept them here until my friend, Mr Holmes, should have seen them in your presence.'

'Why in my presence, sir?'

'In case he wished to ask any questions.'

'What is the use of asking me questions when I tell you I know nothing whatever about it?'

'Quite so, madam,' said Holmes in his soothing way. 'I have no doubt that you have been annoyed more than enough already over this business.'

'Indeed I have, sir. I am a quiet woman and live a retired life. It is something new for me to see my name in the papers and to find the police in my house. I won't have those things in here, Mr Lestrade. If you wish to see them you must go to the outhouse.'

It was a small shed in the narrow garden which ran behind the house. Lestrade went in and brought out a yellow cardboard box, with a piece of brown paper and some string. There was a bench at the end of the path, and we all sat down while Homes examined one by one, the articles which Lestrade had handed to him.

'The string is exceedingly interesting,' he remarked, holding it up to the light and sniffing at it. 'What do you make of this string, Lestrade?'

'It has been tarred.'

'Precisely. It is a piece of tarred twine. You have also, no doubt, remarked that Miss Cushing has cut the cord with a scissors, as can be seen by the double fray on each side. This is of importance.'

'I cannot see the importance,' said Lestrade.

'The importance lies in the fact that the knot is left intact, and that this knot is of a peculiar character.'

'It is very neatly tied. I had already made a note of that effect,' said Lestrade complacently.

'So much for the string, then,' said Holmes, smiling, 'now for the box wrapper. Brown paper, with a distinct smell of coffee. What, did you not observe it? I think there can be no doubt of it. Address printed in rather straggling characters: "Miss S. Cushing, Cross Street, Croydon". Done with a broad-pointed pen, probably a J, and with very inferior ink. The word "Croydon" has been originally spelled with an "i", which has been changed to "y". The parcel was directed, then, by a man – the printing is distinctly masculine – of limited education and unacquainted with the town of Croydon. So far, so good! The box is a yellow, half-pound honeydew box, with nothing distinctive save two thumb marks at the left bottom corner. It is filled with rough salt of the quality used for preserving hides and other of the coarser commercial purposes. And embedded in it are these very singular enclosures.'

He took out the two ears as he spoke, and laying a board across his knee he examined them minutely, while Lestrade and I, bending forward on each side of him, glanced alternately at these dreadful relics and at the thoughtful, eager face of our companion. Finally he returned them to the box once more and sat for a while in deep meditation.

'You have observed, of course,' said he at last, 'that the ears are not a pair.'

'Yes, I have noticed that. But if this were the practical joke of some students from the dissecting rooms, it would be as easy for them to send two odd ears as a pair.'

'Precisely. But this is not a practical joke.'

'You are sure of it?'

'The presumption is strongly against it. Bodies in the dissecting rooms are injected with preservative fluid. These ears bear no signs of this. They are fresh, too. They have been cut off with a blunt instrument, which would hardly happen if a student had done it. Again, carbolic or rectified spirits would be the preservatives which would suggest themselves to the medical mind, certainly not rough salt. I repeat that there is no practical joke here, but that we are investigating a serious crime.'

A vague thrill ran through me as I listened to my companion's words and saw the stern gravity which had hardened his features. This brutal preliminary seemed to shadow forth some strange and inexplicable horror in the background. Lestrade, however, shook his head like a man who is only half convinced.

'There are objections to the joke theory, no doubt,' said he, 'but there are much stronger reasons against the other. We know that this woman has led a most quiet and respectable life at Penge and here for the last twenty years. She has hardly been away from her home for a day during that time. Why on earth, then, should any criminal send her the proofs of his guilt, especially as, unless she is a most consummate actress, she understands quite as little of the matter as we do?'

'That is the problem which we have to solve,' Holmes answered, 'and for my part I shall set about it by presuming that my reasoning is correct, and that a double murder has been committed. One of these ears is a woman's, small, finely formed, and pierced for an earring. The other is a man's, sun-burned, discoloured, and also pierced for an earring. These two people are presumably dead, or we should have heard their story before now. Today is Friday. The packet was posted on Thursday morning. The tragedy, then, occurred on Wednesday or Tuesday, or earlier. If the two people were murdered, who but their murderer would have sent this sign of his work to Miss Cushing? We may take it that the sender of the packet is the man whom we want. But he must have some strong reason for sending Miss Cushing this packet. What reason then? It must have been to tell her that the deed was done! Or to pain her, perhaps. But in that case she knows who it is. Does she know? I doubt it. If she knew, why should she call the police in? She might have buried the ears, and no one would have been the wiser. That is what she would have done if she had wished to shield the criminal. But if she does not wish to shield him she would give his name. There is a tangle here which needs straightening out.' He had been talking in a high, quick voice, staring blankly up over the garden fence, but now he sprang briskly to his feet and walked towards the house.

'I have a few questions to ask Miss Cushing,' said he.

'In that case I may leave you here,' said Lestrade, 'for I have another small business on hand. I think that I have nothing further to learn from Miss Cushing. You will find me at the police station.'

'We shall look in on our way to the train,' answered Holmes. A moment later he and I were back in the front room, where the impassive lady was still quietly working away at her antimacassar. She put it down on her lap as we entered and looked at us with her frank, searching blue eyes.

'I am convinced, sir,' she said, 'that this matter is a mistake, and that the parcel was never meant for me at all. I have said this several times to the gentleman from Scotland Yard, but he simply laughs at me. I have not an enemy in the world, as far as I know, so why should anyone play me such a trick?'

'I am coming to be of the same opinion, Miss Cushing,' said Holmes, taking a seat beside her. 'I think that it is more than probable—' He paused, and I was surprised, on glancing round, to see that he was staring with singular intentness at the lady's profile. Surprise and satisfaction were both for an instant to be read upon his eager face, though when she glanced round to find out the cause of his silence he had become as demure as ever. I stared hard myself at her flat, grizzled hair, her trim cap, her little gilt earrings, her placid features; but I could see nothing which could account for my companion's evident excitement.

'There were one or two questions—'

'Oh, I am weary of questions!' cried Miss Cushing impatiently.

'You have two sisters, I believe.'

'How could you know that?'

'I observed the very instant that I entered the room that you have a portrait group of three ladies upon the mantelpiece, one of whom is undoubtedly yourself, while the others are so exceedingly like you that there could be no doubt of the relationship.'

'Yes, you are quite right. Those are my sisters, Sarah and Mary.'

'And here at my elbow is another portrait, taken at Liverpool, of your younger sister, in the company of a man who appears to be a steward by his uniform. I observe that she was unmarried at the time.'

'You are very quick at observing.'

'That is my trade.'

'Well, you are quite right. But she was married to Mr Browner a few days afterwards. He was on the South American line when that was taken, but he was so fond of her that he couldn't abide to leave her for so long, and he got into the Liverpool and London boats.'

'Ah, the *Conqueror*, perhaps?'

'No, the *May Day*, when last I heard. Jim came down here to see me once. That was before he broke the pledge; but afterwards he would always take drink when he was ashore, and a little drink would send him stark, staring mad. Ah! It was a bad day that ever he took a glass in his hand again. First he dropped me, then he quarrelled with Sarah, and now that Mary has stopped writing we don't know how things are going with them.'

It was evident that Miss Cushing had come upon a subject on which she felt very deeply. Like most people who lead a lonely life, she was shy at first, but ended by becoming extremely communicative. She told us many details about her brother-in-law the steward, and then wandering off on the subject of her former lodgers, the medical students, she gave us a long account of their delinquencies, with their names and those of their hospitals. Holmes listened attentively to everything, throwing in a question from time to time.

'About your second sister, Sarah,' said he. 'I wonder,

since you are both maiden ladies, that you do not keep house together.'

'Ah! You don't know Sarah's temper or you would wonder no more. I tried it when I came to Croydon, and we kept on until about two months ago, when we had to part. I don't want to say a word against my own sister, but she was always meddlesome and hard to please, was Sarah.'

'You say that she quarrelled with your Liverpool relations.'

'Yes, and they were the best of friends at one time. Why, she went up there to live in order to be near them. And now she has no word hard enough for Jim Browner. The last six months that she was here she would speak of nothing but his drinking and his ways. He had caught her meddling, I suspect, and given her a bit of his mind, and that was the start of it.'

'Thank you, Miss Cushing,' said Holmes, rising and bowing. 'Your sister Sarah lives, I think you said, at New Street, Wallington? Goodbye, and I am very sorry that you should have been troubled over a case with which, as you say, you have nothing whatever to do.'

There was a cab passing as we came out, and Holmes hailed it.

'How far to Wallington?' he asked.

'Only about a mile, sir.'

'Very good. Jump in, Watson. We must strike while the iron is hot. Simple as the case is, there have been one or two very instructive details in connection with it. Just pull up at a telegraph office as you pass, cabby.'

Holmes sent off a short wire and for the rest of the drive lay back in the cab, with his hat tilted over his nose to keep the sun from his face. Our driver pulled up at a house which was not unlike the one which we had just quitted. My companion ordered him to wait, and had his hand upon the knocker, when the door opened and a grave young gentleman in black, with a very shiny hat, appeared on the step.

'Is Miss Cushing at home?' asked Holmes.

'Miss Sarah Cushing is extremely ill,' said he. 'She has been suffering since yesterday from brain symptoms of great severity. As her medical adviser, I cannot possibly take the responsibility of allowing anyone to see her. I should recommend you to call again in ten days.' He drew on his gloves, closed the door, and marched off down the street.

'Well, if we can't we can't,' said Holmes, cheerfully.

'Perhaps she could not or would not have told you much.'

'I did not wish her to tell me anything. I only wanted to look at her. However, I think that I have got all that I want. Drive us to some decent hotel, cabby, where we may have some lunch, and afterwards we shall drop down upon friend Lestrade at the police station.'

We had a pleasant little meal together, during which Holmes would talk about nothing but violins, narrating with great exultation how he had purchased his own Stradivarius, which was worth at least five hundred guineas, at a Jew broker's in Tottenham Court Road for fifty-five shillings. This led him to Paganini, and we sat for an hour over a bottle of claret while he told me anecdote after anecdote of that extraordinary man. The afternoon was far advanced and the hot glare had softened into a mellow glow before we found ourselves at the police station. Lestrade was waiting for us at the door.

'A telegram for you, Mr Holmes,' said he.

'Ha! It is the answer!' He tore it open, glanced his eyes over it, and crumpled it into his pocket. 'That's all right,' said he.

'Have you found out anything?'

'I have found out everything!'

'What!' Lestrade stared at him in amazement. 'You are joking.'

'I was never more serious in my life. A shocking crime has been committed, and I think I have now laid bare every detail of it.'

'And the criminal?'

Holmes scribbled a few words upon the back of one of his visiting cards and threw it over to Lestrade.

'That is the name,' he said. 'You cannot effect an arrest until tomorrow night at the earliest. I should prefer that you do not mention my name at all in connection with the case, as I choose to be only associated with those crimes which present some difficulty in their solution. Come on, Watson.' We strode off together to the station, leaving Lestrade still staring with a delighted face at the card which Holmes had thrown him.

'The case,' said Sherlock Holmes as we chatted over our cigars that night in our rooms at Baker Street, 'is one where, as in the investigations which you have chronicled under the names of "A Study in Scarlet" and "The Sign of Four", we have been compelled to reason backward from effects to causes. I have written to Lestrade asking him to supply us with the details which are now wanting, and which he will only get after he has secured his man. That he may be safely trusted to do, for although he is absolutely devoid of reason, he is as tenacious as a bulldog when he once understands what he has to do, and indeed, it is just this tenacity which has brought him to the top at Scotland Yard.'

'Your case is not complete, then?' I asked.

'It is fairly complete in essentials. We know who the author of the revolting business is, although one of the victims still escapes us. Of course, you have formed your own conclusions.'

'I presume that this Jim Browner, the steward of a Liverpool boat, is the man whom you suspect?'

'Oh! It is more than a suspicion.'

'And yet I cannot see anything save very vague indications.'

'On the contrary, to my mind nothing could be more clear. Let me run over the principal steps. We approached the case, you remember, with an absolutely blank mind, which is always an advantage. We had formed no theories. We were simply there to observe and to draw inferences from our observations. What did we see first? A very placid and respectable lady, who seemed quite innocent of any secret, and a portrait which showed me that she had two younger sisters. It instantly flashed across my mind that the box might have been meant for one of these. I set the idea aside as one which could be disproved or confirmed at our leisure. Then we went to the garden, as you remember, and we saw the very singular contents of the little yellow box.

'The string was of the quality which is used by sail-makers aboard ship, and at once a whiff of the sea was perceptible in our investigation. When I observed that the knot was one which is popular with sailors, that the parcel had been posted at a port, and that the male ear was pierced for an earring which is so much more common among sailors than landsmen, I was quite certain that all the actors in the tragedy were to be found among our seafaring classes.

'When I came to examine the address of the packet I observed that it was to Miss S. Cushing. Now, the oldest sister would, of course, be Miss Cushing, and although her initial was "S" it might belong to one of the others as well. In that case we should have to commence our investigation from a fresh basis altogether. I therefore went into the house with the intention of clearing up this point. I was about to assure Miss Cushing that I was convinced that a mistake had been made when you may remember that I came suddenly to a stop. The fact was that I had just seen something which filled me with surprise and at the same time narrowed the field of our inquiry immensely.

'As a medical man, you are aware, Watson, that there is no part of the body which varies so much as the human ear. Each ear is as a rule quite distinctive and differs from all other ones. In last year's *Anthropological Journal* you will find two short monographs from my pen upon the subject. I had, therefore, examined the ears in the box with the eyes of an expert and had carefully noted their anatomical peculiarities. Imagine my surprise, then, when on looking at Miss Cushing I perceived that her ear corresponded exactly with the female ear which I had just inspected. The matter was entirely beyond coincidence. There was the same shortening of the pinna, the same broad curve of the upper lobe, the same convolution of the inner cartilage. In all essentials it was the same ear.

'In the first place, her sister's name was Sarah, and her address had until recently been the same, so that it was quite obvious how the mistake had occurred and for whom the packet was meant. Then we heard of this steward, married to the third sister, and learned that he had at one time been so intimate with Miss Sarah that she had actually gone up to Liverpool to be near the Browners, but a quarrel had afterwards divided them. This quarrel had put a stop to all communications for some months, so that if Browner had occasion to address a packet to Miss Sarah, he would undoubtedly have done so to her old address.

'And now the matter had begun to straighten itself out wonderfully. We had learned of the existence of this steward, an impulsive man, of strong passions – you remember that he threw up what must have been a very superior berth in order to be nearer to his wife – subject, too, to occasional fits of hard drinking. We had reason to believe that his wife had been murdered, and that a man – presumably a seafaring man – had been murdered at the same time. Jealousy, of course, at once suggests itself as the motive for the crime. And why should these proofs of the deed be sent to Miss Sarah Cushing? Probably because during her residence in Liverpool she had some hand in bringing about the events which led to the tragedy. You will observe that this line of boats call at Belfast, Dublin and Waterford; so that, presuming that Browner had committed the deed and had embarked at once upon his steamer, the *May Day*, Belfast would be the first place at which he could post his terrible packet.

'A second solution was at this stage obviously possible, and although I thought it exceedingly unlikely, I was determined to elucidate it before going further. An unsuccessful lover might have killed Mr and Mrs Browner, and the male ear might have belonged to the husband. There were many grave objections to this theory, but it was conceivable. I therefore sent off a telegram to my friend Algar, of the Liverpool force, and asked him to find out if Mrs Browner were at home, and if Browner had departed in the *May Day*. Then we went on to Wallington to visit Miss Sarah.

'I was curious, in the first place, to see how far the family ear had been reproduced in her. Then, of course, she might give us very important information, but I was not sanguine that she would. She must have heard of the business the day before, since all Croydon was ringing with it, and she alone could have understood for whom the packet was meant. If she had been willing to help justice she would probably have communicated with the police already. However, it was clearly our duty to see her, so we went. We found that the news of the arrival of the packet – for her illness dated from that time – had such an effect upon her as to bring on brain fever. It was clearer than ever that she understood its full significance, but equally clear that we should have to wait some time for any assistance from her.

'However, we were really independent of her help. Our answers were waiting for us at the police station, where I had directed Algar to send them. Nothing could be more conclusive. Mrs Browner's house had been closed for more than three days, and the neighbours were of opinion that she had gone south to see her relatives. It had been ascertained at the shipping offices that Browner had left aboard of the *May Day*, and I calculate that she is due in the Thames tomorrow night. When he arrives he will be met by the obtuse but resolute Lestrade, and I have no doubt that we shall have all our details filled in.'

Sherlock Holmes was not disappointed in his expectations. Two days later he received a bulky envelope, which contained a short note from the detective, and a typewritten document, which covered several pages of foolscap.

'Lestrade has got him all right,' said Holmes, glancing up at me. 'Perhaps it would interest you to hear what he says.

'My dear Mr Holmes:

'In accordance with the scheme which we had formed in order to test our theories [the "we" is rather fine, Watson, is it not?] I went down to the Albert Dock yesterday at 6 pm, and boarded the SS *May Day*, belonging to the Liverpool, Dublin, and London Steam Packet Company. On enquiry, I found that there was a steward on board of the name of James Browner and that he had acted during the voyage in such an extraordinary manner that the captain had been compelled to relieve him of his duties. On descending to his berth, I found him seated upon a chest with his head sunk upon his hands, rocking himself to and fro. He is a big, powerful chap, clean-shaven, and very swarthy – something like Aldrige, who helped us in the bogus laundry affair. He jumped up when he heard my business, and I had my whistle to my lips to call a couple of river police, who were round the corner, but he seemed to have no heart in him, and he held out his hands quietly enough for the darbies. We brought him along to the cells, and his box as well, for we thought there might be something incriminating; but, bar a big sharp knife such as most sailors have, we got nothing for our trouble. However, we find that we shall want no more evidence, for on being brought before the inspector at the station he asked leave to make a statement, which was, of course, taken down, just as he made it, by our shorthand man. We had three copies typewritten, one of which I enclose. The affair proves, as I always thought it would, to be an extremely simple one, but I am obliged to you for assisting me in my investigation. With kind regards,

'Yours very truly,

'G. Lestrade.

'Hum! The investigation really was a very simple one,' remarked Holmes, 'but I don't think it struck him in that light when he first called us in. However, let us see what Jim Browner has to say for himself. This is his statement as made before Inspector Montgomery at the Shadwell Police Station, and it has the advantage of being verbatim.

'Have I anything to say? Yes, I have a deal to say. I have to make a clean breast of it all. You can hang me, or you can leave me alone. I don't care a plug which you do. I tell you I've not shut an eye in sleep since I did it, and I don't believe I ever will again until I get past all waking. Sometimes it's his face, but most generally it's hers. I'm never without one or the other before me. He looks frowning and black-like, but she has a kind o' surprise upon her face. Ay, the white lamb, she might well be surprised when she read death on a face that had seldom looked anything but love upon her before.

'But it was Sarah's fault, and may the curse of a broken man put a blight on her and set the blood rotting in her veins!

It's not that I want to clear myself. I know that I went back to drink, like the beast that I was. But she would have forgiven me; she would have stuck as close to me as a rope to a block if that woman had never darkened our door. For Sarah Cushing loved me – that's the root of the business – she loved me until all her love turned to poisonous hate when she knew that I thought more of my wife's footmark in the mud than I did of her whole body and soul.

'There were three sisters altogether. The old one was just a good woman, the second was a devil, and the third was an angel. Sarah was thirty-three, and Mary was twenty-nine when I married. We were just as happy as the day was long when we set up house together, and in all Liverpool there was no better woman than my Mary. And then we asked Sarah up for a week, and the week grew into a month, and one thing led to another, until she was just one of ourselves.

'I was blue ribbon at that time, and we were putting a little money by, and all was as bright as a new dollar. My God, whoever would have thought that it could have come to this? Whoever would have dreamed it?

'I used to be home for the weekends very often, and sometimes if the ship were held back for cargo I would have a whole week at a time, and in this way I saw a deal of my sister-in-law, Sarah. She was a fine tall woman, black and quick and fierce, with a proud way of carrying her head, and a glint from her eye like a spark from a flint. But when little Mary was there I had never a thought of her, and that I swear as I hope for God's mercy.

'It had seemed to me sometimes that she liked to be alone with me, or to coax me out for a walk with her, but I had never thought anything of that. But one evening my eyes were opened. I had come up from the ship and found my wife out, but Sarah at home. "Where's Mary?" I asked. "Oh, she has gone to pay some accounts." I was impatient and paced up and down the room. "Can't you be happy for five minutes without Mary, Jim?" says she. "It's a bad compliment to me that you can't be contented with my society for so short a time." "That's all right, my lass," said I, putting out my hand towards her in a kindly way, but she had it in both hers in an instant, and they burned as if they were in a fever. I looked into her eyes and I read it all there. There was no need for her to speak, nor for me either. I frowned and drew my hand away. Then she stood by my side in silence for a bit, and then put up her hand and patted me on the shoulder. "Steady old Jim!" said she, and with a kind o' mocking laugh, she ran out of the room.

'Well, from that time Sarah hated me with her whole heart and soul, and she is a woman who can hate, too. I was a fool to let her go on biding with us – a besotted fool – but I never said a word to Mary, for I knew it would grieve her. Things went on much as before, but after a time I began to find that there was a bit of a change in Mary herself. She had always been so trusting and so innocent, but now she became queer and suspicious, wanting to know where I had been and what I had been doing, and whom my letters were from, and what I had in my pockets, and a thousand such follies. Day by day she grew queerer and more irritable, and we had ceaseless rows about nothing. I was fairly puzzled by it all. Sarah avoided me now, but she and Mary were just insep-arable. I can see now how she was plotting and scheming and poisoning my wife's mind against me, but I was such a blind beetle that I could not understand it at the time. Then I broke my blue ribbon and began to drink again, but I think I should not have done it if Mary had been the same as ever. She had some reason to be disgusted with me now, and the gap between us began to be wider and wider. And then this Alec Fairbairn chipped in, and things became a thousand times blacker.

'It was to see Sarah that he came to my house first, but soon it was to see us, for he was a man with winning ways, and he made friends wherever he went. He was a dashing, swaggering chap, smart and curled, who had seen half the world and could talk of what he had seen. He was good company, I won't deny it, and he had wonderful polite ways with him for a sailor man, so that I think there must have been a time when he knew more of the poop than the fore-castle. For a month he was in and out of my house, and never once did it cross my mind that harm might come of his soft, tricky ways. And then at last something made me suspect, and from that day my peace was gone forever.

'It was only a little thing, too. I had come into the parlour unexpected, and as I walked in at the door I saw a light of welcome on my wife's face. But as she saw who it was it faded again, and she turned away with a look of disappointment. That was enough for me. There was no one but Alec Fair-bairn whose step she could have mistaken for mine. If I could have seen him then I should have killed him, for I have always been like a madman when my temper gets loose. Mary saw the devil's light in my eyes, and she ran forward with her hands on my sleeve. "Don't, Jim, don't!" says she. "Where's

Sarah?" I asked. "In the kitchen," says she. "Sarah," says I as I went in, "this man Fairbairn is never to darken my door again." "Why not?" says she. "Because I order it." "Oh!" says she, "if my friends are not good enough for this house, then I am not good enough for it either." "You can do what you like," says I, "but if Fairbairn shows his face here again I'll send you one of his ears for a keepsake." She was frightened by my face, I think, for she never answered a word, and the same evening she left my house.

'Well, I don't know now whether it was pure devilry on the part of this woman, or whether she thought that she could turn me against my wife by encouraging her to misbehave. Anyway, she took a house just two streets off and let lodgings to sailors. Fairbairn used to stay there, and Mary would go round to have tea with her sister and him. How often she went I don't know, but I followed her one day, and as I broke in at the door Fairbairn got away over the back garden wall, like the cowardly skunk that he was. I swore to my wife that I would kill her if I found her in his company again, and I led her back with me, sobbing and trembling, and as white as a piece of paper. There was no trace of love between us any longer. I could see that she hated me and feared me, and when the thought of it drove me to drink, then she despised me as well.

'Well, Sarah found that she could not make a living in Liverpool, so she went back, as I understand, to live with her sister in Croydon, and things jogged on much the same as ever at home. And then came this week and all the misery and ruin.

'It was in this way. We had gone on the *May Day* for a

round voyage of seven days, but a hogshead got loose and started one of our plates, so that we had to put back into port for twelve hours. I left the ship and came home, thinking what a surprise it would be for my wife, and hoping that maybe she would be glad to see me so soon. The thought was in my head as I turned into my own street, and at that moment a cab passed me, and there she was, sitting by the side of Fairbairn, the two chatting and laughing, with never a thought for me as I stood watching them from the footpath.

'I tell you, and I give you my word for it, that from that moment I was not my own master, and it is all like a dim dream when I look back on it. I had been drinking hard of late, and the two things together fairly turned my brain. There's something throbbing in my head now, like a docker's hammer, but that morning I seemed to have all Niagara whizzing and buzzing in my ears.

'Well, I took to my heels, and I ran after the cab. I had a heavy oak stick in my hand, and I tell you I saw red from the first; but as I ran I got cunning, too, and hung back a little to see them without being seen. They pulled up soon at the railway station. There was a good crowd round the booking office, so I got quite close to them without being seen. They took tickets for New Brighton. So did I, but I got in three carriages behind them. When we reached it they walked along the Parade, and I was never more than a hundred yards from them. At last I saw them hire a boat and start for a row, for it was a very hot day, and they thought, no doubt, that it would be cooler on the water.

'It was just as if they had been given into my hands. There was a bit of a haze, and you could not see more than a few hundred yards. I hired a boat for myself, and I pulled after them. I could see the blur of their craft, but they were going nearly as fast as I, and they must have been a long mile from the shore before I caught them up. The haze was like a curtain all round us, and there were we three in the middle of it. My God, shall I ever forget their faces when they saw who was in the boat that was closing in upon them? She screamed out. He swore like a madman and jabbed at me with an oar, for he must have seen death in my eyes. I got past it and got one in with my stick that crushed his head like an egg. I would have spared her, perhaps, for all my madness, but she threw her arms round him, crying out to him, and calling him "Alec". I struck again, and she lay stretched beside him. I was like a wild beast then that had tasted blood. If Sarah had been there, by the Lord, she should have joined them. I pulled out my knife, and – well, there! I've said enough. It gave me a kind of savage joy when I thought how Sarah would feel when she had such signs as these of what her meddling had brought about. Then I tied the bodies into the boat, stove a plank, and stood by until they had sunk. I knew very well that the owner would think that they had lost their bearings in the haze, and had drifted off out to sea. I cleaned myself up, got back to land, and joined my ship without a soul having a suspicion of what had passed. That night I made up the packet for Sarah Cushing, and next day I sent it from Belfast.

'There you have the whole truth of it. You can hang me, or do what you like with me, but you cannot punish me as I have been punished already. I cannot shut my eyes but I see those two faces staring at me – staring at me as they stared when my boat broke through the haze. I killed them quick, but they are killing me slow; and if I have another night of it I shall be either mad or dead before morning. You won't put me alone into a cell, sir? For pity's sake don't, and may you be treated in your day of agony as you treat me now.

'What is the meaning of it, Watson?' said Holmes solemnly as he laid down the paper. 'What object is served by this circle of misery and violence and fear? It must tend to some end, or else our universe is ruled by chance, which is unthinkable. But what end? There is the great standing perennial problem to which human reason is as far from an answer as ever.'

The Silver Curtain

Carter Dickson

The croupier's wrist moved with such fluent ease as to seem boneless. Over the green baize its snaky activity never hesitated, never wavered, never was still. His rake, like an enormous butter-pat, attracted the cards, flicked them up, juggled them, and slid them in a steady stream through the slot of the table.

No voice was raised in the Casino at La Bandelette. There was much casualness; hardly any laughter. The tall red curtains and the padded red floors closed in a sort of idle concentration at a dozen tables. And out of it, at table number six, the croupier's monotone droned on.

'*Six mille. Banco? Six mille. Banco? Banco?*'

'*Banco,*' said the young Englishman across the table. The cards, white and grey, slipped smoothly from the shoe. And the young man lost again.

The croupier hadn't time to notice much. The people

round him, moving in hundreds through the season, were hardly human beings at all. There was a calculating machine inside his head; he heard its clicks, he watched the run of its numbers, and it was all he had time for. Yet so acutely were his senses developed that he could tell almost within a hundred francs how much money the players at his table still retained. The young man opposite was nearly broke.

(Best be careful. This perhaps means trouble.)

Casually the croupier glanced round his table. There were five players, all English, as was to be expected. There was the fair-haired girl with the elderly man, obviously her father, who had a bald head and looked ill; he breathed behind his hand. There was the very heavy, military-looking man whom someone had addressed as Colonel March. There was the fat, sleek, swarthy young man with the twisty eyebrows (dubious English?), whose complacency had grown with his run of luck and whose wallet stuffed with *mille* notes lay at his elbow. Finally, there was the young man who lost so much.

The young man got up from his chair.

He had no poker face. The atmosphere about him was so desperately embarrassed that the fair-haired girl spoke.

'Leaving, Mr Winton?' she asked.

'Er – yes,' said Mr Winton. He seemed grateful for that little help thrown into his disquiet. He seized at it; he smiled back at her. 'No luck yet. Time to get a drink and offer up prayers for the next session.'

(Look here, thought Jerry Winton, why stand here explaining? It's not serious. You'll get out of it, even if it does mean a nasty bit of trouble. They all know you're broke. Stop standing here laughing like a gawk, and get away from the table. He looked into the eyes of the fair-haired girl, and wished he hadn't been such an ass.)

'Get a drink,' he repeated.

He strode away from the table with (imagined) laughter following him. The sleek young man had lifted a moon-face and merely looked at him in a way that roused Jerry Winton's wrath.

Curse La Bandelette and baccara and everything else.

'There,' reflected the croupier, 'is a young man who will have trouble with his hotel. *Banco? Six mille. Banco?*'

In the bar, which adjoined the casino rooms, Jerry Winton crawled up on one of the high stools, called for an Armagnac, and pushed his last hundred-franc note across the counter. His head was full of a row of figures written in the spidery style of France. His hotel bill for a week would come to – what? Four, five, six thousand francs? It would be presented tomorrow, and all he had was his return ticket to London by plane.

In the big mirror behind the bar a new image emerged from the crowd. It was that of the fat, sleek, oily-faced young man who had cleaned up such a packet at the table, and who was even now fingering his wallet lovingly before he put it away. He climbed up on a stool beside Jerry. He called for mineral water: how shrewd and finicky-crafty these expert gamblers were! He relighted the stump of a cigar in one corner of his mouth.

Then he spoke.

'Broke?' he enquired off-handedly.

Jerry Winton glared at his reflection in the mirror.

'I don't see,' Jerry said, with a slow and murderous choosing of words, 'that that's anybody's business except mine.'

'Oh, that's all right,' said the stranger, in the same unpleasantly off-handed tone. He took several puffs at his cigar; he drank a little mineral water. He added: 'I expect it's pretty serious, though? Eh?'

'If the matter,' said Jerry, turning round, 'is of so much interest to you: no, it's not serious. I have plenty of money back home. The trouble is that this is Friday night, and I can't get in touch with the bank until Monday.' Though this was quite true, he saw the other's fishy expression grow broader. 'It's a damned nuisance, because they don't know me at the hotel. But a nuisance is all it is. If you think I'm liable to go out in the garden and shoot myself, stop thinking it.'

The other smiled sadly and fishily, and shook his head.

'You don't say? I can't believe that, now can I?'

'I don't care what you believe.'

'You should care,' said his companion, unruffled. As Jerry slid down from the stool, he reached out and tapped Jerry on the arm. 'Don't be in such a rush. You say you're a boy Croesus. All right: you're a boy Croesus. *I* won't argue with you. But tell me: how's your nerve?'

'My what?'

'Your nerve. Your courage,' explained his companion, with something like a sneer.

Jerry Winton looked back at the bland, self-assured face poised above the mineral water. His companion's feet were entangled with the legs of the bar stool; his short upper lip was lifted with acute self-confidence; and a blank eye jeered down.

'I thought I'd ask,' he pursued. 'My name is Davos, Ferdie Davos. Everybody knows me.' He swept his hand towards the crowd. 'How'd you like to make ten thousand francs?'

'I'd like it a whole lot. But I don't know whether I'd like to make it out of any business of yours.'

Davos was unruffled. 'It's no good trying to be on your dignity with me. It don't impress me and it won't help you. I still ask: how would you like to make ten thousand francs? That would more than cover what you owe or are likely to owe, wouldn't it? I thought so. Do you or don't you want to make ten thousand francs?'

'Yes, I do,' Jerry snarled back.

'All right. See a doctor.'

'*What?*'

'See a doctor,' Davos repeated coolly. 'A nerve tonic is what you want: pills. No, I'm not wise-cracking.' He looked at the clock, whose hands stood at five minutes to eleven. 'Go to this address – listen carefully while I tell you – and there'll be ten thousand in it for you. Go to this address in about an hour. No sooner, no later. Do your job properly, and there may be even more than ten thousand in it for you. Number two, Square St Jean, Avenue des Phares, in about an hour. We'll see how your nerve is then.'

La Bandelette, 'the fillet', that strip of silver beach along the channel, is full of flat-roofed and queerly painted houses which give it the look of a town in a Walt Disney film. But the town itself is of secondary consideration. The English colony, which is of a frantic fashionableness, lies among great trees behind. Close to the Casino de la Forêt are three great hotels, gay with awning and piling sham Gothic turrets into the sky. The air is aromatic; open carriages clop and jingle along broad avenues; and the art of extracting money from guests has become so perfected that we find our hands going to our pockets even in sleep.

This sleep is taken by day. By night, when La Bandelette is sealed up except for the Casino, the beam of the great island lighthouse sweeps the streets. It dazzles and then dies, once every twenty seconds. And, as Jerry Winton strode under the trees towards the Avenue of the Lighthouses, its beam was beginning to be blurred by rain.

Square St Jean, Avenue des Phares. Where? And why?

If Davos had approached him in any other way, Jerry admitted to himself, he would have paid no attention to it. But he was annoyed and curious. Besides, unless there were a trick in it, he could use ten thousand francs. There was probably a trick in it. But who cared?

It was the rain that made him hesitate. He heard it patter in the trees, and deepen to a heavy rustling, as he saw the sign-board pointing to the Avenue des Phares. He was without hat or coat. But by this time he meant to see the thing through. Ahead of him was a street of fashionable villas, lighted by mere sparks of gas. An infernally dark street. Something queer, and more than queer, about this. Total strangers didn't ask you how strong your nerves were, and then offer you ten thousand francs on top of it, for any purpose that would pass the customs. Which was all the more reason why ...

Then he saw Davos.

Davos did not see him. Davos was ahead of him, walking fast and with little short steps along the dim street. The white beam of the lighthouse shone out overhead, turning the rain to silver; and Jerry could see the gleam of his polished black hair and the light tan topcoat he was now wearing. Pulling up the collar of his dinner jacket, Jerry followed.

A few yards farther on Davos slackened his pace. He peered round and up. On his left was the entrance to a court-yard, evidently the Square St Jean. But to call it a 'square' was noble overstatement; it was only a cul-de-sac some twenty feet wide by forty feet deep.

Two of its three sides were merely tall, blank brick walls. The third side, on the right, was formed of a tall flat house all of whose windows were closely shuttered. But there was at least a sign of life about the house. Over its door burned a dim white globe, showing that there was a doctor's brass nameplate beside the door. A sedate house with blue-painted shutters in the bare cul-de-sac – and Davos was making for it.

All this Jerry saw at a glance. Then he moved back from the cul-de-sac. The rain was sluicing down on him, blur-ring the dim white globe with shadow and gleam. Davos had almost reached the doctor's door. He had paused, as though to consider or look at something; and then …

Jerry Winton later swore that he had taken his eyes off Davos only for a second. This was true. Jerry, in fact, had glanced back along the Avenue des Phares behind him and was heartened to see the figure of a policeman some distance away. What made him look quickly back again was a noise from the cul-de-sac, a noise that was something between a cough and a scream, bubbling up horribly under the rain; and afterwards the thud of a body on asphalt.

One moment Davos had been on his feet. The next moment he was lying on his side on the pavement, and kicking.

Overhead the beam of the lighthouse wheeled again. Jerry, reaching Davos in a run of half a dozen long strides, saw the whole scene picked out by that momentary light. Davos's fingers still clutched, or tried to clutch, the well-filled wallet Jerry had last seen at the Casino. His tan topcoat was now dark with rain. His heels scraped on the pavement, for he had been stabbed through the back of the neck with a heavy knife whose polished-metal handle projected four inches. Then the wallet slipped out of his fingers, and splashed into a puddle, for the man died.

Jerry Winton looked, and did not believe his own eyes. Mechanically he reached down and picked up the wallet out of the puddle, shaking it. He backed away as he heard running footfalls pound into the cul-de-sac, and he saw the flying waterproof of a policeman.

'Halt there!' the law shouted in French. The policeman, a dim shape under the waterproof, pulled up short and stared. After seeing what was on the pavement, he made a noise like a man hit in the stomach.

Jerry pulled his wits together and conned over his French for the proper phrases.

'His – this wallet,' said Jerry, extending it.

'So I see.'

'He is dead.'

'That would appear obvious,' agreed the other, with a kind of snort. 'Well! Give it to me. Quick, quick, quick! His wallet.'

The policeman extended his hand, snapping the fingers. He added: 'No stupidities, if you please! I am prepared for you.'

'But I didn't kill him.'

'That remains to be seen.'

'Man, you don't think—?'

He broke off. The trouble was that it had happened too rapidly. Jerry's feeling was that of one who meets a super-salesman and under whirlwind tactics is persuaded to buy some huge and useless article before he realises what the talk is all about.

For here was a minor miracle. He had seen the man Davos stabbed under his eyes. Davos had been stabbed by a straight blow from behind, the heavy knife entering in a straight line sloping a little upwards, as though the blow had been struck from the direction of the pavement. Yet at the same time Davos had been alone in an empty cul-de-sac as bare as a biscuit box.

'It is not my business to think,' said the policeman curtly. 'I make my notes and I report to my *commissaire*. Now!' He withdrew into the shelter of the dim-lit doorway, his wary eye fixed on Jerry, and whipped out his notebook. 'Let us have no nonsense. You killed this man and attempted to rob him. I saw you.'

'No!'

'You were alone with him in this court. I saw as much myself.'

'Yes, that is true.'

'Good; he admits it! You saw no one else in the court?'

'No.'

'*Justement*. Could any assassin have approached without being seen?'

Jerry, even as he saw the bleak eye grow bleaker, had to admit that this was impossible. On two sides were blank brick walls; on the third side was a house whose door or windows, he could swear, had not opened a crack. In the second's space of time while he looked away, no murderer could have approached, stabbed Davos, and got back to cover again. There was no cover. This was so apparent that Jerry could not even think of a reasonable lie. He merely stuttered.

'I do not know what happened,' he insisted. 'One minute he was there, and then he fell. I saw nobody.' Then a light opened in his mind. 'Wait! That knife there – it must have been thrown at him.'

Rich and sardonic humour stared at him from the doorway. 'Thrown, you say? Thrown from where?'

'I don't know,' admitted Jerry. The light went out. Again he stared at blank brick walls, and at the house from whose sealed front no knife could have been thrown.

'Consider,' pursued his companion, in an agony of logic, 'the position of the knife. This gentleman was walking with his back to you?'

'Yes.'

'Good; we progress.' He pointed. 'The knife enters the back of his neck in a straight line. It enters from the direction where you were standing. Could it have been thrown past you from the entrance to the court?'

'No. Impossible.'

'No. That is evident,' blared his companion. 'I cannot listen to any more stupidities. I indulge you because you are English and we have orders to indulge the English. But this goes beyond reason! You will go with me to the Hôtel de Ville. Look at the notecase in his hand. Does he offer it to you and say: "Monsieur, honour me by accepting my notecase"?'

'No. He had it in his own hand.'

'He had it in his own hand, say you. Why?'

'I don't know.'

Jerry broke off, both because the story of his losses at the Casino must now come out with deadly significance, and because they heard the rattle of a door being unlocked. The door of the doctor's house opened; and out stepped the fair-haired girl whom Jerry had last seen at the Casino.

Beside the door the brass nameplate read, 'Dr Edouard Hébert', with consulting hours inscribed underneath, and an aggressive, 'Speaks English'. Behind the girl, craning his neck, stood a bristly middle-aged man of immense dignity. His truculent eyeglasses had a broad black ribbon which seemed to form a kind of electrical circuit with the ends of his brushed-up moustache.

But Jerry Winton was not looking at Dr Hébert. He was looking at the girl. In addition to a light fur coat, she now wore a cream-coloured scarf drawn over her hair; she had in one hand a tiny box, wrapped in white paper. Her smooth, worried face, her long, pale-blue eyes, seemed to reflect the expression of the dead man staring back at her from the pavement. She jerked back, bumping into the policeman. She put her hand on Dr Hébert's arm. With her other hand she pointed sharply to Davos.

'That's the man!' she cried.

M. Goron, prefect of police, was a comfortable man, a round, cat-like, amiable sort of man, famous for his manners. Crime, rare in La Bandelette, distressed him. But he was also an able man. At one o'clock in the morning he sat in his office at the town hall examining his fingernails and creaking back and forth in a squeaky swivel chair whose noise had begun to get on Jerry Winton's nerves.

The girl, who for the tenth time had given her name as Eleanor Hood, was insistent.

'M. Goron!'

'Mademoiselle?' said the prefect politely, and seemed to wake out of a dream.

Eleanor Hood turned round and gave Jerry Winton a despairing look.

'I only wish to know,' she urged, in excellent French, 'why we are here, Dr Hébert and I. And Mr Winton too, if it comes to that.' This time the look she gave Jerry was one of smiling companionship: a human sort of look, which warmed that miscreant. 'But as for us – why? It is not as though we were witnesses. I have told you why I was at Dr Hébert's house.'

'Mademoiselle's father,' murmured M. Goron.

'Yes. He is ill. Dr Hébert has been treating him for several days, and he had another attack at the Casino tonight. Mr Winton will confirm that.'

Jerry nodded. The old boy at the table, he reflected, had certainly looked ill.

'I took my father back to our hotel, the Brittany, at half past eleven,' the girl went on, speaking with great intensity. 'I tried to communicate with Dr Hébert by telephone. I could not reach him. So I went to his house; it is only a short distance from the hotel. On the way I kept seeing that man – the man you call Davos. I thought he was following me. He seemed to be looking at me from behind every tree. That is why I said, "That's the man", when I saw him lying on the pavement with his eyes open. His eyes did not even blink when the rain struck them. It was a horrible sight. I was upset. Do you blame me?'

M. Goron made a sympathetic noise.

'I reached Dr Hébert's house at perhaps twenty minutes to twelve. Dr Hébert had retired, but he consented to go with me. I waited while he dressed. We went out, and on the doorstep we found – what you know. Please believe that is all I know about it.'

She had a singularly expressive voice and personality. She was either all anxiety or all persuasiveness, fashioning the clipped syllables. When she turned her wrist, you saw Davos lying in the rain and the searchlight wheeling over-head. Then she added abruptly in English, looking at Jerry:

'He was a nasty little beast; but I don't for a moment believe you killed him.'

'Thanks. But why?'

'I don't know,' said Eleanor simply. 'You just couldn't have!'

'Now there is logic!' cried M. Goron, giving his desk an admiring whack.

M. Goron's swivel chair creaked with pleasure. There were many lights in his office, which smelt of creosote. On the desk in front of him lay Davos's sodden wallet and (curiously) the tiny round box, wrapped in a spill of paper, which Eleanor Hood had been carrying. M. Goron never spoke to

Jerry, never looked at him; ignored him as completely and blandly as though he were not there.

'But,' he continued, growing very sober again, 'you will forgive me, mademoiselle, if I pursue this matter further. You say that Dr Hébert has been treating your father?'

'Yes.'

M. Goron pointed to the small box on the table.

'With pills, perhaps?'

'Ah, my God!' said Dr Hébert, and slapped his forehead tragically.

For several minutes Jerry had been afraid that the good doctor would have an apoplectic stroke. Dr Hébert had indicated his distinguished position in the community. He had pointed out that physicians do not go out in the middle of the night on errands of mercy, and then get dragged off to police stations; it is bad for business. His truculent eyeglasses and moustache bristling, he left off his stiff pacing of the room only to go and look the prefect in the eye.

'I *will* speak,' he said coldly, from deep in his throat.

'As monsieur pleases.'

'Well, it is as this lady says! Why are we here? Why? We are not witnesses.' He broke off, and slapped at the shoulders of his coat as though to rid himself of insects. 'This young man here tells us a story which may or may not be true. If it is true, I do not see why the man Davos should have given him *my* address. I do not see why Davos should have been knifed on my doorstep. I did not know the man Davos, except as a patient of mine.'

'Ah!' said the prefect. 'You gave him pills, perhaps?'

Dr Hébert sat down.

'Are you mad on the subject of pills?' he enquired, with restraint. 'Because this young man' — again he looked with disfavour at Jerry — 'tells you that Davos made some drunken mention of "pills" at the Casino tonight, is that why you pursue the subject?'

'It is possible.'

'It is ridiculous,' said Dr Hébert. 'Do you even question my pills on the desk there? They are for Miss Hood's father. They are ordinary tablets, with digitalin for the heart. Do you think they contain poison? If so, why not test them?'

'It is an idea,' conceded M. Goron.

He picked up the box and removed the paper.

The box contained half a dozen sugar-coated pellets. With great seriousness M. Goron put one of the tablets into his mouth, tasted it, bit it, and finally appeared to swallow it.

'No poison?' asked the doctor.

'No poison,' agreed M. Goron. The telephone on his desk rang. He picked it up, listened for a moment with a dreamy smile, and replaced it. 'Now this is really excellent!' he beamed, rubbing his hands. 'My good friend Colonel March, of the English police, has been making investigations. He was sent here when a certain form of activity in La Bandelette became intolerable both to the French and English authorities. You perhaps noticed him at the Casino tonight, all of you?'

'I remember,' said Jerry suddenly. 'Very large bloke, quiet as sin.'

'An apt description,' said the prefect.

'But—' began Dr Hébert.

'I said "all of you", Dr Hébert,' repeated the prefect. 'One small question is permitted? I thank you. When mademoiselle telephoned to your house at eleven-thirty tonight, you were not there. You were at the Casino, perhaps?'

Dr Hébert stared at him.

'It is possible. But—'

'You saw M. Davos there, perhaps?'

'It is possible.' Still Dr Hébert stared at him with hideous perplexity. 'But, M. Goron, will you have the goodness to explain this? You surely do not suspect either mademoiselle or myself of having any concern with this business? You do not think that either mademoiselle or I left the house at the time of the murder?'

'I am certain you did not.'

'You do not think either mademoiselle or myself went near a door or a window to get at this accursed Davos?'

'I am certain you did not,' beamed the prefect.

'Well, then?'

'But there, you see,' argued M. Goron, lifting one finger for emphasis, 'we encounter a difficulty. We are among thorns. For this would mean that M. Winton must have committed the murder. And that,' he added, looking at Jerry, 'is absurd. We never for a moment believed that M. Winton had anything to do with this; and my friend Colonel March will tell you why.'

Jerry sat back and studied the face of the prefect, wondering if he had heard aright. He felt like an emotional punching bag. But with great gravity he returned the prefect's nod as a *sergent de ville* opened the door of the office.

'We will spik English,' announced M. Goron, bouncing up. 'This is my friend Colonel March.'

''Evening,' said the colonel. His large, speckled face was as bland as M. Goron's; his fists were on his hips. He looked first at Eleanor, then at Jerry, then at Dr Hébert. 'Sorry you were put to this inconvenience, Miss Hood. But I've seen your father, and it will be all right. As for you, Mr Winton, I hope they have put you out of your misery?'

'Misery?'

'Told you you're not headed for Devil's Island, or anything of the sort? We had three very good reasons for believing you had nothing to do with this. Here is the first reason.'

Reaching into the pocket of his dinner jacket, he produced an article which he held out to them. It was a black leather notecase, exactly like the one already on M. Goron's desk. But whereas the first was stuffed with *mille* notes, this one had only a few hundred francs in it.

'We found this second notecase in Davos's pocket,' said Colonel March.

He seemed to wait for a comment, but none came.

'Well, what about it?' Jerry demanded, after a pause.

'Oh, come! Two notecases! Why was Davos carrying two notecases? Why should any man carry two notecases? That is my first reason. Here is my second.'

From the inside pocket of his coat, with the air of a conjurer, he drew out the knife with which Davos had been stabbed.

A suggestive sight. Now cleansed of blood, it was a long, thin, heavy blade with a light metal handle and cross-piece. As Colonel March turned it round, glittering in the light, Jerry Winton felt that its glitter struck a chord of familiarity in his mind: that a scene from the past had almost come back to him: that, for a swift and tantalizing second, he had almost grasped the meaning of the whole problem.

'And now we come to my third reason,' said Colonel March. 'The third reason is Ferdie Davos. Ferdie was a hotel thief. A great deal too clever for us poor policemen. Eh, Goron? Though I always told him he was a bad judge of men. At the height of the summer season, at hotels like the Brittany and the Donjon, he had rich pickings. He specialised in necklaces; particularly in pearl necklaces. Kindly note that.'

A growing look of comprehension had come into Eleanor Hood's face. She opened her mouth to speak, and then checked herself.

'His problem,' pursued Colonel March, 'was how to smuggle the stolen stuff over to England, where he had a market for it. He couldn't carry it himself. In a little place like La Bandelette, Goron would have had him turned inside out if he had as much as taken a step towards Boulogne. So he had to have accomplices. I mean accomplices picked from among the hordes of unattached young men who come here every season. Find some young fool who's just dropped more than he can afford at the tables; and he may grab at the chance to earn a few thousand francs by a little harmless customs bilking. You follow me, Mr Winton?'

'You mean that I was chosen——?'

'Yes.'

'But, good lord, how? I couldn't smuggle a pearl necklace through the customs if my life depended on it.'

'You could if you needed a tonic,' Colonel March pointed

out. 'Davos told you so. The necklace would first be taken to pieces for you. Each pearl would be given a thick sugar-coating, forming a neat medicinal pill. They would then be poured into a neat bottle or box under the prescription of a well-known doctor. At the height of the tourist rush, the customs can't curry-comb everybody. They would be looking for a pearl-smuggler: not for an obviously respectable young tourist with stomach trouble.'

Eleanor Hood, with sudden realisation in her face, looked at the box of pills on M. Goron's desk.

'So *that* is why you tasted my pills!' she said to the prefect of police, who made deprecating noises. 'And kept me here for so long. And—'

'Mademoiselle, I assure you!' said M. Goron. 'We were sure there was nothing wrong with those pills!' He somewhat spoiled the gallant effect of this by adding: 'There are not enough of them, for one thing. But, since you received them from Dr Hébert after office hours, you had to be investigated. The trick is neat, *hein*? I fear the firm of Hébert and Davos have been working it for some time.'

They all turned to look at Dr Hébert.

He was sitting bolt upright, his chin drawn into his collar as though he were going to sing. On his face was a look of what can only be called frightened scepticism. Even his mouth was half open with this effect, or with unuttered sounds of ridicule.

'We were also obliged to delay you all,' pursued M. Goron, 'until my men found Madame Fley's pearls, which were stolen a week ago, hidden in Dr Hébert's surgery. I repeat: it was a neat trick. We might never have seen it if Davos had not incautiously hinted at it to M. Winton. But then Davos was getting a bit above himself.' He added: 'That, Colonel March thinks, is why Dr Hébert decided to kill him.'

Still Dr Hébert said nothing.

It was, in fact, Jerry Winton who spoke. 'Sir, I don't hold any brief for this fellow. I should think you were right. But how could he have killed Davos? He couldn't have!'

'You are forgetting,' said Colonel March, as cheerfully as though the emotional temperature of the room had not gone up several degrees, 'you are forgetting the two notecases. Why was Davos carrying two notecases?'

'Well?'

'He wasn't,' said Colonel March, with his eye on Hébert. 'Our good doctor here was, of course, the brains of the partnership. He supplied the resources for Ferdie's noble front. When Ferdie played baccara at the Casino, he was playing with Dr Hébert's money. And, when Dr Hébert saw Ferdie at the Casino tonight, he very prudently took away the large sum you saw in Ferdie's notecase at the tables. When Ferdie came to the doctor's house at midnight, he had only his few hundred francs commission in his own notecase, which was in his pocket.

'You see, Dr Hébert needed that large sum of money in his plan to kill Ferdie. He knew what time Ferdie would call at his house. He knew Mr Winton would be close behind Ferdie. Mr Winton would, in fact, walk into the murder and get the blame. All Dr Hébert had to do was take that packet of *mille* notes, stuff them into another notecase just like Ferdie Davos's, and use it as a trap.'

'A trap?' repeated Eleanor.

'A trap,' said Colonel March.

'Your presence, Miss Hood,' he went on, 'gave the doctor an unexpected alibi. He left you downstairs in his house. He went upstairs to "get dressed". A few minutes before Davos was due to arrive, he went quietly up to the roof of his house – a flat roof, like most of those in La Bandelette. He looked down over the parapet into that cul-de-sac, forty feet below. He saw his own doorstep with the lamp burning over it. He dropped that notecase over the parapet, so that it landed on the pavement before his own doorstep.

'Well?' continued Colonel March. 'What would Davos do? What would *you* do, if you walked along a pavement and saw a notecase bulging with thousand-franc notes lying just in front of you?'

Again Jerry Winton saw that dim cul-de-sac. He heard the rain splashing; he saw it moving and gleaming past the door-lamp, and past the beam of the lighthouse overhead. He saw the jaunty figure of Davos stop short as though to look at something—

'I imagine,' Jerry said, 'that I'd bend over and pick up the notecase.'

'Yes,' said Colonel March. 'That's the whole sad story. You would bend over so that your body was parallel with the ground. The back of your neck would be a plain target to anybody standing forty feet up above you, with a needle-sharp knife whose blade is much heavier than the handle. The murderer has merely to drop that knife: stretch out his fingers and drop it. Gravity will do the rest.

'My friend, you looked straight at that murder; and you never saw it. You never saw it because a shifting, gleaming

72

wall of rain, a kind of silver curtain, fell across the door-lamp and the beam of the lighthouse. It hid the fall of a thin, long blade made of bright metal. Behind that curtain moved invisibly our ingenious friend Dr Hébert, who, if he can be persuaded to speak—'

Dr Hébert could not be persuaded to speak, even when they took him away. But Eleanor Hood and Jerry Winton walked home through the summer dawn, under a sky coloured with a less evil silver; and they had discovered any number of mutual acquaintances by the time they reached the hotel.

The Mouse Trap

Michael Innes

'Is that Sir John Appleby?' the voice asked. And it added, 'Of Scotland Yard?'

'Appleby speaking. But you've been put through to me at my home address.'

'I know, I know. And I'm most terribly sorry.' The voice – it appeared to be that of a lowland Scot – was quite at ease in its apology. 'I hope I haven't fetched you from your dinner.'

Appleby, who found that he had brought his table napkin with him to the telephone, said nothing. He had received this sort of call before.

'My only warrant for breaking in upon your privacy, Sir John, is a common friend. Lord Arthur Spendlove.'

'Ah, yes.' Appleby didn't precisely kindle. This gambit, too, he was familiar with.

'Arthur has told me how absolutely one can rely upon your discretion. I ought to say that my name is Macrae – Robert

Macrae.' The voice paused very briefly, as if upon this information Appleby ought decidedly not to have cast about in his mind. And, in point of fact, the name did ring a bell. Robert Macrae was a very distinguished industrial chemist, and the head of a firm of high scientific repute. 'Discretion,' the voice went on, 'is the essential thing. I want to consult you in the strictest confidence.'

'My dear sir, you speak as if I were a family solicitor or a physician or a private inquiry agent. As it happens, I'm an Assistant Commissioner of Police. I can't possibly undertake to entertain confidential communications.'

'Quite so, quite so.' The voice was now betraying a shade of agitation. 'But this is so *very* difficult a matter. Threats. Menaces. Or can it be a joke? Your experience could advise me. I'd hate to visit disgrace on what may be a mere whim or prank. But there are circumstances that make me … apprehensive. Could you run down?'

'Run down?' Appleby was so surprised that he repeated the words mechanically.

'Yes – and at once.' The voice gave an address. 'That's on the river, you know, just short of Bainton. Say forty minutes.' Suddenly the voice spoke on a new queer note. 'My God – it may be life or death to me!'

'If you consider yourself to be in some immediate danger, Dr Macrae, you should contact your local police station at once.'

'No, no – that's just what I want to avoid. But you'll come?'

'Yes, I'll come.' In saying this, Appleby felt fleetingly that he was acting almost as oddly as Macrae was. Without ceremony, he put down the receiver. Five minutes later, he was driving rapidly west.

An estate agent would have described Dr Macrae's house as standing in its own grounds. In the deepening summer dusk Appleby could just distinguish that these seemed to consist mostly of shrubberies, together with a tree-shaded lawn running down to the river at the back. A burglar's paradise, he told himself professionally as he took the last curve of the drive. The house itself was large and gloomy, and from this aspect showed only a single light – a feeble glimmer in a porch before what must be the front door. The effect wasn't welcoming.

Not that the place was at all tumbledown. There was plenty of fresh paint in a forbidding chocolate tone, and through the open doors of a garage Appleby had glimpsed a couple of opulent cars. Their owner was presumably a wealthy man. But there was no sign that he was a particularly cheerful one.

Appleby rang the bell. It was of the antique sort that peals loud and long in some remote kitchen. There was rather a lengthy wait and then the front door opened. An ancient female servant, heavily armoured in starched linen before and on top, peered at the visitor suspiciously. 'Who are ye for?' she asked in a strong Scottish accent.

'Good evening. I am Sir John Appleby. I have an appointment with Dr Macrae.'

'An appointment?' The old woman seemed to regard this claim as an occasion of increased misgiving. 'Come in, then. But ye'll hae to see Miss Hatt.'

'My appointment is with Dr Macrae himself.'

'Naebody sees the Doctor until Miss Hatt's had a worrd wi' him. This way.'

Appleby found himself in a high, dusky hall. The panelled walls were ornamented with enormous oil paintings of deer and Highland cattle, interspersed with claymores, dirks and the species of small round shield conventionally associated with Rob Roy Macgregor. It was apparent that Dr Macrae cherished his Caledonian ancestry. They moved down a long corridor and came to a closed door at the end. In the room beyond, a man was talking, fluently and incisively, to the accompaniment of a clattering typewriter. The old woman opened the door and motioned Appleby forward. 'A gentleman to see the Doctor,' she said.

The typewriter stopped, but the voice – a Scottish one – continued. It was advancing cogent reasons for being unable to subscribe to a charity organisation. Then the voice stopped too. Miss Hatt had silenced it by turning a switch on her dictaphone. 'Your name?' she said.

'Sir John Appleby.'

'You have an appointment with Dr Macrae?'

'He made an appointment with me by telephone, just an hour ago.'

Miss Hatt, although her speech was quite dauntingly severe, was personable and in early middle age. She suggested the possession of high professional proficiency, together with certain quite different qualities which might declare themselves upon appropriate occasions. At the moment, she appeared rather at a loss. Appleby guessed that his name had conveyed quite a lot to her. There was nothing surprising about that. But he rather wondered why she was so clearly perplexed by his visit. There might be half a dozen occasions for it, after all. 'Then will you wait a moment,' she asked, 'while I tell Dr Macrae you are here?'

Briskly and competently, Miss Hatt rose and left the room. Her manner was entirely as it should be; nevertheless Appleby found himself obscurely called upon to notice that her figure was excellent and her complexion really beautiful. He waited in solitude and patience – for he wasn't, as it happened, without something to think about. He waited rather a long time. And then Miss Hatt came in again. She was still brisk and competent – which made it a little odd that the beautiful complexion had vanished. Her face was pale and seemed faintly moist. 'Did you *know*?' she asked.

'I beg your pardon?'

'You *are* Sir John Appleby – of the police? When you sent me to find Dr Macrae, you knew that ... he was dead?'

The queerness of this question was almost as surprising as the news it conveyed. But it wasn't quite crazy. It was, in fact, just the sort of logic one sometimes gets from persons suffering from severe shock. 'Nothing of the sort, madam. Put such an idea out of your head.' Appleby walked up to the woman and looked at her searchingly but sympathetically. 'You have actually found Dr Macrae dead?' he asked. 'You are certain of it?'

She turned and gestured him out of the room. He could hear her taking a deep, gasping breath, as if determined to regain control of herself. 'You will be certain yourself in a moment, Sir John. Dr Macrae has been ... he has been murdered.'

They went down another corridor and through a couple of baize-covered doors. The dead man appeared to have prized seclusion. His study was a book-lined apartment, sombre like everything else in this house, and fronting the lawn that ran down to the river. A french window was open upon the warm July night, and directly before this the body of Robert Macrae sat at a large desk. Appleby walked round this. 'Or perhaps,' he heard Miss Hatt say behind him, 'it might be suicide?'

It certainly hadn't been that. Macrae had been shot clean through the forehead at just short of point-blank range. His assailant had presumably walked up to the french window out of the darkness, killed his man, and walked away again. Appleby frowned. He didn't like the simplicity of the thing. It is the elaborately conceived murder that it is easier to get a grip on. 'Suicide?' he said, and turned to Miss Hatt. He spoke as if with an entirely open mind. 'It comes into your head as likely? Was Dr Macrae a sick man, or worried?'

'His arthritis was troubling him, and he found it rather difficult to get about. But I don't think it seriously worried him. Of course, he had been working very hard. He and Mr Ivor – that is his nephew, Ivor Macrae – have been on the verge of some extremely important discovery – a chemical process which would revolutionise man-made fibres.'

'I see. Does Mr Ivor Macrae live here?'

'No, not now.' Miss Hatt hesitated. 'Only Mr Colin lives in the house. He is Mr Ivor's brother.'

'And also a chemist?'

'Colin – Mr Colin – is an author.'

'Ah, an author.' Appleby, intent on examining the body,

seemed to repeat the word absently. But he was really wondering if he had been right in detecting a note of warmth in Miss Hatt's voice. 'But Mr Ivor too lived here until recently?'

Miss Hatt nodded. She was standing quite still near the door. It wasn't necessary to tell her not to wander about. As well as a good figure she had a good head. 'Yes,' she said. 'But now Mr Ivor has a cottage of his own just up the river. He had a – a dispute with his uncle. It has been a great worry to Dr Macrae, particularly as they work so closely together at the laboratories.'

'A professional dispute?'

'No. It has been entirely a family matter. Mr Ivor's father left a peculiar will, giving the control of very considerable property to Dr Macrae during his lifetime. Mr Ivor has felt the position to be increasingly absurd. As a result there was – well, almost a quarrel.'

Appleby looked hard at Miss Hatt. 'And now' – and he pointed with a certain grimness at the dead man – 'Mr Ivor will get what he has wanted?'

'I suppose so.'

'And Mr Colin too?'

Just perceptibly, Miss Hatt hesitated. She was still quite startlingly pale. 'Oh, certainly. But, of course, he didn't break with his uncle in any way. I don't think property and money mean very much to Mr Colin Macrae. As I've said, he is an author – an artist.'

'That makes a difference, no doubt.' Permitting himself this fleeting irony, Appleby took a prowl around the room. 'Is Mr Colin at home now?'

Miss Hatt was about to reply when there was an

interruption. Abruptly out of the night, a man had appeared at the french window. 'Hullo,' he said. 'Who's t-t-talking about m-me?'

It couldn't be said, Appleby reflected a few minutes later, that Colin Macrae took his uncle's sudden and shocking death very hard. But then it seemed likely that he didn't take things in general that way. He was easy-going, loquacious despite his pronounced stammer, and possessed of a personal modesty that Appleby didn't seem to recall as a very regular endowment of authors. And there was certainly something between him and Miss Hatt. He would do a lot for her, Appleby guessed. And perhaps she would do even more for him.

'B-b-but doesn't Ivor know?' Colin turned enquiringly to Miss Hatt. 'He hasn't b-been over?'

'Certainly he has been over. I came upon him with Dr Macrae in this room half an hour ago.' Miss Hatt was now impassive. 'So it surprised me that Dr Macrae had made an appointment with Sir John. But when I came to tell Dr Macrae of Sir John's arrival, Mr Ivor, of course, wasn't here. There was only … the body.'

A moment's silence succeeded upon this. It was broken by Appleby. 'When he came to see his uncle, Mr Ivor was in the habit of simply walking in?'

'Yes. Or sometimes he would drop down the river in his dinghy and walk across the lawn.'

'He had that familiar habit, despite the quarrel?'

'I wouldn't c-c-call it a quarrel.' Colin Macrae had broken in, suddenly eager. 'It's t-t-too strong a word. But Ivor is no good at p-personal relations. Too intellectual and h-h-highly strung. B-brains all the time. Archaeology instead of g-g-golf. Chess problems, and competitions in high-brow weeklies, instead of thrillers and the p-p-pools. The P-p-proceedings of the Royal Society as a b-bed-time book.' Colin paused, as if vaguely aware of rambling. 'N-n-not quarrelsome – n-n-not really.'

'But he *did* quarrel with Dr Macrae, all the same.' Miss Hatt's impassivity had hardened.

'Were they quarrelling when you came upon them half an hour ago?' Appleby asked this question gently.

Miss Hatt had one of her moments of fleeting irresolution. 'Dr Macrae was denying something. I heard him say, rather hotly, "I don't know what you're talking about." I had taken Dr Macrae one or two letters to sign. But it was clearly an awkward moment, and I came away at once.'

Again there was a silence. This time it was broken by the *purr-purr* of a telephone on the desk. There was something indefinably sinister in this summons addressed to an ear now sealed by death. Appleby brought a handkerchief from his pocket and picked up the receiver gingerly in its folds. He listened for some moments in silence. 'Unfortunately not,' he said. 'I am, in fact, a police officer ... I regret to have to tell you of Dr Macrae's sudden death ... Yes, death ... Yes, I think you very usefully might ... At once? But certainly. Come right over now.' He put down the receiver and stood motionless for a moment, frowning. He might have been trying to make sense of something he had heard. 'Somebody called Cokayne,' he said presently. 'Declares himself to have rung up Dr Macrae because he felt uneasy.'

'Uneasy?' Miss Hatt spoke sharply.

'Yes – but he didn't explain himself further. He's coming along, however, straight away. A colleague, I gather.'

'The principal research assistant, working closely with Dr Macrae and Mr Ivor. He lives in the village.' Miss Hatt was now composed and once more entirely business-like. 'Ought we not to try to contact Mr Ivor, Sir John?'

'His cottage is on the telephone? Then would you mind, Miss Hatt, going to another instrument, and trying to get him on that? I want this one handled as little as possible. And get the local police station at the same time, and tell the fellow on duty what's happened. And tell him that I'm here. He'll know how to proceed.' Appleby waited until the secretary had left the room, and then turned to Colin Macrae. 'Is there – or was there – anything very valuable in this room?'

Colin shook his head. 'I d-d-don't think so. All my uncle's things were s-s-solid, but not really good. He had no t-t-taste whatever.' Colin paused to glance at the body. 'And the s-s-set-up doesn't suggest his coming upon a thief.'

'Perfectly true.' Appleby was now systematically searching the room. 'There's nothing,' he said suddenly and sharply, 'you ought to tell me?'

'I d-d-don't think so.' Colin seemed unperturbed by the abrupt question.

'Do you think Miss Hatt knows anything?'

'It's not my business to speak for her.'

'But you might be described as in one another's confidence?'

'That's quite irrelevant. I won't d-discuss it.'

Appleby looked curiously at Colin Macrae. 'Very well.

But we don't yet know what *is* relevant. This is a complicated affair.'

'I'd have thought it rather a s-s-simple one.'

'That was my way of thinking, until a few minutes ago.' Appleby was walking over to the fireplace – in which, despite the mildness of the summer night, a low fire was burning. 'But now I've changed my mind.' For a moment he stood quite still, staring into the small dull glow. Suddenly he stooped and fished something from a corner of the grate. It was a piece of charred paper.

'Have you found a c-c-clue, Sir John?' Colin Macrae, who a moment before had been reticent and dry, now spoke almost mockingly.

'It looks to be precisely that, doesn't it?' Appleby's reply was in the same tone. Nevertheless it was with an absorbed seriousness that he carried his find to a table, smoothed it out, and studied it. He studied it for a long time. Then he brought a notebook from his pocket, tore out a couple of leaves, and with these covered all but a narrow strip of the paper. 'What I have found is part of a letter,' he said. 'Would you mind coming over and looking at it?'

Colin crossed the room silently and looked. Having done so, he showed no disposition to speak.

'Perhaps you can tell me whose writing this is?'

'It isn't c-c-clear to me that I ought to offer an opinion – or discuss the matter f-further with you at all, Sir John.'

'I'm not asking for an opinion. I'm asking for assured knowledge, if you happen to have it.'

'V-v-very well. It is my brother's writing – Ivor's writing.'

'Thank you. And can you—'

Appleby paused as Miss Hatt entered the room again. They both turned to her expectantly. 'I got the police,' she said. 'But there was no reply from Mr Ivor. I wonder whether—'

Suddenly she broke off with a startled cry. Following her gaze, both men swung round.

Someone else was now standing in the french window. It was a young woman. She could scarcely have been more than twenty. She was staring at the dead man with a look of transfixed horror. And then she cried out. 'Ivor ... Ivor – where are you?' She looked round the brightly lit room helplessly, and began to sway oddly on her feet. Making a dive forward, Appleby caught her as she fainted away.

The local police had come, and with them the police surgeon. Presently there would be detectives and photographers. Appleby had dismissed Miss Hatt and Colin Macrae for the moment, and had himself withdrawn into another room. The latest arrival had been quickly restored to consciousness. But there seemed to be no reason why she should be interviewed in the presence of the corpse. Her name was Joyce Hereward. Once calm and reassured, she gave an entirely coherent account of herself. But she remained in a considerable state of anxiety, all the same.

'Ivor Macrae and I are engaged. We are to be married this autumn. I live with my parents just beyond the village. Ivor and I go on the river a lot. He has a dinghy for messing about, and also a small motor-launch. This evening we were going to take a late picnic out in the launch. So I told my parents, and walked over to the cottage.'

Joyce Hereward paused. She had felt it important, Appleby thought, to get in that bit about her parents. She was very young, and almost certainly wholly ingenuous. 'You had arranged this picnic some time ago?' Appleby asked.

'Yes, indeed. I've been looking forward to it all week!' For the first time Miss Hereward faintly smiled. 'But just as we set out, Ivor was brought a telephone message, asking him to call on his uncle. We decided to do it on the way. So we tied up at the landing-stage here, and Ivor walked up to the house. I waited in the launch. We thought he wouldn't be long.'

'There was no suggestion that you might come up to the house too?'

'No. Of course I know – I mean I knew – Dr Macrae. But we thought it would just be business. And then there was the fact—' The girl hesitated and fell awkwardly silent.

'You mean the fact that your uncle and your fiancé had ceased to be on very good terms?'

'Yes.' She nodded, at once apprehensive and grateful. 'So I stopped. But it was quite a long time, after all. And then I thought I heard somebody – a man – cry out for help. It was getting nearly dark. I tried to persuade myself that what I had heard was something quite different – just somebody giving an ordinary sort of shout. So I went on waiting. But Ivor didn't come, and didn't come. Suddenly I became frightened. So I landed and walked up to the house. The light in the study window seemed to – to suggest security, and I made straight for it. I told myself I'd find Dr Macrae and Ivor just talking away. But you know what I *did* find.'

Appleby nodded kindly. 'Yes, indeed. And I am very sorry that you had the shock.'

Suddenly the girl's lip quivered. 'But Ivor! Please, please, what has happened to him?'

It took Appleby a second to know how to meet this appeal. 'That,' he said gravely, 'is something that I think we shall know quite soon.'

'He wouldn't be ... suspected? Ivor could never do a thing like that.'

'I'm afraid that everybody concerned, Miss Hereward, must in some degree be suspected – until we clear the matter up.'

'Can I help?' She was suddenly eager.

And once more Appleby produced his crumpled piece of paper. This time he concealed no part of it. 'Is this your fiancé's handwriting?'

She glanced at it only for a moment. 'Yes, it is.' She looked pitifully up at him, as if hoping to discover that this was good news. What she saw made her shrink a little. 'It can't mean anything bad?'

'Its meaning – or its significance – is obscure to me, Miss Hereward. And that, perhaps, is something. For it ought, you see, to be as damnably clear as daylight.'

'You mean—?'

Appleby shook his head. And as he did so, the front doorbell pealed. 'At least,' he said, 'we're making progress. For here, I think, is the last of our *dramatis personae*. Will you go and join Miss Hatt for a little? I must see this fellow on his own.'

Charles Cokayne was smooth and featureless. Quite soon after a casual meeting, one would probably recall only that he had a cold grey eye.

'Why was I uneasy?' He made a small restrained gesture. 'It is this family quarrel. For months it has been upsetting the relations of Dr Macrae with his nephew Ivor. That has been very bad for our work.'

'And the work is very important just now? There is a big discovery pending?'

Cokayne smiled faintly. 'That is the sort of story that is always going round. One day – perhaps, yes. But my chiefs, I think, had still rather a long way to go. And the friction between them didn't help.'

'I see. And your uneasiness—'

'What I have feared is the secretary here, Miss Hatt. She is secretly passionate on Colin Macrae's behalf. And I believe her to be very unscrupulous. Yesterday I heard from Ivor Macrae that she had betrayed herself in a flash of temper as keyed up to any mischief. So I have been worried. And this evening I thought I would ring up Dr Macrae, and then come across and have a serious word with him about the situation.'

'You were on terms with him that made that an appropriate course? He would have welcomed your intervention and counsel?'

Cokayne made his small gesture again. 'I could only hope so, Sir John.'

'You had no worries, no suspicions, about Ivor Macrae?'

'But certainly not!' Cokayne was emphatic. 'Ivor is rash, and he had this open break with his uncle. But I have worked for him and with him for years, and I would never believe ill of him.'

'That is very gratifying.' And once again Appleby fished the enigmatic scrap of paper from his pocket. 'You would agree that this fragment of a letter is in Ivor Macrae's hand? I wonder, Mr Cokayne, if you would oblige me by reading it – aloud?'

Cokayne raised his eyebrows – as well he might at this slightly strange request. Appleby wondered whether the action didn't reveal in the eyes themselves some glint of excitement. In Cokayne's hand, however, there was no tremor as he took the charred and crumpled paper. And what he read was in an even, carefully expressionless voice:

'My dear Uncle,
'You have twenty-four hours. If this surprises you, the fault is mine for hesitating as I have done. But if you have come to think of me as a man who cannot make up his mind, then you are, believe me, fatally wrong. Give up what you have unjustly taken, or you will not live to enjoy even what is rightfully yours. And decide within, I say, twenty ...'

There was a moment's silence when Cokayne had finished reading the fragment. Then Appleby, who had been listening with a curiously strained attention, took back the paper. 'Well,' he asked, 'does this sound as if it's Miss Hatt who's for the Old Bailey?'

'No ... it doesn't.' Cokayne spoke hesitantly, as if his mind were groping its way into a new situation. 'It sounds like something quite different.'

'And that is?'

'Insanity!' Cokayne came out with the word vehemently. 'Ivor Macrae could never turn into a calculating criminal – but he might, I suppose, turn into a madman. We can all testify that he is an intensely highly strung intellectual type, who might conceivably—'

'Quite so.' Appleby cut this short almost harshly. 'The question is, where are we now? What happens to a man who writes this' – and he tapped the paper – 'proceeds to act on it lethally, and then, on retrieving it, tosses it carefully to the side of a feeble fire?'

Cokayne produced a handkerchief and nervously dabbed at his lips and forehead. 'It's too terrible. It's an abomination. And that poor girl to whom he's engaged! But there's only one answer to your question. A man in that position has no future. And he'd be very mad indeed if he didn't know it.'

'But you'd call this whole notion of Dr Macrae's wrongfully holding on to family property a bit crazy?'

'I know nothing about the rights and wrongs of the matter. But, looking at it in the light of what's happened, I can see that Ivor has been quite irrationally obsessed with it … I suppose a search is being organised?'

'Not yet. But it will be, within the next ten minutes.' Appleby spoke grimly. 'And I think that – dead or alive – we'll find Ivor Macrae quite soon.'

'If I can give any help, I'll be glad. Miss Hatt has my telephone number.'

'Thank you.' Appleby, as if he had lost interest in Charles Cokayne, was already moving towards the door, with the charred letter held slightly out before him. It was almost as if he felt it to be in the strictest sense a clue, which his hand must follow if he was to gain the heart of the labyrinth.

Colin Macrae, Miss Hatt and Joyce Hereward were together

in a large, bleak drawing room at the front of the house. If it wasn't cheerful, at least it didn't harbour a corpse. The two women were conversing in low tones, and Colin was moodily turning the pages of a weekly paper. The young girl sprang to her feet as soon as Appleby entered. 'Is there any news?'

'No – but it isn't news that's needed, Miss Hereward. It's some piece of logical inference – probably perfectly simple in itself – that I just haven't got round to.' As he made this candid report, Appleby moved restlessly across the room. 'Mr Macrae, what do you think of that fellow Cokayne?'

'I d-d-don't like him.' The answer was prompt.

'Then you'll be glad to know I've discovered something he may have difficulty in accounting for. Unfortunately it seems inconsequent. It just doesn't fit in with … this.' And Appleby tossed his letter on the table. 'By the way, you'd better read the whole of it.'

Colin Macrae threw down his weekly and moved over to read the letter. 'I c-c-can't believe it,' he said.

For a moment the two men looked at the fragmentary letter in silence. And then Appleby stiffened. 'I can!' he exclaimed. 'I believe I can – at last.'

'You mean you know what h-happened?'

'I think I do. I think the explanation may have been – well, under your very nose not long ago. Just let me take a look—' Appleby broke off as the door opened and a police sergeant came hurriedly into the room. 'Yes?'

'We've lost our man, sir.' The sergeant was rueful. 'He was on the drive, and must have tumbled to what was happening, and taken alarm at it. We think he slipped into the shrubbery and doubled back towards the river. One of our constables says he heard someone trying to start up a motor-launch there.'

'That's bad.' Appleby wasted no further time in recrimination, but turned to Colin Macrae. 'You keep a launch here yourselves?'

'Yes – and it's in g-g-good order. I w-was out in it this afternoon.'

'If we can get it moving within three or four minutes, we've some chance of averting a tragedy. Lead the way.'

And they all tumbled from the room. But Appleby – rather surprisingly – spared seconds to sweep up a pile of newspapers and periodicals that lay on a window seat. He was still clutching these as he doubled across the lawn.

Ivor Macrae's launch had vanished; it seemed plain that somebody had made his escape in it. But there appeared to be a chance that he was not yet far away, since the sound of an engine could just be heard fading down the river. The fugitive – Appleby thought grimly as he watched Colin unlock a boathouse – was doing rather more than just bolting. In fact he was still out to win. And that had meant an operation – at which Appleby could at last pretty confidently guess – by which his departure had been hazardously delayed. But if he now succeeded in doing what he was minded to do, he might get away with a lot. For it mightn't be very easy to prove—

Colin's launch glided to the landing-stage and Appleby jumped in. Joyce Hereward did the same, and there was no time to expostulate. The engine roared and the vessel leapt forward. In the same instant Colin switched on a powerful searchlight in its bow, and a long reach of the river before them flashed into view. Here and there were the dim lights of vessels moored or anchored, and a few craft were still cruising through the soft summer night. Their own speed increased; a long curling wake was flying out from their stern; now and then Appleby thought he could hear indignant shouts. No doubt they were causing a sort of disturbance that the Thames Conservancy Board wouldn't much care for. But it wasn't a moment for worrying about that.

'Ten minutes!' Bending slightly forward, Colin was shouting in Appleby's ear. 'We'll b-b-be up with him inside that.'

Appleby nodded, and felt in his pocket for a torch. Switching it on, and wedging himself securely against a thwart, he began rapidly to sort through his bundle of papers and journals. He caught Joyce Hereward staring at him in astonishment. 'All right!' he called to her. 'I'm pretty sure. But I just want to be certain ... Ah!' He had found what he wanted, and within a couple of seconds he appeared to be satisfied. 'Really simple – as all truly devilish plans are.' He glanced at her with compassion. 'I'm afraid there's – well, a crisis ahead. It will come when that launch passes under the first bridge.'

'But that's almost at once! The railway—'

Colin Macrae gave a shout. 'There he is! But he's crazy. He'll k-kill himself and—'

'The bridge!' Joyce Hereward was pointing forward. Appleby could now see, first, the fugitive launch, leaping and swerving madly on the surface of the river; and then, dimly and uncertainly beyond, two stone arches. A moment later the leading launch had plunged beneath one of them, seeming to miss by a hair's breadth the massive central pier. And in the same instant something could be seen hurled overboard.

Colin had cut out his engine, and their own speed was slackening. Appleby got to his feet, scanning the surface of the water. 'There!' he cried – and dived. And even as he hit the water, he knew that the girl – as if prompted by some flash of intuition – had dived too.

When Colin Macrae, having lost sufficient speed to turn, swept back up river, it was to find Appleby and Joyce Hereward supporting in the water the inert body of a young man. With a good deal of difficulty, they were all got on board.

'Is he—?' The girl, kneeling in a puddle in the launch, looked imploringly at Appleby as he presently knelt beside the unconscious figure of Ivor Macrae.

And Appleby smiled. 'A little the worse for wear, Miss Hereward. But he's decidedly alive – and a perfectly innocent and honourable man.'

Miss Hatt, not having been in at what was so nearly the death of Ivor, had to be given explanations next day.

'You remember the charred letter?' Appleby asked. 'In it, the writer described himself as a man who couldn't make up his mind. Now, who is famous for just that?'

'Hamlet.' Miss Hatt answered without a moment's hesitation.

'Precisely. And the simple explanation of the whole thing ought to have jumped at me at once. But it didn't – until, in the drawing room last night, I saw Colin happening to turn over a copy of a weekly paper: *The New Spokesman*. And then I remembered. Ivor was in the habit of doing the competitions in that sort of paper. So I grabbed a pile of recent ones as I ran for that launch. And this is what I found, in the last *Spokesman* but one. Listen.' And Appleby read:

'Prince Hamlet, having set the players to present *The Murder of Gonzago* and thus neatly caught the conscience of the king, unfortunately falls a prey to hysteria and loses his grip of the situation. A prize of two guineas is offered for a letter addressed by the Prince to his uncle at this point, cogently arguing that the game is up and he had better abdicate quietly.'

Miss Hatt needed only a second to consider. 'Cokayne found Ivor's unfinished attempt at the competition?'

'Just that. And he saw that it could be passed off as an incriminating letter from Ivor to *his* uncle, which would fit neatly into this bit of trouble about family property. That gave him his idea.'

'I see. But what was his motive?'

'You set me on the track of that yourself. Dr Macrae and Ivor were on the verge of perfecting a valuable chemical process, and Cokayne was their chief assistant. If he could liquidate both of them he would be able, after a discreet interval, to come forward with it as his own. I noticed that when I mentioned this piece of research to him, he at once played it down. His cunning was notable all the way through. He professed that it was you he suspected, and he gave Ivor a high character – while at the same time starting the notion that he might be subject to serious mental disturbance. But his real flair was for timing. His mouse trap was a much more intricate affair than Hamlet's. And it almost came off pat.'

Miss Hatt considered. 'His first job was to get Ivor and yourself onstage at just the right moment?'

'Precisely … And while getting Ivor with a false message was comparatively easy, the getting me out here was tricky. The request was so queer – so cool, you might say – that I rather surprised myself by agreeing to it.'

'Why did he have to have you at all, Sir John?'

'He wanted an expert who wouldn't miss that letter planted in the fireplace. And, of course, the notion of Dr Macrae's sending an alarmed appeal to the police was a useful one. What he didn't reckon on was my hearing Dr Macrae's real voice on your dictaphone. I felt at once it didn't square with the voice on the telephone. There was a moment when I thought of Colin Macrae as having conceivably sent that, but I at once realised that his stammer ruled him out as impersonating his uncle. Then when Cokayne rang up and I took the call, I had an obscure feeling that here the actual voice might be. But it was only when I'd got Cokayne to read the letter aloud that I was certain. It was my first important discovery. Cokayne was deeply, although still quite obscurely, implicated.

'And now, consider the sequence of events. Ivor arrived by launch and went up to his uncle's study, where you saw him. The uncle and nephew were at cross-purposes – and what you heard, of course, was Dr Macrae denying that he had sent any summons. But before they got any further, Cokayne, lurking in the garden, gave his dramatic shout for help. Ivor dashed out, while Dr Macrae, being crippled, stayed put. Cokayne stunned Ivor, returned to the study, shot Dr Macrae, and planted the letter. Then he returned to Ivor, and hauled him down to the river. His plan was to take him away in his own craft and stage a suicide by drowning. But it had to be near a bridge.'

'A bridge?' Miss Hatt, although so acute, was at a loss here.

'Because of that blow on Ivor's head. It must appear that he had thrown himself down from a height, and hit a pier or buttress. And now there was a first hitch: Joyce Hereward. Her presence in the launch was the unexpected factor. So Cokayne hauled Ivor into shadow, tied him up, and waited. And the wait was his undoing. He became nervous and felt – as criminals so often do – that he must have a look at the scene of the crime and make sure that all was going according to plan there. So he hurried home and made that odd call about being uneasy. He certainly *was* uneasy. Then he waited a little longer, and came up to the house. The discovery that the girl was now there, and the launch therefore deserted, gave him fresh confidence. So he played his part very well.'

'He certainly did. But he must have been on tenterhooks to get away.'

'Quite so. And he must have made a shrewd guess that he'd be watched, and that the position was pretty desperate. But if he could just get Ivor where he still wanted him, he had a chance of pulling the thing off even now. There was still that damning letter. But he failed.'

Miss Hatt was silent for a moment. 'We are to be faced with the horrors of a murder trial?'

'No.' Appleby shook his head seriously. 'You haven't heard the end. After hurling Ivor overboard, Cokayne lost his nerve completely. As a result, he smashed the launch to matchwood against the next bridge, and was drowned. The engineer – as Hamlet, once more, has it – was hoist with his own petard.'

The Mystery of the Russian Prince

Baroness Orczy

1

There had been a great deal of talk about that time, in newspapers and among the public, of the difficulty an inexperienced criminal finds in disposing of the evidences of his crime – notably of course of the body of his victim. In no case perhaps was this difficulty so completely overcome – at any rate as far as was publicly known – as in that of the murder of the individual known as Prince Orsoff. I am thus qualifying his title because as a matter of fact the larger public never believed that he was a genuine Prince – Russian or otherwise – and that even if he had not come by such a violent and tragic death the Smithsons would never have seen either their £10,000 again, or poor Louisa's aristocratic bridegroom.

I had been thinking a great deal about this mysterious affair; indeed it had been discussed at most of the literary and journalistic clubs as a possible subject for a romance or drama, and it was with deliberate intent that I walked over to Fleet Street that afternoon in order to catch the Man in the Corner in his accustomed tea shop and get him to give me his views on the subject of the mystery that to this very day surrounds the murder of the Russian Prince.

'Let me just put the whole case before you,' the funny creature began as soon as I had led him to talk upon the subject, 'as far as it was known to the general public. It all occurred in Folkestone, you remember, where the wedding of Louisa Smithson, the daughter of a late retired grocer, to a Russian Prince whom she had met abroad, was the talk of the town.

'It was on a lovely day in May, and the wedding ceremony was to take place at Holy Trinity Church. The Smithsons – mother and daughter – especially since they had come into a fortune, were very well known in Folkestone, and there was a large crowd of relatives and friends inside the church and another out in the street to watch the arrival of guests and to see the bride. There were camera men and newspaper men, and hundreds of idlers and visitors, and the police had much ado to keep the crowd in order.

'Mrs Smithson had already arrived looking gorgeous in what I understand is known as amethyst *crêpe-de-chine*, and there was a marvellous array of Bond Street gowns and gorgeous headgears, all of which kept the lookers-on fully occupied during the traditional quarter of an hour's grace usually accorded to the bride. But presently those fifteen minutes became twenty, the clergy had long since arrived, the guests had all assembled, the bridesmaids were waiting in the porch: but there was no bridegroom. Neither he nor his best man had arrived; and now it was half an hour after the time appointed for the ceremony, and, oh, horror! – the bride's car was in sight. The bride in church waiting for the bridegroom! – such an outrage had not been witnessed in Folkestone within the memory of the oldest inhabitant. One of the guests went at once to break the news to the elderly relative who had arranged to give the bride away, and who was with her in the car, while another, a Mr Sutherland Ford, jumped into the first available taxi, having volunteered to go to the station in order to ascertain whether there had been any breakdown on the line, as the bridegroom was coming down by train from London with his best man.

'The bride, hastily apprised of the extraordinary contretemps, remained in the car, with the blinds pulled down, well concealed from the prying eyes of the crowd, while the fashionable guests, relatives and friends had perforce to possess their souls in patience.

'And presently the news fell like a bombshell in the midst of this lively throng. A taxi drove up and from it alighted first Mr Sutherland Ford, who had volunteered to go to the station for information, and then John and Henry Carter, the two latter beautifully got up, in frock coats, striped trousers, top hats, and flowers in their buttonholes, looking obviously like belated wedding guests. But still no bridegroom, and no best man. The three gentlemen, paying no heed to the shower of questions that assailed them, as soon as they had jumped out of the taxi ran straight into the church, leaving everyone's curiosity unsatisfied and public excitement at fever pitch. "It was John and Henry Carter," the ladies whispered agitatedly; "fancy their being asked to the wedding!"

'And those who were in the know whispered to those who were less favoured that young Henry had at one time been engaged to Louisa Smithson, before she met her Russian Prince, and that when she threw him over he was in such dire despair that his friends thought he would commit suicide.

'A moment or two later Mrs Smithson was seen hurriedly coming out of church, her face pale and drawn, and her beautiful hat all awry. She made straight for the bride's car, stepped into it, and the car immediately drove off, while the wedding guests trooped out of the church and the terrible news spread like wildfire through the crowd and was presently all over the town. It seems that when the midday train, London to Folkestone, stopped at Swanley Junction, two passengers who were about to enter a first-class compartment in one of the corridor carriages were horrified to find it in a terrible state of disorder. They hastily called the guard, and on examination the carriage looked indeed as if it had been the scene of a violent struggle: the door on the off side was unlatched, two of the window straps were wrenched off, the antimacassars were torn off the cushions, one of the luggage racks was broken and the net hung down in strips, and over some of the cushions were marks unmistakably made by a bloodstained hand.

'The guard immediately locked the compartment and sent for the local police. No one was allowed in or out of the station until every passenger on the train had satisfied the police as to his or her identity. Thus the train was held up for over two hours while preliminary investigations were going on. There appeared no doubt that a terrible murder had been committed, and telephonic communication all along the line presently established the fact that it must have been done somewhere in the neighbourhood of Sydenham Hill, because a group of men who were at work on the up side of the line at Penge when the down train came out of the tunnel noticed that the door of one of the first-class carriages was open. It swung to again just before the train steamed through the station. A preliminary search was at once made in and about the tunnel; it revealed on the platform of Sydenham Hill station a first-class single ticket of that day's issue, London to Folkestone, crushed and stained with blood, and on the permanent way, close to the entrance of the tunnel on the Penge side, a soft black hat, and a broken pair of pince-nez. But as to the identity of the victim there was for the moment no clue.

'After a couple of wearisome and anxious hours the passengers were allowed to proceed on their journey. Among these passengers, it appears, were John and Henry Carter, who were on their way to the Smithson wedding. Until they arrived in Folkestone they had no more idea than the police who the victim of the mysterious train murder was: but in the station they caught sight of Mr Sutherland Ford, whom they knew slightly. Mr Ford was making agitated enquiries as to any possible accident on the line. The Carters put him *au fait* of what had occurred, and as there was no sign of the Russian Prince among the passengers who had just arrived, all three men came to the horrifying conclusion that it was indeed the bridegroom-elect who had been murdered. They communicated at once with the police, and there were more investigations and telephonic messages up and down the line before the Carters and Mr Ford were at last allowed to proceed to the church and break the awful news to those most directly concerned.

'And in this tragic fashion did Louisa Smithson's wedding day draw to its end; nor, as far as the public was concerned, was the mystery of that terrible murder ever satisfactorily cleared up. The local police worked very hard and very systematically, but, though presently they also had the help of one of the ablest detectives from Scotland Yard, nothing was seen or found that gave the slightest clue either as to the means which the murderer or murderers adopted for removing the body of their victim, or in what manner they made good their escape.'

The body of the Russian Prince was never found, and, as far as the public knows, the murderer is still at large; and although, as time went on, many strange facts came to light, they only helped to plunge that extraordinary crime into darker mystery.

2

'The facts in themselves were curious enough, you will admit,' the Man in the Corner went on after a while; 'many of these were never known to the public, while others found their way into the columns of the halfpenny press, who battened on the "Mystery of the Russian Prince" for weeks on end, and, as far as the unfortunate Smithsons were concerned, there was not a reader of the *Express Post* and kindred newspapers who did not know the whole of their family history.

'It seems that Louisa Smithson is the daughter of a grocer in Folkestone who had retired from business just before the War, and with his wife and his only child led a meagre and obscure existence in a tiny house in Warren Avenue somewhere near the tram road. They were always supposed to be very poor, but suddenly old Smithson died and it turned out that he had been a miser, for he left the handsome little fortune of £15,000 to be equally divided between his daughter and his widow.

'At once Mrs Smithson and Louisa found themselves the centre of an admiring throng of friends and relatives, all eager to help them spend their money for their especial benefit; but Mrs Smithson was shrewd enough not to allow herself to be exploited by those who in the past had never condescended to more than a bowing acquaintance with her. She turned her back on most of those sycophants, but at the same time she was determined to do the best for herself and Louisa, and to this end she admitted into her councils her sister, Margaret Penny, who was saleswoman at a fashionable shop in London, and who immediately advised a journey up to town so that the question of clothes might at once be satisfactorily settled.

'In addition to valuable advice on that score, this Miss Penny seems to have succeeded in completely turning her sister's head. Certain it is that Mrs Smithson left Folkestone a quiet, sensible, motherly woman, and that she returned, six weeks later, an arrogant, ill-mannered parvenue, who seemed to think that the possession of a few thousand pounds entitled her to ride roughshod over the feelings and sentiments of those who had less money than herself.

'She began by taking a suite of rooms at the Splendid Hotel for herself, her daughter and her maid, then she sold her house in Warren Avenue, bought a car, and, though she and Louisa were of course in deep mourning, they were to be seen everywhere in wonderful Bond Street dresses and marvellous feathered hats. Finally they announced their intention of spending the coming winter on the Riviera, probably Monte Carlo.

'All this extravagant behaviour made some people smile, others shrugged their shoulders and predicted disaster: but there was one who suffered acutely through this change in the fortune of the Smithsons. This was Henry Carter, a young clerk employed in an insurance office in London. He and his brother were Folkestone men, sons of a local tailor in a very small way of business, who had been one of old Smithson's rare friends. The elder Carter boy had long since cut his stick and was said to be earning a living in London by freelance journalism. The younger one, Henry, remained to help his father with the tailoring. He was a constant visitor in the little house in Warren Avenue, and presently became engaged to Louisa. There could be no question of an imme-diate marriage, of course, as Henry had neither money nor prospects; however, presently old Carter died, the tailor-ing business was sold for a couple of hundred pounds, and Henry went up to London to join his brother and to seek his fortune. Presently he obtained a post in an insurance office, but his engagement to Louisa subsisted: the young people were known to be deeply in love with one another and Henry spent most weekends and all his holidays in Folkestone in order to be near his girl.

'Then came the change in the fortune of the Smithsons and an immediate coolness in Louisa's manner towards young Henry. It was all very well in the past to be engaged to the son of a jobbing tailor, while one was poor oneself, and one had neither wit nor good looks, but now …!

'In fact already when they were in London Mrs Smithson had intimated to Henry Carter that his visits were none too welcome, and when he appealed to Louisa she put him off with a few curt words. The young man was in despair, and, indeed, his brother actually feared at one time that he would commit suicide.

'It was soon after Christmas of that same year that the curtain was rung up on the first act of the mysterious tragedy which was destined to throw a blight for ever after upon the life of Louisa Smithson. It began with the departure of herself and her mother for the Continent, where they intended to remain until the end of March. For the first few weeks their friends had no news of them, but presently Miss Margaret Penny, who had kept up a desultory correspondence with a pal of hers in Folkestone, started to give glowing accounts of the Smithsons' doings in Monte Carlo. They were staying at the Hôtel de Paris, paying two hundred francs a day for their rooms alone. They were lunching and dining out every day of the week; they had been introduced to one or two of the august personages who usually graced the Riviera with their presence at this time of the year; and they had met a number of interesting people. According to Miss Penny's account, Louisa Smithson was being greatly admired, and in fact several titled gentlemen of various nationalities had professed themselves deeply enamoured of her.

'All this Miss Penny recounted in her letters to her friends, with a wealth of detail and a marvellous profusion of adjectives, and finally in one of her letters there was mention of a certain Russian grandee – Prince Orsoff by name – who was paying Louisa marked attention. He also was staying at the "Paris", appeared very wealthy, and was obviously of very high rank for he never mixed with the crowd which was more than usually brilliant this year in Monte Carlo. This exclusiveness on his part was all the more flattering to the Smithsons, and, when he apprised them of his intention to spend the season in London, they had asked him to come and visit them in Folkestone, where Mrs Smithson intended to take a house presently and there to entertain lavishly during the summer.

'After this preliminary announcement from Miss Penny, Louisa herself wrote a letter to Henry Carter. It was quite a pleasant chatty letter, telling him of their marvellous doings abroad, and of her own social successes. It did not do more, however, than vaguely hint at the Russian Prince, his distinguished appearance and obvious wealth. Nevertheless it plunged the unfortunate young man into the utmost depths of despair, and according to his brother John's subsequent account the latter had a terrible time with young Henry that winter. John himself was very busy with journalistic work which kept him away sometimes for days and weeks on end from the little home in London which the two brothers had set up for themselves with the money derived from the sale of the tailoring business. And Henry's state of mind did at times seriously alarm his brother, for he would either threaten to do away with himself, or vow that he would be even with that accursed foreigner.

'At the end of March, the Smithsons returned to England. During the interval Mrs Smithson had made all arrangements for taking "The Towers", a magnificently furnished house facing the Leas at Folkestone, and here she and Louisa installed themselves preparatory to launching their invitations for the various tea- and tennis-parties, dinners and dances which they proposed to give during the summer.

'One might really quite truthfully say that the eyes of all Folkestone were fixed upon the two ladies. Their Paris dresses, their hats, their jewellery was the chief subject of conversation at tea-tables, and of course everyone was talking about the Russian Prince, who – Mrs Smithson had confided this to a bosom friend – was coming over to England for the express purpose of proposing to Louisa.

'There was quite a flutter of excitement on a memorable Friday afternoon when it was rumoured that Henry Carter had come down for a weekend, and had put up at a small hotel down by the harbour. Of course, he had come to see Louisa Smithson; everyone knew that, and no doubt he wished to make a final appeal to her love for him, which could not be entirely dead yet. Within twenty-four hours, however, it was common gossip that young Henry had presented himself at The Towers and been refused admittance. The ladies were out, the butler said, and he did not know when they would be home. This was on the Saturday. On the Sunday Henry walked about on the Leas all morning in the hope of seeing Louisa or her mother, and as he failed to do so he called again in the early part of the afternoon: he was told the ladies were resting. Later he came again and the ladies had gone out, and on the Monday, as presumably business called him back to town, he left by the early-morning train, without having seen his former fiancée. Indeed people from that moment took it for granted that young Henry had formally been given his congé.

'Towards the middle of April Prince Orsoff arrived in London. Within two days he telephoned to Mrs Smithson to ask her when he might come to pay his respects. A day was fixed and he came to The Towers to lunch. He came again, and at his third visit he formally proposed to Miss Louisa Smithson and was accepted. The wedding was to take place almost immediately, and the very next day the exciting announcement had gone the round of the Smithsons' large circle of friends, not only in Folkestone but also in London.

'The effect of the news appears to have been staggering as far as the unfortunate Henry Carter was concerned. In the picturesque language of Mrs Hicks, the middle-aged charlady who "did" for the two brothers in their little home in Chelsea, "'e carried on something awful". She even went so far as to say that she feared he might "put 'is 'ead in the gas oven", and that, as Mr John was away at the time, she took the precaution every day when she left to turn the gas off at the meter.

'The following weekend Henry came down to Folkestone and again took up his quarters in the small hotel by the harbour. On the Saturday afternoon he called at The Towers and refused to take "No" for an answer when he asked to see Miss Smithson. Indeed he seems literally to have pushed his way into the drawing room where the ladies were having tea. According to statements made subsequently by the butler, there ensued a terrible scene between Henry and his former fiancée, at the very height of which, as luck would have it, who should walk in but Prince Orsoff.

'That elegant gentleman, however, seems to have behaved on that trying occasion with perfect dignity and tact, making it his chief business to reassure the ladies and paying no heed to Henry's recriminations, which presently degenerated into vulgar abuse and ended in violent threats. At last, with the aid of the majestic butler, the young man was thrust out of the house, but even on the doorstep he turned and raised a menacing fist in the direction of Prince Orsoff and said loudly enough for more than one person to hear:

'"Wait! I'll be even with that —— foreigner yet."

'It must indeed have been a terrifying scene for two sensitive and refined ladies like Mrs and Miss Smithson to witness. Later on, after the Prince himself had taken his leave, the butler was rung for by Mrs Smithson who told him that under no circumstances was Mr Henry Carter ever to be admitted inside The Towers.

'However, a Sunday or two afterwards, Mr John Carter called and Mrs Smithson saw him. He said that he had come down expressly from London in order to apologise for his brother's conduct. Harry, he said, was deeply contrite that he should thus have lost control over himself; his broken heart was his only excuse. After all, he had been and still was deeply in love with Louisa, and no man, worth his salt, could see the girl he loved turning her back on him without losing some of that equanimity which should of course be the characteristic of every gentleman.

'In fact Mr John Carter spoke so well and so persuasively that Mrs Smithson and Louisa, who were at bottom a quite worthy pair of women, agreed to let bygones be bygones, and said that, if Henry would only behave himself in the future, there was no reason why he should not remain their friend.

'This appeared a quite satisfactory state of things, and over in the little house in Chelsea Mrs Hicks gladly noted that "Mr 'Enry seemed more like 'isself afterwards". The very next weekend the two brothers went down to Folkestone together, and they called at The Towers so that Henry might offer his apologies in person. The two gentlemen on that occasion were actually asked to stay to tea.

'Indeed it seems as if Henry had entirely turned over a new leaf, and when presently the gracious invitation came for both brothers to come to the wedding they equally graciously accepted.

3

'The day fixed for the happy event was now approaching. The large circle of acquaintances, friends and hangers-on which the Smithsons had gathered around them were all agog with excitement, and wedding presents were pouring in by every post. A kind of network of romance had been woven around the personalities of the future bride, her mother and the Russian Prince. The wealth of the Smithsons had been magnified a hundredfold, and Prince Orsoff was reputed to be a brother of the late czar, who had made good his escape out of Russia bringing away with him most of the crown jewels, which he would presently bestow upon his wife.

'And so on, ad infinitum.

'And upon the top of all that excitement and that gossip,

and marvellous tales akin to the *Arabian Nights*, came the wedding day with its awful culminating tragedy.

'The Russian Prince had been murdered and his body so cleverly disposed of that in spite of the most strenuous efforts on the part of the police not a trace of it could be found.

'That robbery had been the main motive of the crime was quickly enough established. The Smithsons – mother and daughter – had at once supplied the detective in charge of the case with proofs as to that. It seems that as soon as the unfortunate Prince had become engaged to Louisa he asked that the marriage should take place without delay. He explained that his dearest friend, Mr Schumann, the great international financier, had offered him shares in one of the greatest postwar undertakings which had ever been floated in Europe, and which would bring in to the fortunate shareholders a net income of not less than £10,000 yearly for every £10,000 invested; Mr Schumann himself owned one half of all the shares and had, by a most wonderful act of disinterested generosity, allowed his bosom friend, Prince Orsoff, to have a few – a concession, by the way, which he had only granted to two other favoured personages, one being the Prince of Wales and the other the President of the French Republic. Of course to receive £10,000 yearly for every £10,000 invested was too wonderful for words; the President of the French Republic had been so delighted with this chance of securing a fortune that he had put two million francs into the concern, and the Prince of Wales had put in £500,000.

'And it was so wonderfully secure, as otherwise the British Government would not have allowed the Prince of Wales to invest such a vast sum of money if the business was only speculative. Security and fortune beyond the dreams of thrift! It was positively dazzling. No wonder that this vision of untold riches made poor Mrs Smithson's mouth water, the more so as she was quite shrewd enough to realise that at the rate she was going her share in the £15,000 left by the late worthy grocer would soon fade into nothingness. In the past few months she and Louisa had spent considerably over £4,000 between them, and once her daughter was married to a quasi-royal personage, good old Mrs Smithson did not see herself retiring into comparative obscurity on a few hundred a year to be jeered at by all her friends.

'So she and Louisa talked the matter over together, and then they talked it over with Prince Orsoff on the occasion of his visit about ten days before the wedding. The Prince at first was very doubtful if the great Mr Schumann would be willing to make a further sacrifice in the cause of friendship. He was an international financier, accustomed to deal in millions; he would not look favourably – the Prince feared – at a few thousand. Mrs Smithson's entire fortune now only consisted of about £5,000; this she was unwilling to admit to the wealthy and aristocratic future son-in-law. So the two ladies decided to pool their capital and then they begged that Prince Orsoff should ask the great Mr Schumann whether he would condescend to receive £10,000 for investment in Mrs Smithson's name in his great undertaking.

'Fortunately the great financier did condescend to do this – he really was more of a philanthropist than a business man – but, of course, he could not be kept waiting; the money must reach him in Paris not later than May the 20th, which was the very day fixed for the wedding. It was all terribly difficult, and Mrs Smithson was at first in despair as she feared she could not arrange to sell out her securities in time, and the difficulties were increased a hundredfold because, as Prince Orsoff explained to her, Mr Schumann would even at the eleventh hour refuse to allow her to participate in the huge fortune if he found that she had talked about the affair over in England. The business had to be kept a profound secret for international reasons; in fact, if any detail relating to the business and to Mr Schumann's participation in it were to become known, the whole of Europe would once more be plunged into war.

'To make a long story short, Mrs Smithson and Louisa sold out all their securities, amounting between them to £10,000. Then they went up to London, drew the money out of their bank, changed it themselves into French money – so as to make it more convenient for Mr Schumann – and handed the entire sum over to Prince Orsoff on the eve of the wedding. Of course such fatuous imbecility would be unbelievable if it did not occur so frequently: vain, silly women who have never moved outside their own restricted circle are always the ready prey of plausible rascals.

'Anyway, in this case the Smithsons returned to Folkestone that day, perfectly happy and with never a thought of anything but contentment for the present and prosperity in the future. The wedding was to be the next day; the bridegroom-elect was coming down by the midday train with his best man, whom he vaguely described as secretary to the Russian Embassy, and the bridal pair would start for Paris by the afternoon boat.

'All this the Smithsons related to the police inspector in

charge of the case and subsequently to the Scotland Yard detective, with a wealth of details and a profusion of lamentations not unmixed with expletives directed against the unknown assassin, and thief. For indeed there was no doubt in the minds of Louise and her mother that the unfortunate Prince, on whom the girl still lavished the wealth of her trustful love, had been murdered for the sake of the vast wealth which he had upon his person. It must have amounted to millions of francs, Mrs Smithson declared, for he had the Prince of Wales's money upon him also, and probably that of the President of the French Republic, and at first she and Louisa fastened their suspicions upon the anonymous best man, the so-called secretary of the Russian Embassy. Even when they were presently made to realise that there was no such thing as a Russian Embassy in London these days, and that minute enquiries both at home and abroad regarding the identity of a Prince Orsoff led to no result whatever, they repudiated with scorn the suggestion put forth by the police that their beloved Russian Prince was nothing more or less than a clever crook who had led them by the nose, and that in all probability he had not been murdered in the train but had succeeded in jumping out of it and making good his escape across country.

'This the Smithson ladies would not admit for a moment, and with commendable logic they argued that if Prince Orsoff had been a crook and had intended to make away with their money he could have done that easily enough without getting into a train at Victoria and jumping out of it at Sydenham Hill.

'Pressed with questions, however, the ladies were forced

to admit that they knew absolutely nothing about Prince Orsoff, they had never been introduced to any of his relations, nor had they met any of his friends. They did not even know where he had been staying in London. He was in the habit of telephoning to Louisa every morning, and any arrangements for his visits down to The Towers or the ladies' trips up to town were made in that manner. As a matter of fact Louisa and her future husband had not met more than a dozen times altogether, on some five or six occasions in Monte Carlo, and not more than six in England. It had been a case of love at first sight.

'The question of Mr Schumann's vast undertaking was first discussed at The Towers. After that the ladies wrote to their bank to sell out their securities, and subsequently went up to town for a couple of days to draw out their money, change it into French currency, and finally hand it over to Prince Orsoff. On that occasion he had met them at Victoria Station and taken them to a quiet hotel in Kensington, where he had engaged a suite of rooms for them. All financial matters were then settled in their private sitting room. In answer to enquiries at that hotel, one or two of the employees distinctly remembered the foreign-looking gentleman who had called on Mrs and Miss Smithson, lunched with them in their sitting room that day, and saw them into their cab when they went away the following afternoon. One or two of the station porters at Victoria also vaguely remembered a man who answered to the description given of Prince Orsoff by the Smithson ladies: tall, with a slight stoop, wearing pince-nez, and with a profusion of dark, curly hair, bushy eyebrows, long dark moustache, and old-fashioned imperial, which made him distinctly noticeable, he could not very well have passed unperceived.

'Unfortunately, on the actual day of the murder, not one man employed at Victoria Station could swear positively to having seen him, either alone or in the company of another foreigner; and the latter has remained a problematic personage to this day.

'But the Smithson ladies remained firm in their loyalty to their Russian Prince. Had they dared they would openly have accused Henry Carter of the murder; as it was they threw out weird hints and insinuations about Henry, who had more than once sworn that he would be even with his hated rival, and who had actually travelled down in the same train as the Prince on that fateful wedding morning, together with his brother John, who no doubt helped him in his nefarious deed. I believe that the unfortunate ladies actually spent some of the money which now they could ill spare in employing a private detective to collect proofs of Henry Carter's guilt.

'But not a tittle of evidence could be brought against him. To begin with, the train in which the murder was supposed to have been committed was a nonstop to Swanley. Then how could the Carters have disposed of the body? The Smithsons suggested a third miscreant as a possible confederate; but the same objection against that theory subsisted in the shape of the disposal of the body. The murder – if murder there was – occurred in broad daylight in a part of the country that certainly was not lonely. It was not possible to suppose that a man would stand waiting on the line close to Sydenham Hill station until a body was flung out to him from the passing train, and then drag that body about until he found a suitable place in which to bury it: and all that without being seen by the workmen on the line or employees on the railway, or in fact any passer-by. Therefore the hypothesis that Henry Carter or his brother murdered the Russian Prince with or without the help of a confederate was as untenable as that the Prince had travelled from Victoria to Sydenham Hill and there jumped out of the train, at risk of being discovered in the act, rather than disappear quietly in London, shave off his luxuriant hair, or assume any other convenient disguise, until he found an opportunity for slipping back to the Continent.

'But the Smithsons remained firm in their belief in the genuineness of their Prince and in their conviction that he had been murdered – if not by the Carters, then by the mysterious secretary to the Russian Embassy or any other Russian or German emissary, for political reasons.

'And thus the public was confronted with the two hypotheses, both of which led to a deadlock. No sensible person doubted that the so-called Russian Prince was a crook and that he had a confederate to help him in his clever plot, but the mystery remained as to how the rascal or rascals disappeared so completely as to checkmate every investigation. The travelling by train that morning and setting the scene for a supposed murder was, of course, part of the plan, but it was the plan that was so baffling, because to an ordinary mind that disappearance could have been effected so much more easily and with far less risk without the train journey.

'Of course there was not a single passenger on that train who was not the subject of the closest watchfulness on the part of the police, but there was not one – not excluding the Carters – who could by any possible chance have known that the Prince carried a large sum of money upon his person. He was not likely to have confided the fact to a stranger, and the mystery of the vanished body was always there to refute the theory of an ordinary murderous attack for motives of robbery.'

4

The Man in the Corner ceased talking and became once more absorbed in his favourite task of making knots in a bit of string.

'I see in the papers,' I now put in thoughtfully, 'that Miss Louisa Smithson has overcome her grief for the loss of her aristocratic lover by returning to the plebeian one.'

'Yes,' the funny creature replied drily, 'she is marrying Henry Carter. Funny, isn't it? But women are queer fish! One moment she looked on the man as a murderer, now, by marrying him, she actually proclaims her belief in his innocence.'

'It certainly was abundantly proved,' I rejoined, 'that Henry Carter could not possibly have murdered Prince Orsoff.'

'It was also abundantly proved,' he retorted, 'that no one murdered the so-called Prince.'

'You think, of course, that he was an ordinary impostor?' I asked.

'An impostor, yes,' he replied, 'but not an ordinary one. In fact I take off my hat to as clever a pair of scamps as I have ever come across.'

'A pair?'

'Why, yes! It could not have been done alone.'

'But the police ...'

'The police,' the spook-like creature broke in with a sharp cackle, 'know more, in this case, than you give them credit for. They know well enough the solution of the puzzle which appears so baffling to the public, but they have not sufficient proof to effect an arrest. At one time they hoped that the scoundrels would presently make a false move and give themselves away, in which case they could be prosecuted for defrauding the Smithsons of £10,000, but this eventuality has become complicated through the masterstroke of genius which made Henry Carter marry Louisa Smithson.'

'Henry Carter?' I exclaimed. 'Then you do think the Carters had something to do with the case?'

'They had everything to do with the case. In fact, they planned the whole thing in a masterly manner.'

'But the Russian Prince at Monte Carlo?' I argued. 'Who was he? If he was a confederate where has he disappeared to?'

'He is still engaged in the freelance journalism,' the Man in the Corner replied drily, 'and in his spare moments changes parcels of French currency back into English notes.'

'You mean the brother!' I ejaculated with a gasp.

'Of course I mean the brother,' he retorted drily, 'who else could have been so efficient a collaborator in the plot? John Carter was comparatively his own master. He lived with Henry in the small house in Chelsea, waited on by a char-woman who came by the day. It was generally given out that his reporting work took him frequently and for lengthened stays out of London. The brothers, remember, had inherited a few hundred from their father, while the Smithsons had inherited a few thousand. We must suppose that the idea of relieving those ladies of those thousands occurred to them as soon as they realised that Louisa, egged on by her mother, would cold-shoulder her fiancé.

'John Carter, mind you, must be a very clever man, else he could not have carried out all the details of the plot with so much sang-froid. We have been told, if you remember, that he had, early in life, cut his stick and gone to seek fortune in London, therefore the Smithsons, who had never been out of Folkestone, did not know him intimately. His make-up as the Prince must have been very good, and his histrionic powers not to be despised: his profession and life in London no doubt helped him in these matters. Then, remember also that he took very good care not to be a great deal in the Smithsons' company – even in Monte Carlo he only let them see him less than half a dozen times, and as soon as he came to England he hurried on the wedding as much as he could.

'Another fine stroke was Henry's apparent despair at being cut out of Louisa's affections and his threats against his successful rival: it helped to draw suspicion on himself – suspicion which the scoundrels took good care could easily be disproved. Then take a pair of vain, credulous, unintelligent women, and a smart rascal who knows how to flatter them, and you will see how easily the whole plot could be worked. Finally, when John Carter had obtained possession of the money, he and Henry arranged the supposed tragedy in the train and the Russian Prince's disappearance from the world as suddenly as he had entered it.'

I thought the matter over for a moment or two. The solution of the mystery certainly appealed to my dramatic sense.

'But,' I said at last, 'one wonders why the Carters took the trouble to arrange a scene of a supposed murder in the train: they might quite well have been caught in the act, and in any case it was an additional unnecessary risk. John Carter might quite well have been content to shed his role of Russian Prince, without such an elaborate setting.'

'Well,' he admitted, 'in some ways you are right there, but it is always difficult to gauge accurately the mentality of a clever scoundrel. In this case I don't suppose that the Carters had quite made up their minds about what they would do when they left London, but that the plan was in their heads is proved by the hat, pince-nez and railway ticket which they took with them when they started, and which, if you remember, were found on the line: but it was probably only because the train was comparatively empty, and they had both time and opportunity in the nonstop train, that they decided to carry their clever comedy through.

'Then think what an immense advantage in their future plans would be the Smithsons' belief in the death of their Prince. Probably Louisa would never have dreamed of marrying if she thought her aristocratic lover was an impostor and still alive; she would never have let the matter rest; her mind would for ever have been busy with trying to trace him, and bring him back, repentant, to her feet. You know what women are when they are in love with that type of scoundrel, they cling to them with the tenacity of a leech. But once she believed the man to be dead, Louisa Smithson gradually got over her grief and Henry Carter wooed and won her on the rebound. She was poor now, and her friends had quickly enough deserted her; she was touched by the fidelity of her simple lover, and he thus consolidated his position and made the future secure.

'Anyway,' the Man in the Corner concluded, 'I believe that it was with a view to making a future marriage possible between Louisa and Henry that the two brothers organised the supposed murder. Probably if the train had been full and they had seen danger in the undertaking they would not have done it. But the *mise-en-scène* was easily enough set and it certainly was an additional safeguard. Now in another week or so Louisa Smithson will be Henry Carter's wife, and presently you will find that, John in London, and Henry and his wife, will be quite comfortably off. And after that, whatever suspicions Mrs Smithson might have of the truth, her lips would have to remain sealed. She could not very well prosecute her only child's husband.

'And so the matter will always remain a mystery to the public: but the police know more than they are able to admit because they have no proof.

'And now they never will have. But as to the murder in the train, well! – the murdered man never existed.'

The Border-Line Case

Margery Allingham

DATE: Aug. 8, 1933.

VENUE: London.

OFFICIALS: Chief Detective Inspector Stanislaus Oates of the Central Division of the Criminal Investigation Department, Scotland Yard.

PRIVATE NOTES: My first "armchair" investigation. Extraordinary blind spot in Oates's mentality where women are concerned.

Sorry for the girl.

The Border-Line Case

It was so hot in London that night we slept with the wide skylight in our city studio open and let the soot-blacks fall in on us willingly, so long as they brought with them a single stirring breath to move the stifling air. Heat hung on the dark horizons and beneath our particular bowl of sky the city fidgeted, breathless and uncomfortable.

The early editions of the evening papers carried the story of the murder. I read it when they came along about three o'clock on the following afternoon. My mind took in the details lazily, for my eyelids were sticky and the printed words seemed remote and unrelated to reality.

It was a straightforward little incident, or so I thought it, and when I had read the guarded half-column I threw the paper over to Albert Campion, who had drifted in to lunch and stayed to sit quietly in a corner, blinking behind his spectacles, existing merely, in the sweltering day.

The newspapers called the murder the "Coal Court Shooting Case", and the facts were simple.

At one o'clock in the morning, when Vacation Street, N.E., had been a deserted lane of odoriferous heat, a policeman on the beat had seen a man stumble and fall to the pavement. The intense discomfort of the night being uppermost in his mind, he had not unnaturally diagnosed a case of ordinary collapse and, after loosening the stranger's collar, had summoned the ambulance.

When the authorities arrived, however, the man was pronounced to be dead and the body was taken to the mortuary, where it was discovered that death had been due to a bullet wound neatly placed between the shoulder blades. The bullet had made a small hole and, after perforating the left lung, had furrowed the heart itself, finally coming to rest in the bony structure of the chest.

Since this was so, and the fact that the police constable had heard no untoward sound, it had been reasonable to believe that the shot had been fired at some little distance from a gun with a silencer.

Mr Campion was only politely interested. The afternoon certainly was hot and the story as it then appeared was hardly original or exciting. He sat on the floor reading it patiently, his long thin legs stretched out in front of him.

"Someone died at any rate," he remarked at last and added after a pause: "poor chap! Out of the frying pan… Dear me, I suppose it's the locality which predisposes one to think of that. Ever seen Vacation Street, Margery?"

I did not answer him. I was thinking how odd it was that a general irritant like the heat should make the dozens of situations arising all round one in the great city seem suddenly almost personal. I found I was desperately sorry for the man who had been shot, whoever he was.

It was Stanislaus Oates who told us the real story behind the half column in the evening paper. He came in just after four looking for Campion. He was a detective inspector in those days and had just begun to develop the habit of chatting over his problems with the pale young man in the horn-rimmed spectacles. Theirs was an odd relationship. It was certainly not a case of the clever amateur and the humble policeman: rather the irritable and pugnacious policeman taking it out of the inoffensive, friendly representative of the general public.

On this occasion Oates was rattled.

"It's a case right down your street," he said briefly to Campion as he sat down. "Seems to be a miracle, for one thing."

He explained after a while, having salved his conscience by pointing out that he had no business to discuss the case and excusing himself most illogically on grounds of the heat.

"It's 'low-class' crime," he went on briskly. "Practically gang shooting. And probably quite uninteresting to all of you, who like romance in your crimes. However, it's got me right down on two counts: the first because the man who shot the fellow who died couldn't possibly have done so, and second because I was wrong about the girl. They're so true to type, these girls, that you can't even rely on the proverbial exception."

He sighed as if the discovery had really grieved him.

We heard the story of Josephine as we sat round in the paralysingly hot studio and, although I never saw the girl then or afterwards, I shall not forget the scene; the three of us listening, breathing rather heavily, while the inspector talked.

She had been Donovan's girl, so Oates said, and he painted a picture of her for us: slender and flat chested, with black hair and eyes like a Russian madonna's in a transparent face. She wore blouses, he said, with lace on them and gold ornaments, little chains and crosses and frail brooches whose security was reinforced by gilt safety pins. She was only twenty, Oates said, and added enigmatically that he would have betted on her but that it served him right and showed him there was no fool like an old one.

He went on to talk about Donovan, who, it seemed, was thirty-five and had spent ten years of his life in jail. The inspector did not seem to think any the less of him for that. The fact seemed to put the man in a definite category in his mind and that was all.

"Robbery with violence and the R.O. boys," he said with a wave of his hand and smiled contentedly as though he had made everything clear. "She was sixteen when he found her and he's given her hell ever since."

While he still held our interest he mentioned Johnny Gilchick. Johnny Gilchick was the man who was dead.

Oates, who was never more sentimental than was strictly reasonable in the circumstances, let himself go about Josephine and Johnny Gilchick. It was love, he said—love, sudden, painful and ludicrous; and he admitted that he liked to see it.

"I had an aunt once who used to talk about the Real Thing," he explained, "and embarrassingly silly the old lady sounded, but after seeing those two youngsters meet and flame and go on until they were a single fiery entity—youngsters who were pretty ordinary tawdry material without it—I find myself sympathising with her if not condoning the phrase."

He hesitated and his smooth grey face cracked into a depreciating smile.

"Well, we were both wrong, anyway," he murmured, "my aunt and I. Josephine let her Johnny down just as you'd expect her to and after he got what was coming to him and was lying in the mortuary he was born to lie in she upped and perjured her immortal soul to swear his murderer an alibi. Not that her testimony is of much value as evidence. That's beside the point. The fact remains that she's certainly done her best. You may think me sentimental, but it depresses me. I thought that girl was genuine and my judgment was out."

Mr Campion stirred.

"Could we have the details?" he asked politely. "We've only seen the evening paper. It wasn't very helpful."

Oates glared at him balefully.

"Frankly, the facts are exasperating," he said. "There's little catch in them somewhere. It must be something so simple that I missed it altogether. That's really why I've come to look for you. I thought you might care to come along and take a glance at the place. What about it?"

There was no general movement. It was too hot to stir. Finally the inspector took up a piece of chalk and sketched a rough diagram on the bare boards of the model's throne.

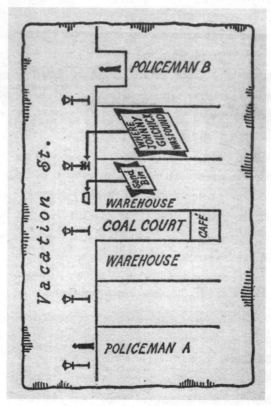

Vacation St., Coal Court

"This is Vacation Street," he said, edging the chalk along a crack. "It's the best part of a mile long. Up this end, here by the chair, it's nearly all wholesale houses. This sand bin I'm sketching in now marks the boundary of two police divisions. We'll take that as the starting point. Well, here, ten yards to the left, is the entrance to Coal Court, which is a cul-de-sac composed of two blank backs of warehouse buildings and a café at the far end. The café is open all night. It serves the printers from the two big presses further down the road. That's its legitimate trade. But it is also a sort of unofficial headquarters for Donovan's mob. Josephine sits at the desk downstairs and keeps an eye on the door. God knows what hours she keeps. She always seems to be there."

He paused and there came into my mind a recollection of the breathless night through which we had all passed, and I could imagine the girl sitting there in the stuffy shop with her thin chest and her great black eyes.

The inspector was still speaking.

"Now," he said, "there's an upstairs room in the café. It's on the second floor. That's where our friend Donovan spent most of his evening. I expect he had a good few friends with him and we shall locate them all in time."

He bent over the diagram.

"Johnny Gilchick died here," he said, drawing a circle about a foot beyond the square which indicated the sand bin. "Although the bobby was right down the road, he saw him pause under the lamppost, stagger and fall. He called the constable from the other division and they got the ambulance. All that is plain sailing. There's just one difficulty. Where was Donovan when he fired the shot? There were two policemen in the street at the time, remember. At the moment of the actual shooting one of them, the Never Street man, was making a round of a warehouse yard, but the other, the Phyllis Court chap, was there on the spot, not forty yards away, and it was he who actually saw Johnny Gilchick fall, although he heard no shot. Now I tell you, Campion, there's not an ounce of cover in the whole of that street. How did Donovan get out of the café, where did he stand to shoot Johnny neatly through the back, and how did he get back again without being seen? The side walls of the cul-de-sac are solid concrete backs of warehouses, there is no way round from the back of the café, nor could he possibly have gone over the roofs. The warehouses tower over the café like liners over a tug. Had he come out down the road one or other of the bobbies must have been certain to have seen him. How did he do it?"

"Perhaps Donovan didn't do it," I ventured and received a pitying glance for my temerity.

"That's the one fact," said the inspector heavily. "That's the only thing I do know. I know Donovan. He's one of the few English mob boys who carry guns. He served five years with the gangs in New York before Repeal and he has the misfortune to take his liquor in bouts. After each bout he has a period of black depression, during which he may do anything. Johnny Gilchick used to be one of Donovan's mob and when Johnny fell for the girl he turned in the gang, which was adding insult to injury where Donovan was concerned."

He paused and smiled.

"Donovan was bound to get Johnny in the end," he said. "It was never anything but a question of time. The whole mob expected it. The neighbourhood was waiting for it. Donovan had said openly that the next time Johnny dropped into the café would be his final appearance there. Johnny called last night, was ordered out of the place by the terrified girl, and finally walked out of the cul-de-sac. He turned the corner and strolled down the road. Then he was shot by Donovan. There's no way round it, Campion. The doctors say that death was as near instantaneous as may be. Johnny Gilchick could not have walked three paces with that bullet in his back. As for the gun, that was pretty obviously Donovan's too. We haven't actually picked it up yet, but we know he had one of the type we are after. It's a clear case, a straightforward case, if only we knew where Donovan stood when he fired the shot."

Mr Campion looked up. His eyes were thoughtful behind his spectacles.

"The girl gave Donovan an alibi?" he enquired.

Oates shrugged his shoulders. "Rather," he said. "She was passionate about it. He was there the whole time, every minute of the time, never left the upper room once in the whole evening. I could kill her and she would not alter her story; she'd take her dying oath on it and so on and so on. It didn't mean anything either way. Still, I was sorry to see her doing it, with her boy friend barely cold. She was sucking up to the mob, of course; probably had excellent reasons for doing so. Yet, as I say, I was sorry to hear her volunteering the alibi before she was asked."

"Ah! She volunteered it, did she?" Campion was interested.

Oates nodded and his small grey eyes widened expressively.

"Forced it on us. Came roaring round to the police station with it. Threw it off her chest as if she were doing something fine. I'm not usually squeamish about that sort of thing but it gave me a distinct sense of distaste, I don't mind telling you. Frankly, I gave her a piece of my mind. Told her to go and look at the body, for one thing."

"Not kind of you," observed Mr Campion mildly. "And what did she do?"

"Oh, blubbered herself sick, like the rest of 'em." Oates was still disgruntled. "Still, that's not of interest. What girls like Josephine do or don't do doesn't really matter. She was saving her own skin. If she hadn't been so enthusiastic about it I'd have forgiven her. It's Donovan who is important. Where was Donovan when he fired?"

The shrill chatter of the telephone answered him and he glanced at me apologetically.

"I'm afraid that's mine," he said. "You didn't mind, did you? I left the number with the sergeant."

He took off the receiver and as he bent his head to listen his face changed. We watched him with an interest it was far too hot to dissemble.

"Oh," he said flatly after a long pause. "Really? Well, it doesn't matter either way, does it? ... Still, what did she do it for? ... What? ... I suppose so.... Yes? ... Really?"

He seemed suddenly astounded as his informant at the other end of the wire evidently came out with a second piece of information more important than the first.

"You can't be certain... you are? ... What?"

The faraway voice explained busily. We could hear its steady drone. Inspector Oates's exasperation grew.

"Oh all right, all right," he said at last. "I'm crackers …
we're all crackers … have it your own damned way!"

With which vulgar outburst he rang off.

"Alibi sustained?" enquired Mr Campion.

"Yes." The inspector grunted out the word. "A couple of
printers who were in the downstairs room swear he did not
go through the shop all the evening. They're sound fellows.
Make good witnesses. Yet Donovan shot Johnny. I'm certain
of it. He shot him clean through the concrete angle of a piano
warehouse as far as I can see." He turned to Campion almost
angrily. "Explain that, can you?"

Mr Campion coughed. He seemed a little embarrassed.

"I say, you know," he ventured, "there are just two things
that occur to me."

"Then out with them, son." The inspector lit a cigarette
and wiped his face. "Out with them. I'm not proud."

Mr Campion coughed. "Well, the—er—heat, for one
thing, don't you know," he said with profound uneasiness.
"The heat and one of your concrete walls."

The inspector swore a little and apologised.

"If anyone could forget this heat he's welcome," he said.
"What's the matter with the wall too?"

Mr Campion bent over the diagram on the boards of the
throne. He was very apologetic.

"Here is the angle of the warehouse," he said, "and here is
the sand bin. Here to the left is the lamppost where Johnny
Gilchick was found. Further on to the left is the P.C. from
Never Street examining a courtyard and temporarily off the
scene, while to the right, on the other side of the entrance to
Coal Court, is another constable, P.C. someone-or-other,

of Phyllis Court. One is apt to—er—think of the problem as though it were contained in four solid walls, two concrete walls, two policemen."

He hesitated and glanced timidly at the inspector.

"When is a policeman not a concrete wall, Oates? In—er—well, in just such heat ... do you think, or don't you?"

Oates was staring at him, his eyes narrowed.

"Damn it!" he said explosively. "Damn it, Campion, I believe you're right. I knew it was something so simple that it was staring me in the face."

They stood together looking down at the diagram. Oates stooped to put a chalk cross at the entrance to the cul-de-sac.

"It was *that* lamppost," he said. "Give me that telephone. Wait till I get hold of that fellow."

While he was carrying on an excited conversation we demanded an explanation from Mr Campion and he gave it to us at last, mild and apologetic as usual.

"Well, you see," he said, "there's the sand bin. The sand bin marks the boundary of two police divisions. Policeman A, very hot and tired, sees a man collapse from the heat under a lamppost on his own territory. The man is a little fellow and it occurs to Policeman A that it would be a simple matter to move him to the next lamppost on the other side of the sand bin, where he would automatically become the responsibility of Policeman B, who is even now approaching. Policeman A achieves the change and is bending over the prostate figure when his colleague comes up. Since he knows nothing of the bullet wound, the entrance to the cul-de-sac, with its clear view to the café second-floor room, has no significance in his mind. Today, when its full importance must have dawned upon him, he evidently thinks it best to hold his tongue."

Oates came back from the phone triumphant.

"The first bobby went on leave this morning," he said. "He was an old hand. He must have spotted the chap was dead, took it for granted it was the heat, and didn't want to be held up here by the inquest. Funny I didn't see that in the beginning."

We were all silent for some moments.

"Then—the girl?" I began at last.

The inspector frowned and made a little grimace of regret.

"A pity about the girl," he said. "Of course it was probably an accident. Our man who saw it happen said he couldn't be sure."

I stared at him and he explained, albeit a little hurriedly.

"Didn't I tell you? When my sergeant phoned about the alibi he told me. As Josephine crossed the road after visiting the mortuary this morning she stepped under a bus … Oh yes, instantly."

He shook his head. He seemed uncomfortable.

"She thought she was making a gesture when she came down to the station, don't you see. The mob must have told her to swear that no one had been in the upstairs room; that must have been their first story until they saw how the luck lay. So when she came beetling down to us she must have thought she was risking her life to give her Johnny's murderer away, while instead of that she was simply giving the fellow an alibi…. Funny the way things happen, isn't it?"

He glanced at Campion affectionately.

"It's because you don't get your mind cluttered up with

the human element that you see these things so quickly," he said. "You see everything in terms of A and B. It makes all the difference."

Mr Campion, the most gentle of men, made no comment at all.

A Good Hanging

Ian Rankin

1

It was quite some time since a scaffold had been seen in Parliament Square. Quite some time since Edinburgh had witnessed a hanging, too, though digging deeper into history the sight might have been common enough. Detective Inspector John Rebus recalled hearing some saloon-bar story of how criminals, sentenced to hang, would be given the chance to run the distance of the Royal Mile from Parliament Square to Holyrood, a baying crowd hot on their heels. If the criminal reached the Royal Park before he was caught, he would be allowed to remain there, wandering in safety so long as he did not step outside the boundary of the park itself. True or not, the tale conjured up the wonderful image of rogues and vagabonds trapped within the confines of Arthur's Seat, Salisbury Crags and Whinny Hill. Frankly, Rebus would have preferred the noose.

'It's got to be a prank gone wrong, hasn't it?'

A prank. Edinburgh was full of pranks at this time of year. It was Festival time, when young people, theatrical people, flooded into the city with their enthusiasm and their energy. You couldn't walk ten paces without someone pressing a handbill upon you or begging you to visit their production. These were the 'Fringe lunatics' as Rebus had not very originally, but to his own satisfaction, termed them. They came for two or three or four weeks, mostly from London and they squeezed into damp sleeping bags on bedsit floors throughout the city, going home much paler, much more tired and almost always the poorer. It was not unusual for the unlucky Fringe shows, those given a venue on the outskirts, those with no review to boast of, starved of publicity and inspiration, for those unfortunate shows to play to single-figure audiences, if not to an audience of a single figure.

Rebus didn't like Festival time. The streets became clogged, there seemed a despair about all the artistic fervour and, of course, the crime rate rose. Pickpockets loved the Festival. Burglars found easy pickings in the overpopulated, underprotected bedsits. And, finding their local pub taken over by the 'Sassenachs', the natives were inclined to throw the occasional punch or bottle or chair. Which was why Rebus avoided the city centre during the Festival, skirting around it in his car, using alleyways and half-forgotten routes. Which was why he was so annoyed at having been called here today, to Parliament Square, the heart of the Fringe, to witness a hanging.

'Got to be a prank,' he repeated to Detective Constable Brian Holmes. The two men were standing in front of a scaffold, upon which hung the gently swaying body of a young man. The body swayed due to the fresh breeze which was sweeping up the Royal Mile from the direction of Holyrood Park. Rebus thought of the ghosts of the Royal Park's inmates. Was the wind of their making? 'A publicity stunt gone wrong,' he mused.

'Apparently not, sir,' Holmes said. He'd been having a few words with the workmen who were trying to erect a curtain of sorts around the spectacle so as to hide it from the view of the hundreds of inquisitive tourists who had gathered noisily outside the police cordon. Holmes now consulted his notebook, while Rebus, hands in pockets, strolled around the scaffold. It was of fairly ramshackle construction, which hadn't stopped it doing its job.

'The body was discovered at four-fifty this morning. We don't think it had been here long. A patrol car passed this way at around four and they didn't see anything.'

'That doesn't mean much,' Rebus interrupted in a mutter.

Holmes ignored the remark. 'The deceased belonged to a Fringe group called Ample Reading Time. They come from the University of Reading, thus the name.'

'It also makes the acronym ART,' Rebus commented.

'Yes, sir,' said Holmes. His tone told the senior officer that Holmes had already worked this out for himself. Rebus wriggled a little, as though trying to keep warm. In fact, he had a summer cold.

'How did we discover his identity?' They were in front of the hanging man now, standing only four or so feet below him. Early twenties, Rebus surmised. A shock of black curly hair.

'The scaffold has a venue number pinned to it,' Holmes was saying. 'A student hall of residence just up the road.'

'And that's where the ART show's playing?'

'Yes, sir.' Holmes consulted the bulky Fringe programme which he had been holding behind his notebook. 'It's a play of sorts called *Scenes from a Hanging*.' The two men exchanged a look at this. 'The blurb,' Holmes continued, consulting the company's entry near the front of the programme, 'promises "thrills, spills and a live hanging on stage".'

'A live hanging, eh? Well, you can't say they didn't deliver. So, he takes the scaffold from the venue, wheels it out here – I notice it's on wheels, presumably to make it easier to trundle on and off the stage – and in the middle of the night he hangs himself, without anyone hearing anything or seeing anything.' Rebus sounded sceptical.

'Well,' said Holmes, 'be honest, sir.' He was pointing towards and beyond the crowd of onlookers. 'Does anything look suspicious in Edinburgh at this time of year?'

Rebus followed the direction of the finger and saw that a twelve-foot-high man was enjoying a grandstand view of the spectacle, while somewhere to his right someone was juggling three saucepans high into the air. The stilt-man walked towards the pans, grabbed one from mid-air and set it on his head, waving down to the crowd before moving off. Rebus sighed.

'I suppose you're right, Brian. Just this once you may be right.'

A young DC approached, holding a folded piece of paper towards them. 'We found this in his trousers back-pocket.'

'Ah,' said Rebus, 'the suicide note.' He plucked the sheet from the DC's outstretched hand and read it aloud.

'"Pity it wasn't *Twelfth Night*".'

Holmes peered at the line of type. 'Is that it?'

'Short but sweet,' said Rebus. '*Twelfth Night*. A play by Shakespeare and the end of the Christmas season. I wonder which one he means?' Rebus refolded the note and slipped it into his pocket. 'But is it a suicide note or not? It could just be a bog-standard note, a reminder or whatever, couldn't it? I still think this is a stunt gone wrong.' He paused to cough. He was standing beside the cobblestone inset of the Heart of Midlothian, and like many a Scot before him, he spat for luck into the centre of the heart-shaped stones. Holmes looked away and found himself gazing into the dead man's dulled eyes. He turned back as Rebus was fumbling with a handkerchief.

'Maybe,' Rebus was saying between blows, 'we should have a word with the rest of the cast. I don't suppose they'll have much to keep them occupied.' He gestured towards the scaffold. 'Not until they get back their prop. Besides, we've got a job to do, haven't we?'

2

'Well, I say we keep going!' the voice yelled. 'We've got an important piece of work here, a play people should *see*. If anything, David's death will bring audiences *in*. We shouldn't be pushing them away. We shouldn't be packing our bags and crawling back south.'

'You sick bastard.'

Rebus and Holmes entered the makeshift auditorium as the speaker of these last three words threw himself forwards and landed a solid punch against the side of the speech-maker's face. His glasses flew from his nose and slid along the floor, stopping an inch or two short of Rebus's scuffed leather shoes. He stooped, picked up the spectacles and moved forward.

The room was of a size, and had an atmosphere, that would have suited a monastery's dining hall. It was long and narrow, with a stage constructed along its narrow face and short rows of chairs extending back into the gloom. What windows there were had been blacked out and the hall's only natural light came from the open door through which Rebus had just stepped, to the front left of the stage itself.

There were five of them in the room, four men and a woman. All looked to be in their mid- to late twenties. Rebus handed over the glasses.

'Not a bad right hook that,' he said to the attacker, who was looking with some amazement at his own hand, as though hardly believing it capable of such an action. 'I'm Inspector Rebus, this is Detective Constable Holmes. And you are?'

They introduced themselves in turn. Sitting on the stage was Pam, who acted. Beside her was Peter Collins, who also acted. On a chair in front of the stage, legs and arms crossed and having obviously enjoyed tremendously the one-sided bout he had just witnessed, sat Marty Jones.

'I don't act,' he said loudly. 'I just design the set, build the bloody thing, make all the props and work the lights and the music during the play.'

'So it's your scaffold then?' commented Rebus. Marty Jones looked less confident.

'Yes,' he said. 'I made it a bit too bloody well, didn't I?'

'We could just as easily blame the rope manufacturer, Mr Jones,' Rebus said quietly. His eyes moved to the man with the spectacles, who was nursing a bruised jaw.

'Charles Collins,' the man said sulkily. He looked towards where Peter Collins sat on the stage. 'No relation. I'm the director. I also wrote *Scenes from a Hanging*.'

Rebus nodded. 'How have the reviews been?'

Marty Jones snorted.

'Not great,' Charles Collins admitted. 'We've only had four,' he went on, knowing if he didn't say it someone else would. 'They weren't exactly complimentary.'

Marty Jones snorted again. Stiffening his chin, as though to take another punch, Collins ignored him.

'And the audiences?' Rebus asked, interested.

'Lousy.' This from Pam, swinging her legs in front of her as though such news was not only quite acceptable, but somehow humorous as well.

'Average, I'd say,' Charles Collins corrected. 'Going by what other companies have been telling me.'

'That's the problem with staging a new play, isn't it?' Rebus said knowledgeably, while Holmes stared at him. Rebus was standing in the midst of the group now, as though giving them a pre-production pep talk. 'Trying to get audiences to watch new work is always a problem. They prefer the classics.'

'That's right,' Charles Collins agreed enthusiastically. 'That's what I've been telling—' with a general nod in everyone's direction, 'them. The classics are "safe". That's why we need to challenge people.'

'To excite them,' Rebus continued, 'to shock them even. Isn't that right, Mr Collins? To give them a spectacle?'

Charles Collins seemed to see where Rebus's line, devious though it was, was leading. He shook his head.

'Well, they got a spectacle all right,' Rebus went on, all enthusiasm gone from his voice. 'Thanks to Mr Jones's scaffold, the people got a shock. Someone was hanged. I think his name's David, isn't it?'

'That's right.' This from the attacker. 'David Caulfield.' He looked towards the writer/director. 'Supposedly a friend of ours. Someone we've known for three years. Someone we never thought could ...'

'And you are?' Rebus was brisk. He didn't want anyone breaking down just yet, not while there were still questions that needed answers.

'Hugh Clay.' The young man smiled bitterly. 'David always said it sounded like "ukulele".'

'And you're an actor?'

Hugh Clay nodded.

'And so was David Caulfield?'

Another nod. 'I mean, we're not really professionals. We're students. That's all. Students with pretensions.'

Something about Hugh Clay's voice, its tone and its slow rhythms, had made the room darken, so that everyone seemed less animated, more reflective, remembering at last that David Caulfield was truly dead.

'And what do you think happened to him, Hugh? I mean, how do you think he died?'

Clay seemed puzzled by the question. 'He killed himself, didn't he?'

'Did he?' Rebus shrugged. 'We don't know for certain. The pathologist's report may give us a better idea.' Rebus turned to Marty Jones, who was looking less confident all the time. 'Mr Jones, could David have operated the scaffold by himself?'

'That's the way I designed it,' Jones replied. 'I mean, David worked it himself every night. During the hanging scene.'

Rebus pondered this. 'And could someone else have worked the mechanism?'

Jones nodded. 'No problem. The neck noose we used was a dummy. The real noose was attached around David's chest, under his arms. He held a cord behind him and at the right moment he pulled the cord, the trapdoor opened and he fell about a yard. It looked pretty bloody realistic. He had to wear padding under his arms to stop bruising.' He glanced at Charles Collins. 'It was the best bit of the show.'

'But,' said Rebus, 'the scaffold could easily be rejigged to work properly?'

Jones nodded. 'All you'd need is a bit of rope. There's plenty lying around backstage.'

'And then you could hang yourself? Really hang yourself?'

Jones nodded again.

'Or someone could hang you,' said Pam, her eyes wide, voice soft with horror.

Rebus smiled towards her, but seemed to be thinking about something else. In fact, he wasn't thinking of anything in particular: he was letting them stew in the silence, letting their minds and imaginations work in whatever way they would.

At last, he turned to Charles Collins. 'Do you think David killed himself?'

Collins shrugged. 'What else?'

'Any particular reason why he would commit suicide?'

'Well,' Collins looked towards the rest of the company. 'The show,' he said. 'The reviews weren't very complimentary about David's performance.'

'Tell me a little about the play.'

Collins tried not to sound keen as he spoke. Tried, Rebus noticed, but failed. 'It took me most of this year to write,' he said. 'What we have is a prisoner in a South American country, tried and found guilty, sentenced to death. The play opens with him standing on the scaffold, the noose around his neck. Scenes from his life are played out around him, while his own scenes are made up of soliloquies dealing with the larger questions. What I'm asking the audience to do is to ask themselves the same questions he's asking himself on the scaffold. Only the answers are perhaps more urgent, more important for him, because they're the last things he'll ever know.'

Rebus broke in. The whole thing sounded dreadful. 'And David would be on stage the entire time?' Collins nodded. 'And how long was that?'

'Anywhere between two hours and two and a half—' with a glance towards the stage, 'depending on the cast.'

'Meaning?'

'Sometimes lines were forgotten, or a scene went missing.' (Peter and Pam smiled in shared complicity.) 'Or the pace just went.'

'"Never have I prayed so ardently for a death to take place", as one of the reviews put it,' Hugh Clay supplied. 'It was a problem of the play. It didn't have anything to do with David.'

Charles Collins looked ready to protest. Rebus stepped in. 'But David's mentions weren't exactly kind?' he hinted.

'No,' Clay admitted, 'They said he lacked the necessary *gravitas*, whatever that means.'

'"Too big a part for too small an actor",' interrupted Marty Jones, quoting again.

'Bad notices then,' said Rebus. 'And David Caulfield took them to heart?'

'David took everything to heart,' explained Hugh Clay. 'That was part of the problem.'

'The other part being that the notices were true,' sniped Charles Collins. But Clay seemed prepared for this.

'"Overwritten and messily directed by Charles Collins",' he quoted. Another fight seemed to be on the cards. Rebus blew his nose noisily.

'So,' he said. 'Notices were bad, audiences were poor. And you didn't decide to remedy this situation by staging a little publicity stunt? A stunt that just happened – nobody's fault necessarily – to go wrong?'

There were shakes of the head, eyes looked to other eyes, seemingly innocent of any such plans.

'Besides,' said Marty Jones, 'you couldn't hang yourself accidentally on that scaffold. You either had to mean to do it yourself, or else someone had to do it for you.'

More silence. An impasse seemed to have been reached. Rebus collapsed noisily into a chair. 'All things considered,' he said with a sigh, 'you might have been better off sticking to *Twelfth Night*.'

'That's funny,' Pam said.

'What is?'

'That's the play we did last year,' she explained. 'It went down very well, didn't it?' She had turned to Peter Collins, who nodded agreement.

'We got some good reviews for that,' he said. 'David was a brilliant Malvolio. He kept the cuttings pinned to his bedroom wall, didn't he, Hugh?'

Hugh Clay nodded. Rebus had the distinct feeling that Peter Collins was trying to imply something, perhaps that Hugh Clay had seen more of David Caulfield's bedroom walls than was strictly necessary.

He fumbled in his pocket, extracting the note from below the handkerchief. Brian Holmes, he noticed, was staying very much in the wings, like the minor character in a minor scene. 'We found a note in David's pocket,' Rebus said without preamble. 'Maybe your success last year explains it.' He read it out to them. Charles Collins nodded.

'Yes, that sounds like David all right. Harking back to past glories.'

'You think that's what it means?' Rebus asked conversationally.

Collins nodded. 'You should know, Inspector, that actors are conceited. The greater the actor, the greater the ego. And David was, I admit, on occasion a very gifted actor.' He was speechifying again, but Rebus let him go on. Perhaps it was the only way a director could communicate with his cast.

'It would be just like David to get depressed, suicidal even, by bad notices, and just like him to decide to stage as showy an exit as he could, something to hit the headlines. I happen to think he succeeded splendidly.'

No one seemed about to contradict him on this, not even

David Caulfield's stalwart defender, Hugh Clay. It was Pam who spoke, tears in her eyes at last.

'I only feel sorry for Marie,' she said.

Charles Collins nodded. 'Yes, Marie's come into her own in *Scenes from a Hanging*.'

'She means,' Hugh Clay said through gritted teeth, 'she feels sorry for Marie because Marie's lost David, not because Marie can no longer act in your bloody awful play.'

Rebus felt momentary bemusement, but tried not to show it. Marty Jones, however, had seen all.

'The other member of ART,' he explained to Rebus. 'She's back at the flat. She wanted to be left on her own for a bit.'

'She's pretty upset,' Peter Collins agreed.

Rebus nodded slowly. 'She and David were ...?'

'Engaged,' Pam said, the tears falling now, Peter Collins's arm snaking around her shoulders. 'They were going to be married after the Fringe was finished.'

Rebus stole a glance towards Holmes, who raised his eyebrows in reply. Just like every good melodrama, the raised eyebrows said. A twist at the end of every bloody act.

3

The flat the group had rented, at what seemed to Rebus considerable expense, was a dowdy but spacious second-floor affair on Morrison Street, just off Lothian Road. Rebus had been to the block before, during the investigation of a housebreaking. That had been years ago, but the only difference in the tenement seemed to be the installation of a communal intercom at the main door. Rebus ignored the entry-phone and pushed at the heavy outside door. As he had guessed, it was unlocked anyway.

'Bloody students,' had been one of Rebus's few voiced comments during the short, curving drive down the back of the Castle towards the Usher Hall and Lothian Road. But then Holmes, driving, had been a student, too, hadn't he? So Rebus had not expanded on his theme. Now they climbed the steep winding stairwell until they arrived at the second floor. Marty Jones had told them that the name on the door was BLACK. Having robbed the students of an unreasonable rent (though no doubt the going rate), Mr and Mrs Black had departed for a month-long holiday on the proceeds. Rebus had borrowed a key from Jones and used it to let Holmes and himself in. The hall was long, narrow and darker than the stairwell. Off it were three bedrooms, a bathroom, a kitchen and the living room. A young woman, not quite out of her teens, came out of the kitchen carrying a mug of coffee. She was wearing a long baggy T-shirt and nothing else, and there was a sleepy, tousled look to her, accompanying the red streakiness of her eyes.

'Oh,' she said, startled. Rebus was quick to respond.

'Inspector Rebus, miss. This is Detective Constable Holmes. One of your friends lent us a key. Could we have a word?'

'About David?' Her eyes were huge, doe-like, her face small and round. Her hair was short and fair, the body slender and brittle. Even in grief – perhaps especially in grief – she was mightily attractive, and Holmes raised his eyebrows again as she led them into the living room.

Two sleeping bags lay on the floor, along with paperback

books, an alarm clock, mugs of tea. Off the living room was a box room, a large walk-in cupboard. These were often used by students to make an extra room in a temporary flat and light coming from the half-open door told Rebus that this was still its function. Marie went into the room and switched off the light, before joining the two policemen.

'It's Pam's room,' she explained. 'She said I could lie down there. I didn't want to sleep in our ... in my room.'

'Of course,' Rebus said, all understanding and sympathy.

'Of course,' Holmes repeated. She signalled for them to sit, so they did, sinking into a sofa the consistency of marshmallow. Rebus feared he wouldn't be able to rise again without help and struggled to keep himself upright. Marie meantime had settled, legs beneath her, with enviable poise on the room's only chair. She placed her mug on the floor, then had a thought.

'Would you like ...?'

A shake of the head from both men. It struck Rebus that there was something about her voice. Holmes beat him to it.

'Are you French?'

She smiled a pale smile, then nodded towards the Detective Constable. 'From Bordeaux. Do you know it?'

'Only by the reputation of its wine.'

Rebus blew his nose again, though pulling the hankie from his pocket had been a struggle. Holmes took the hint and closed his mouth. 'Now then, Miss ...?' Rebus began.

'Hivert, Marie Hivert.'

Rebus nodded slowly, playing with the hankie rather than trying to replace it in his pocket. 'We're told that you were engaged to Mr Caulfield.'

Her voice was almost a whisper. 'Yes. Not officially, you understand. But there was – a promise.'

'I see. And when was this promise made?'

'Oh, I'm not sure exactly. March, April. Yes, early April I think. Springtime.'

'And how were things between David and yourself?' She seemed not quite to understand. 'I mean,' said Rebus, 'how did David seem to you?'

She shrugged. 'David was David. He could be—' she raised her eyes to the ceiling, seeking words, 'impossible, nervous, exciting, foul-tempered.' She smiled. 'But mostly exciting.'

'Not suicidal?'

She gave this serious thought. 'Oh yes, I suppose,' she admitted. 'Suicidal, just as actors can be. He took criticism to heart. He was a perfectionist.'

'How long had you known him?'

'Two years. I met him through the theatre group.'

'And you fell in love?'

She smiled again. 'Not at first. There was a certain … competitiveness between us, you might say. It helped our acting. I'm not sure it helped our relationship altogether. But we survived.' Realising what she had said, she grew silent, her eyes dimming. A hand went to her forehead as, head bowed, she tried to collect herself.

'I'm sorry,' she said, collapsing into sobs. Holmes raised his eyebrows: someone should be here with her. Rebus shrugged back: she can handle it on her own. Holmes's eyebrows remained raised: can she? Rebus looked back at the tiny figure, engulfed by the armchair. Could actors always tell the real world from the illusory?

We survived. It was an interesting phrase to have used. But then she was an interesting young woman.

She went to the bathroom to splash water on her face and while she was gone Rebus took the opportunity to rise awkwardly to his feet. He looked back at the sofa.

'Bloody thing,' he said. Holmes just smiled.

When she returned, composed once more, Rebus asked if David Caulfield might have left a note somewhere. She shrugged. He asked if she minded them having a quick look round. She shook her head. So, never men to refuse a gift, Rebus and Holmes began looking.

The set-up was fairly straightforward. Pam slept in the box room, while Marty Jones and Hugh Clay had sleeping bags on the living-room floor. Marie and David Caulfield had shared the largest of the three bedrooms, with Charles and Peter Collins having a single room each. Charles Collins's room was obsessively tidy; its narrow single bed made up for the night and on the quilt an acting-copy of *Scenes from a Hanging*, covered in marginalia and with several long speeches, all Caulfield's, seemingly excised. A pencil lay on the typescript, evidence that Charles Collins was taking the critics' view to heart himself and attempting to shorten the play as best he could.

Peter Collins's room was much more to Rebus's personal taste, though Holmes wrinkled his nose at the used underwear underfoot, the contents of the hastily unpacked rucksack scattered over every surface. Beside the unmade bed, next to an overflowing ashtray, lay another copy of the play. Rebus flipped through it. Closing it, his attention was caught by some doodlings on the inside cover. Crude heart shapes had been constructed around the words 'I love Edinburgh'. His smile was quickly erased when Holmes held the ashtray towards him.

'Not exactly Silk Cut,' Holmes was saying. Rebus looked. The butts in the ashtrays were made up of cigarette papers wrapped around curled strips of cardboard. They were called 'roaches' by those who smoked dope, though he couldn't remember why. He made a tutting sound.

'And what were we doing in here when we found these?' he asked. Holmes nodded, knowing the truth: they probably couldn't charge Peter Collins even if they'd wanted to, since there was no reason for their being in his room. *We were looking for someone else's suicide note* probably wouldn't impress a latter-day jury.

The double room shared by Marie Hivert and David Caulfield was messiest of all. Marie helped them sift through a few of Caulfield's things. His diary proved a dead end, since he had started it faithfully on 1 January but the entries ceased on 8 January. Rebus, having tried keeping a diary himself, knew the feeling.

But in the back of the diary were newspaper clippings, detailing Caulfield's triumph in the previous year's *Twelfth Night*. Marie, too, had come in for some praise as Viola, but the glory had been Malvolio's. She wept again a little as she read through the reviews. Holmes said that he'd make another cup of coffee. Did he want her to fetch Pam from the theatre? She shook her head. She'd be all right. She promised she would.

While Marie sat on the bed and Holmes filled the kettle, Rebus wandered back into the living room. He peered into the box room, but saw little there to interest him. Finally, he came back to the sleeping bags on the floor. Marie was coming back into the room as he bent to pick up the paperback book from beside one sleeping bag. It was Tom Wolfe's *Bonfire of the Vanities*. Rebus had a hardback copy at home, still unopened. Something fell from the back of the book, a piece of card. Rebus retrieved it from the floor. It was a photograph of Marie, standing on the Castle ramparts with the Scott Monument behind her. The wind blew her hair fiercely against her face and she was attempting to sweep the hair out of her eyes as she grinned towards the camera. Rebus handed the picture to her.

'Your hair was longer then,' he said.

She smiled and nodded, her eyes still moist. 'Yes,' she said. 'That was in June. We came to look at the venue.'

He waved the book at her. 'Who's the Tom Wolfe fan?'

'Oh,' she said, 'it's doing the rounds. I think Marty's reading it just now.' Rebus flipped through the book again, his eyes lingering a moment on the inside cover. 'Tom Wolfe's had quite a career,' he said before placing the book, face down as it had been, beside the sleeping bag. He pointed towards the photograph. 'Shall I put it back?' But she shook her head.

'It was David's,' she said. 'I think I'd like to keep it.'

Rebus smiled an avuncular smile. 'Of course,' he said. Then he remembered something. 'David's parents. Have you been in touch at all?'

She shook her head, horror growing within her. 'Oh God,' she said, 'they'll be devastated. David was very close to his mother and father.'

'Well,' said Rebus, 'give me the details and I'll phone them when I get back to the station.'

She frowned. 'But I don't ... No, sorry,' she said, 'all I know is that they live in Croydon.'

'Well, never mind,' said Rebus, knowing, in fact, that the parents had already been notified, but interested that Caulfield's apparent fiancée should know their address only vaguely. If David Caulfield had been so close to his mother and father, wouldn't they have been told of the engagement? And once told, wouldn't they have wanted to meet Marie? Rebus's knowledge of English geography wasn't exactly *Mastermind* material, but he was fairly sure that Reading and Croydon weren't at what you would call opposite ends of the country.

Interesting, all very interesting. Holmes came in carrying three mugs of coffee, but Rebus shook his head, suddenly the brisk senior officer.

'No time for that, Holmes,' he said. 'There's plenty of work waiting for us back at the station.' Then, to Marie: 'Take care of yourself, Miss Hivert. If there's anything we can do, don't hesitate.'

Her smile was winning. 'Thank you, Inspector.' She turned to Holmes, taking a mug from him. 'And thank you, too, constable,' she said. The look on Holmes's face kept Rebus grinning all the way back to the station.

4

There the grin promptly vanished. There was a message marked URGENT from the police pathologist asking Rebus to call him. Rebus pressed the seven digits on his new-fangled telephone. The thing had a twenty-number memory and somewhere in that memory was the single-digit number that would connect him with the pathologist, but Rebus could never remember which number was which and he kept losing the sheet of paper with all the memory numbers on it.

'It's four,' Holmes reminded him, just as he'd come to the end of dialling. He was throwing Holmes a kind of half-scowl when the pathologist himself answered.

'Oh, yes, Rebus. Hello there. It's about this hanging victim of yours. I've had a look at him. Manual strangulation, I'd say.'

'Yes?' Rebus, his thoughts on Marie Hivert, was waiting for some punchline.

'I don't think you understand me, Inspector. *Manual* strangulation. From the Latin *manus*, meaning the hand. From the deep body temperature, I'd say he died between midnight and two in the morning. He was strung up on that contraption some time thereafter. Bruising around the throat is definitely consistent with thumb-pressure especially.'

'You mean someone strangled him?' Rebus said, really for Holmes's benefit.

'I *think* that's what I've been telling you, yes. If I find out anything more, I'll let you know.'

'Are the forensics people with you?'

'I've contacted the lab. They're sending someone over with some bags, but to be honest, we started off on this one thinking it was simple suicide. We may have inadvertently destroyed the tinier scraps of evidence.'

'Not to worry,' Rebus said, a father-confessor now, easing guilt. 'Just get what you can.'

He put down the receiver and stared at his Detective

Constable. Or, rather, stared *through* him. Holmes knew that there were times for talking and times for silence, and that this fell into the latter category. It took Rebus a full minute to snap out of his reverie.

'Well I'll be buggered,' he said. 'We've been talking with a murderer this morning, Brian. A cold-blooded one at that. And we didn't even know it. I wonder whatever happened to the famous police "nose" for a villain. Any idea?'

Holmes frowned. 'About what happened to the famous police "nose"?'

'No,' cried Rebus, exasperated. 'I mean, any idea who did it?'

Holmes shrugged, then brought the Fringe programme back out from where it had been rolled up in his jacket pocket. He started turning pages. 'I think,' he said, 'there's an Agatha Christie playing somewhere. Maybe we could get a few ideas?'

Rebus's eyes lit up. He snatched the programme from Holmes's hands. 'Never mind Agatha Christie,' he said, starting through the programme himself. 'What we want is Shakespeare.'

'What, *Macbeth*? *Hamlet*? *King Lear*?'

'No, not a tragedy, a good comedy, something to cheer the soul. Ah, here we go.' He stabbed the open page with his finger. '*Twelfth Night*. That's the play for us, Brian. That's the very play for us.'

The problem, really, in the end was: which *Twelfth Night*? There were three on offer, plus another at the Festival proper. One of the Fringe versions offered an update to gangster Chicago, another played with an all-female cast and the third boasted futuristic stage design. But Rebus wanted traditional fare, and so opted for the Festival performance. There was just one hitch: it was a complete sell-out.

Not that Rebus considered this a hitch. He waited while Holmes called his girlfriend, Nell Stapleton, and apologised to her about some evening engagement he was breaking, then the two men drove to the Lyceum, tucked in behind the Usher Hall so as to be almost invisible to the naked eye.

'There's a five o'clock performance,' Rebus explained. 'We should just make it.' They did. There was a slight hold-up while Rebus explained to the house manager that this really was police business and not some last-minute culture beano, and a place was found for them in a dusty corner to the rear of the stalls. The lights were dimming as they entered.

'I haven't been to a play in years,' Rebus said to Holmes, excited at the prospect. Holmes, bemused, smiled back, but his superior's eyes were already on the stage, where the curtain was rising, a guitar was playing and a man in pale pink tights lay across an ornate bench, looking as cheesed off with life as Holmes himself felt. Why did Rebus always have to work from instinct, and always alone, never letting anyone in on whatever he knew or thought he knew? Was it because he was afraid of failure? Holmes suspected it was. If you kept your ideas to yourself, you couldn't be proved wrong. Well, Holmes had his own ideas about this case, though he was damned if he'd let Rebus in on them.

'If music be the food of love ...' came the voice from the stage. And that was another thing – Holmes was starving. It was odds-on the back few rows would soon find his growling stomach competition for the noises from the stage.

'Will you go hunt, my lord?'

'What, Curio?'

'The hart.'

'Why, so I do, the noblest that I have ...'

Holmes sneaked a glance towards Rebus. To say the older man's attention was rapt would have been understating the case. He'd give it until the end of Act One, then sneak out to the nearest chip shop. Leave Rebus to his Shakespeare; Holmes was a nationalist when it came to literature. A pity Hugh MacDiarmid had never written a play.

In fact, Holmes went for a wander, up and down Lothian Road as far as the Caledonian Hotel to the north and Tollcross to the south. Lothian Road was Edinburgh's fast-food centre and the variety on offer brought with it indecision. Pizza, burgers, kebabs, Chinese, baked potatoes, more burgers, more pizza and the once-ubiquitous fish and chip shop (more often now an offshoot of a kebab or burger restaurant). Undecided, he grew hungrier, and stopped for a pint of lager in a noisy barn of a pub before finally settling for a fish supper, naming himself a nationalist in cuisine as well as in writing.

By the time he returned to the theatre, the players were coming out to take their applause. Rebus was clapping as loudly as anyone, enjoyment evident on his face. But when the curtain came down, he turned and dragged Holmes from the auditorium, back into the foyer and out onto the street.

'Fish and chips, eh?' he said. 'Now there's an idea.'

'How did you know?'

'I can smell the vinegar coming off your hands. Where's the chippie?'

Holmes nodded in the direction of Tollcross. They started

walking. 'So did you learn anything?' Holmes asked. 'From the play, I mean?'

Rebus smiled. 'More than I'd hoped for, Brian. If you'd been paying attention, you'd have noticed it, too. The only speech that mattered was way back in Act One. A speech made by the Fool, whose name is Feste. I wonder who played Feste in ART's production last year? Actually, I think I can guess. Come on then, where's this chip shop? A man could starve to death on Lothian Road looking for something even remotely edible.'

'It's just off Tollcross. It's nothing very special.'

'So long as it fills me up, Brian. We've got a long evening ahead of us.'

'Oh?'

Rebus nodded vigorously. 'Hunting the heart, Brian.' He winked towards the younger man. 'Hunting the heart.'

5

The door of the Morrison Street flat was opened by Peter Collins. He looked surprised to see them.

'Don't worry, Peter,' Rebus said, pushing past him into the hall. 'We're not here to put the cuffs on you for possession.' He sniffed the air in the hall, then tutted. 'Already? At this rate you'll be stoned before *News at Ten*.'

Peter blushed.

'All right if we come in?' Rebus asked, already sauntering down the hall towards the living room. Holmes followed him indoors, smiling an apology. Peter closed the door behind them.

'They're mostly out,' Peter called.

'So I see,' said Rebus, in the living room now. 'Hello, Marie, how are you feeling?'

'Hello again, Inspector. I'm a little better.' She was dressed, and seated primly on the chair, hands resting on her knees. Rebus looked towards the sofa, but thought better of sitting down. Instead he rested himself on the sofa's fairly rigid arm. 'I see you're all getting ready to go.'

He nodded towards the two rucksacks parked against the living-room wall. The sleeping bags from the floor had been folded away, as had books and alarm clocks.

'Why bother to stay?' Peter said. He flopped onto the sofa and pushed a hand through his hair. 'We thought we'd drive down through the night. Be back in Reading by dawn with any luck.'

Rebus nodded at this. 'So the show does *not* go on?'

'It'd be a bit bloody heartless, don't you think?' This from Peter Collins, with a glance towards Marie.

'Of course,' Rebus agreed. Holmes had stationed himself between the living-room door and the rucksacks. 'So where is everyone?'

Marie answered. 'Pam and Marty have gone for a last walk around.'

'And Charles is almost certainly off getting drunk some-where,' added Collins. 'Rueing his failed show.'

'And Hugh?' asked Rebus. Collins shrugged.

'I think,' Marie said, 'Hugh went off to get drunk, too.'

'But for different reasons, no doubt,' Rebus speculated.

'He was David's best friend,' she answered quietly.

Rebus nodded thoughtfully. 'Actually, we just bumped into him – literally.'

'Who?' asked Peter.

'Mr Clay. He seems to be in the middle of a pub crawl the length of Lothian Road. We were coming out of a chip shop and came across him weaving his way to the next watering hole.'

'Oh?' Collins didn't sound particularly interested.

'I told him where the best pubs in this neighbourhood are. He didn't seem to know.'

'That was good of you,' Collins said, voice heavy with irony.

'Nice of them all to leave you alone, isn't it though?'

The question hung in the air. At last, Marie spoke. 'What do you mean?'

But Rebus shifted on his perch and left the comment at that. 'No,' he said instead, 'only I thought Mr Clay might have had a better idea of the pubs, seeing how he was here last year, and then again in June to look at the venue. But of course, as he was good enough to explain, he *wasn't* here in June. There were exams. Some people had to study harder than others. Only three of you came to Edinburgh in June.' Rebus raised a finger shiny with chip fat. 'Pam, who has what I'd call a definite crush on you, Peter.' Collins smiled at this, but weakly. Rebus raised a second and then third finger. 'And you two. Just the three of you. That, I presume, is where it started.'

'What?' The blood had drained from Marie's face, making her somehow more beautiful than ever. Rebus shifted again, seeming to ignore her question.

'It doesn't really matter who took that photo of you, the one I found in *Bonfire of the Vanities*.' He was staring at her quite evenly now. 'What matters is that it was there. And on the inside cover someone had drawn a couple of hearts, very similar to some I happened to see on Peter's copy of the play. It matters that on his copy of the play, Peter has also written the words "I love Edinburgh".' Peter Collins was ready to protest, but Rebus studiously ignored him, keeping his eyes on Marie's, fixing her, so that there might only have been the two of them in the room.

'You told me,' he continued, 'that you'd come to Edinburgh to check on the venue. I took that "you" to mean all of you, but Hugh Clay has put me right on that. You came without David, who was too busy studying to make the trip. And you told me something else earlier. You said your relationship with him had "survived". Survived what? I asked myself afterwards. The answer seems pretty straightforward. Survived a brief fling, a fling that started in Edinburgh and lasted the summer.'

Now, only now, did he turn to Peter Collins. 'Isn't that right, Peter?'

Collins, his face mottled with anger, made to rise.

'Sit down,' Rebus ordered, standing himself. He walked towards the fireplace, turned and faced Collins, who looked to be disappearing into the sofa, reducing in size with the passing moments. 'You love Edinburgh,' he went on, 'because that's where your little fling with Marie started. Fair enough, these things are never anyone's fault, are they? You managed to keep it fairly secret. The Tom Wolfe book belongs to you, though, and that photo you'd kept in it — maybe forgetting it was there — that photo might have been a giveaway, but then again it could all be very innocent, couldn't it?

'But it's hard to keep something like that so secret when you're part of a very small group. There were sixteen of you in ART last year; that might have made it manageable. But not when there were only seven of you. I'm not sure who else knows about it. But I am sure that David Caulfield found out.' Rebus didn't need to turn round to know that Marie was sobbing again. He kept staring at Peter Collins. 'He found out, and last night, late and backstage, perhaps drunk, the two of you had a fight. Quite dramatic in its way, isn't it? Fighting over the heroine and all that. But during the fight you just happened to strangle the life out of David Caulfield.' He paused, waiting for a denial which didn't come.

'Perhaps,' he continued, 'Marie wanted to go to the police. I don't know. But if she did, you persuaded her not to. Instead, you came up with something more dramatic. You'd make it look like suicide. And by God, what a suicide, the kind that David himself might just have attempted.' Rebus had been moving forward without seeming to, so that now he stood directly over Peter Collins.

'Yes,' he went on, 'very dramatic. But the note was a mistake. It was a bit too clever, you see. You thought everyone would take it as a reference to David's success in last year's production, but you knew yourself that there was a double meaning in it. I've just been to see *Twelfth Night*. Bloody good it was, too. You played Feste last year, didn't you, Peter? There's one speech of his ... how does it go?'

Rebus seemed to be trying to remember. 'Ah yes: "Many a good hanging prevents a bad marriage." Yes, that's it. And that's when I knew for sure.'

Peter Collins was smiling thinly. He gazed past Rebus

towards Marie, his eyes full and liquid. His voice when he spoke was tender. '"Many a good hanging prevents a bad marriage; and for turning away, let summer bear it out."'

'That's right,' Rebus said, nodding eagerly. 'Summer bore it out, all right. A summer fling. That's all. Not worth killing someone for, was it, Peter? But that didn't stop you. And the hanging was so apt, so neat. When you recalled the Fool's quote, you couldn't resist putting that note in David's pocket.' Rebus was shaking his head. 'More fool you, Mr Collins. More fool you.'

Brian Holmes went home from the police station that night in sombre mood. The traffic was slow, too, with theatregoers threading in and out between the near-stationary cars. He rolled down the driver's-side window, trying to make the interior less stuffy, less choked, and instead let in exhaust fumes and balmy late-evening air. Why did Rebus have to be such a clever bugger so much of the time? He seemed always to go into a case at an odd angle, like someone cutting a paper shape which, apparently random, could then be folded to make an origami sculpture, intricate and recognisable.

'Too clever for his own good,' he said to himself. But what he meant was that his superior was too clever for Holmes's own good. How was he expected to shine, to be noticed, to push forwards towards promotion, when it was always Rebus who, two steps ahead, came up with the answers? He remembered a boy at school who had always beaten Holmes in every subject save History. Yet Holmes had gone to university; the boy to work on his father's farm. Things could change, couldn't they? Though all he seemed to be learning from Rebus was how to keep your thoughts to yourself, how to be devious, how to, well, how to *act*. Though all this were true, he would still be the best understudy he possibly could be. One day, Rebus wouldn't be there to come up with the answers, or – occasion even more to be relished – would be unable to find the answers. And when that time came, Holmes would be ready to take the stage. He felt ready right now, but then he supposed every understudy must feel that way.

A flybill was thrown through his window by a smiling teenage girl. He heard her pass down the line of cars, yelling 'Come and see our show!' as she went. The small yellow sheet of paper fluttered onto the passenger seat and stayed there, face up, to haunt Holmes all the way back to Nell. Growing sombre again, it occurred to him how different things might have been if only Priestley had called the play *A Detective Constable Calls* instead.

Summer Show

Julian Symons

'What do you think of that little lot?' From under the bar counter Joe Grayson drew out six shiny broad beans, green and plump, well over a foot long. 'Too late for entry in the show, but I reckon they'd have taken first prize.'

The little group of farmers round the counter considered the beans solemnly. Francis Quarles looked at the poster behind Grayson's head, which told him that the Mannington Flower and Produce Summer Show was to be held on the following day, with sideshows, stalls. Punch and Judy, fortune-teller, bowling for a pig, and prizes for local fruit, flowers and vegetables.

The men round the counter agreed that the beans looked good. Joe Grayson split one to reveal eight perfectly shaped beans, green and delicate, an equal distance apart in their soft furry beds.

'If they'd all have been like that you'd a won it,' said one of the farmers. 'What do you say, Mr Ashley?'

A cadaverous, pale, dark-featured man with deep-set eyes, who had been sitting on a bench at the other end of the room, came up to the counter.

Quarles's host, a painter named John Tarn, whispered, 'Here's the expert.'

'Shouldn't look at these by rights, since I'm judging,' Ashley said. 'But as you're not entering them, there's no harm in it.' He looked at the open bean, and nodded. Then most delicately, merely using his fingertips, he felt the others. Three he put aside with no comment, but at the fourth he said: 'Soft in the middle.'

He split the bean. It looked identical with the others, but inside there were only five beans instead of eight. 'No good,' Ashley said.

'You're a wonder, Mr Ashley,' said one of the farmers. 'Have a drink.'

'Tell me what that means,' Quarles said to Tarn. 'I'm baffled.'

'They judge beans and peas like this. You make an entry of six bean or pea pods, and they should contain exactly the same number of beans or peas in them. Of course, there are other factors too – tenderness, ripeness, and so on – but the number is important. The judge opens just one pod and he tries to find a faulty one, as Ashley did just then.

'They do say Ashley's infallible, best judge in this part of the country. Queer chap, spent most of his life travelling round the world. Done all sorts of jobs by his own account, from selling vacuum cleaners and building bridges to working in a circus. Then settled down in England, made money as a nurseryman, and retired.'

A big red-faced man pushed open the pub door. 'Evening all,' he said. 'Pint of ale, please, landlord. Looks like a fine day for the show tomorrow.'

There was a chorus of 'Evening, Mr Wayne'. Ashley did not join in it. He thumped his glass of beer on the table still half-full, and walked out of the pub. There was an awkward silence for a moment, then everybody went on talking.

When they were on their way home, Tarn enlightened him as to the reason for Ashley's rudeness. 'A bad business. Ashley's daughter, his only child, was more or less engaged to Wayne's son, and he threw her over. Treated her very badly. She took an overdose of sleeping tablets and died. Wayne's son's married and was farming out in Kenya but Ashley and his wife have never forgiven Wayne – he was against the marriage, thought the two weren't suited. The Ashleys are fanatical about it. They've both got religion late in life, belong to some obscure sect, and they regard Wayne more or less as anti-Christ. There was trouble between them yesterday, when Ashley was helping to put up the tents. Wayne's dressing up as the fortune-teller, and there was a scene because he thought he'd been put rather out of the way. Bad to have that kind of thing in a village.'

The sun was shining when Tarn and Quarles entered the large meadow where the show was being held, half an hour before it was due to open. Colonel Comstock, who had organised it all, greeted Tarn with a worried smile. 'Ashley hasn't turned up yet to judge the beans and peas. Rang up and said he'd been unavoidably delayed. Ah, here he is now. That's good.'

Ashley, grim and hollow-eyed, accompanied by a grey-haired woman, was ushered by Colonel Comstock to the door of a large tent. The two of them went in while Comstock stayed at the entrance talking to Quarles and Tarn.

'This your first experience of a country show, Mr Quarles?' Quarles said it was, 'Lucky to get a fine day for it. Hope Ashley's not going to be long, all the judging should have been done this morning.'

Ashley was not long. After a few minutes his head poked out from inside the tent flap. On tables inside the tent the entries of broad beans, peas and other vegetables were arranged on plates. One pod had been opened from each entry in the broad bean and pea section which Ashley was judging, and he curtly indicated entries to which he had given prizes.

Outside the tent there was a shout, and agitated voices. A young man wearing a steward's badge ran in.

'Is there a doctor here? It's the fortune-teller, Mr Wayne.'

'What's the matter with him? Taken ill?' asked Colonel Comstock.

The young man gulped. 'No, Colonel. There's a knife – through his neck.'

The small fortune-teller's tent was next to the big marquee where Ashley had been judging. Wayne lay sprawled face forward across his table, his crystal ball just in front of him. His tall hat had fallen on the ground by his side. A thin shaft of sunlight through a gap near the top of the tent shone on the knife embedded deep in his neck. Quarles put a hand on the body. It was warm.

'Queer sort of knife,' said Colonel Comstock. 'Never seen one with a handle that looked as light as that. And the blade doesn't even look sharp.'

Quarles touched the edge of the blade. 'It's completely blunt. Does that mean anything to you?'

'Only that tremendous strength must have been needed to drive it deep into his neck like that. How long has he been dead?'

'Not more than five minutes.'

'Then that lets Ashley out,' the Colonel said. 'He's the obvious suspect, but he was in the marquee judging. There's no other way out of it except the entrance where we were standing.'

Quarles's face was grim as they returned to the marquee. He looked hard at the Ashleys. Mrs Ashley, wild-eyed as her husband, returned his stare. Quarles thoughtfully examined the open bean and pea pods and then walked round the inside of the marquee.

When he had reached a point opposite the fortune-teller's tent he got onto a chair and pushed at the apparently unbroken canvas. Suddenly a gap appeared where the guy ropes had not been firmly tightened. This gap was just opposite the larger gap in the fortune-teller's tent. Through it one could see the sprawled body of Wayne.

'You helped to fix these tents, Mr Ashley,' Quarles said. 'You fixed them conveniently for murder.'

'I don't know what you mean. You saw me arrive here. Since then I've been in this tent. You can all testify that I've had no time to do anything but judging – and also that I didn't leave the tent.'

'That's right,' said Colonel Comstock.

'Your wife could have opened these beans and peas and put the prize notices on them,' Quarles said. 'Because you're regarded as infallible your decisions wouldn't be questioned. You'd better open all those pods.'

'Oh, I say now, I don't think we could do that.' The Colonel's sense of propriety was outraged. 'Ashley wouldn't make a mistake.'

'But his wife might.' In a tense silence Quarles broke open the pods of the beans given first prize. Two of the six were much inferior to the one on show.

Colonel Comstock's lips were tightly pursed. He broke open the beans awarded second prize himself and found a pod containing beans large and hard, well past their prime. In one of the pea pods awarded a prize there were discoloured, brownish peas.

'You never judged these, Ashley,' Colonel Comstock said harshly.

'You can think what you like.' Ashley's voice was violent. 'I did what I had to do.'

'The Lord destroyeth evildoers,' his wife said suddenly. 'We are the servants of the Lord.'

'What was your job in that circus, Ashley?' Quarles asked.

'I heard a voice that said, "Kill",' Ashley answered his wife.

Tarn was looking puzzled. 'Whether Ashley judged the entries or not I don't see how he could have killed Wayne. He never left the tent.'

'He didn't need to leave the tent. Yesterday he helped to

fix this marquee and the fortune-teller's tent. You remember Wayne was annoyed about the placing of it. He arranged things so that there was a gap in each tent to the point where Wayne was sitting. Then he threw a knife through the gaps into Wayne's neck. The two of them planned it together. I don't know whether any jury will consider them sane.'

'But to throw a knife in that way would require extraordinary skill.'

'It was a special kind of knife,' Quarles said. 'With a sharp point, a blunt blade, and a specially light handle to ensure balance in the middle. I recognised it as soon as I saw it, and I knew how the murder had been done. It's the kind of knife that's only used in a circus by a professional knife-thrower.'

White Cap

Ethel Lina White

When Tess Leigh washed her hair, one June evening, she involved the issue of life or death ... On the surface it seemed merely a matter of a trivial change of habit. Instead of going bare-headed to work, she had to wear a cap.

The reason was that her thick wavy hair became unruly if she exposed it to the open air too soon after a shampoo.

The turban was made from a white Angora scarf and was ornamented with a lucky brooch of green-and-white enamel in the shape of a sprig of white heather. Inside the band was stitched a laundry-tape marked with her name in red thread.

It was a glorious morning when – disdaining the trams – she set out to walk to the Peninsular Dye-Stuffs Corporation, where she was employed as a stenographer. The industrial town was built upon rolling moorland whose natural beauty had been destroyed; but the Council had acquired a range of hills – the Steepes – as its lungs and playground. About

1,000 feet in height, they were dominated by the mountain peak – the Spike – which rose another 3,000 feet into the air.

Tess walked with the rapid ease of youth, swinging the suitcase which held her holiday-kit. From time to time she looked up at the Spike – sharply outlined against a cloudless blue sky. It helped her forget the smoking chimneys of the factories and also to calm her spirit – for all was not well either with her work or her love.

She had only herself to blame for her heart-trouble. No one at the Peninsular could understand why she had been taken in by the cheap glamour of Clement Dodd. She was attractive, athletic and possessed of a sweet yet strong character. Fearlessly outspoken, she had deep sympathy with the underdog and always rushed in to champion any victim of injustice.

As she approached the majestic pillared entrance to the factory, she felt a reluctance to enter which was becoming a familiar sensation.

She knew that she was not the only employee to feel that suddenly sinking heart and lagging foot, in spite of the fact that old John Aspinall – who founded the Peninsular Works – had striven to make it a model factory. He had arranged for the health, comfort and recreation of his workers. There were extensive grounds, a swimming pool, an excellent canteen and various athletic clubs.

These good things remained after his death when his son – Young John – went to the USA to study American methods, leaving his brother to direct the corporation. Brother Eustace was a lazy, inefficient man who was content to sink to the status of a puppet government after Miss Ratcliffe had bought a controlling interest in the Peninsular.

She was a wealthy, keen-witted woman with a lust for power. Soured by lack of social sovereignty through her failure to marry a titled husband, she strove to become a Power in commerce. Part of her policy was to use the brains and experience of the men employed by the Peninsular. While she was professing interest in them, her keen brain was mincing up their suggestions and theories until they emerged as facts – for which she took all the credit.

Unfortunately the process was accompanied by corresponding human wastage, when gradually the atmosphere became poisoned because employees feared for their jobs. Most of the small fry were too insignificant to be vulnerable, but Tess stood out from the bulk of the stenographer staff, because of an unlucky incident.

The Peninsular ran a rifle club in connection with the municipal shooting range. One day, Miss Ratcliffe visited them and gave what practically amounted to a demonstration in marksmanship. Tess, who was also expert, welcomed her only as a worthy opponent and challenged her to a match which she won by a narrow margin.

'Bad show,' commented her friends. 'After this, she will have her knife in you.'

In addition to anxiety for her job, Tess was beginning to fear that Miss Ratcliffe was developing her specialised interest in Clement Dodd. As chief accountant of the Finance Department, he frequently visited her office although he denied any personal element to Tess.

Tess's frown deepened as she passed through the gates and entered the grounds – gay with lilac and laburnum. Although it was the half-holiday, the model factory repelled her like a prison. As she gazed wistfully up at the soaring Spike, she suddenly saw a bird circling over its rocky summit.

'Don,' she called to a tall stooping man with grey hair and a classical profile, 'Don, do you see what I see?'

He shaded his eyes with a shaking white hand.

'It must be an unusually large bird to be visible at this distance,' he remarked. 'Can it be an eagle?'

'Of course it's an eagle,' cried Tess exultantly. 'Oh, isn't he a real king of birds? So free and splendid. I've a passion for eagles. The sight of one in captivity makes me see red.'

The old man did not respond to her interest for he was gazing eagerly at an impressive black saloon car which had just driven up to the main entrance. As a majestic blonde ascended the steps, he glanced at the clock tower.

'Miss Ratcliffe sets us an example in punctuality,' he remarked. 'In confidence, I have an appointment with her. My poor wife has resented the overtime I have given to the corporation. The fact is I was staying late to work out a system of reorganisation for several of the departments, to submit to Miss Ratcliffe … Now I believe I am going to reap my reward. My letter states that the subject of the interview is "important clerical changes".'

As she looked at his flushed triumphant face, Tess had a sudden pang of misgiving. Originally a schoolmaster, Don was a man of superior education. For the sake of a delicate wife and daughter, he had commercialised his scientific knowledge in the Peninsular Laboratory. He was intensely proud of his intellectual family and his cultured surroundings, where every book and picture was the result of selective taste.

'Don't count on it,' she warned him. 'Everyone knows that Ratcliffe is a rat.'

A short girl with a dark fringe and an important air looked at her sharply as she hurried past. She had chosen an unfortunate moment for her remark, since the energetic damsel was Miss Ratcliffe's secretary. Donovan, too, was visibly distressed by her imprudence.

But Tess smiled at him and entered the great hall to clock in.

A young man came forward to meet Tess as though he had been watching for her arrival. Ted Lockwood made no secret of his feeling for her. It was one of Nature's mysteries why she had rejected him for Clement, since he was so suited to be her opposite number. She had a mechanical mind so could appreciate the fact that he was a clever engineer. Like her, he was a fine athlete while he seasoned his sound qualities with a sense of humour.

'Will madame lunch with me?'

'Sorry, Ted,' replied Tess. 'I'm eating with Clem. Have you seen him around?'

'In the sick bay. He's got a hangover and Matron's fussing over him. If a woman wants to be maternal, it beats me why she doesn't marry and set up her own outfit?'

'Meaning me?' asked Tess with customary bluntness.

'Yes, Tess.' Lockwood's face was grim with resolution. 'Why won't you face the facts? The most successful marriages are founded on mutual interest – and you and I have the same tastes. How will you make out with an artistic bloke like Dodd?'

'Oh, not again, Ted,' pleaded Tess wearily.

She had no further chance to brood for she always worked at high pressure. As the subject of the dictation was technical matter which exacted her entire attention, she welcomed a break, in order to freshen herself with a wash. The men's and women's cloakrooms were built off a central domed hall with a white marble drinking fountain, which was a popular meeting place.

When she entered it, a group of employees were talking in excited undertones as they gathered around Clement Dodd. He was a tall, slim-waisted youth who would have made a pretty girl, but for thin mobile lips. He spoke with a stressed Oxford accent while his manner to women of all ages was that of a courtier.

'Heard the latest casualty?' he asked Tess. 'Poor old Don's got the K.O.'

As Tess stared at him in dismay, he lit a cigarette.

'Afraid he asked for it,' he said casually. 'Too big for his boots. That line does not appeal to our lady-boss.'

'It's a real tragedy,' exclaimed a woman who dyed her grey hairs. 'He was nearly due to retire. Now he'll lose his pension. What will become of him?'

'Hush,' whispered a typist. 'He's coming in.'

His head held high, the old scientist approached the group. He cleared his throat before he made an announcement after the fashion of a headmaster addressing his school.

'I have just resigned my position. I have never been happy in a non-scholastic atmosphere. Now I shall hope to resume my academic career. I wish to take this opportunity to thank you for your loyal support and cooperation.'

Although his lips quivered, he managed to make a grand exit.

As she watched him, Tess grew suddenly hot and giddy.

'It's cruel – hateful – abominable—' she stormed. 'That horrible woman has thrown him out just to save his pension.'

'Cool off, you young volcano.'

Tess felt herself pushed down on a chair. Although she recognised Lockwood's voice, she barely saw him through a shifting mist. She gulped down the glass of water which he drew for her and then gave him a grateful grin.

'Okay?' he asked. 'What was the matter? You went first red and then white.'

'Temper,' she replied frankly. 'Only it's a bit more than that. Just before I left Canada, I was in an air crash. Since then, if I get too steamed up, I have a blackout. The doctor told me I'd grow out of it very soon, but he warned me not to get excited.'

'What's it like?'

'Foul – and frightening. Everything turns black and I drop into a sort of sleep. The doctor explained that sleep was my salvation, but it scares me because when I wake up, I can remember nothing. I go right out.'

The rest of the morning dragged itself out. Worried about Don, she forgot to concentrate on her work with the result that she had the greatest difficulty in reading back her outlines. As she was typing her notes, she noticed that Miss James – Ratcliffe's secretary – had entered the room and was whispering to the supervisor.

Although she vaguely expected it, her heart knocked at the summons.

'Miss Leigh. Please report at once to Miss Ratcliffe.'

Seated at her desk, Miss Ratcliffe looked a model of impersonal Administration – correct to form and polished in every detail. Her dark suit was perfectly built and her silver-blonde wave faultless.

'Miss Leigh?' Her voice was languid. 'Ah yes. I am sorry that your services will not be required after today. You will receive a week's wages in lieu of notice. This is no reflection on your work – but we have to reduce the staff.'

'But Miss Ratcliffe,' gasped Tess, 'there must be some mistake. My speeds are the highest in the office and—'

'This is not a personal matter.'

'But it is personal.' With characteristic courage, Tess dared to interrupt the tyrant. 'If it were not, I should be expected to work out my notice. I have a right to know the reason.'

'The reason is this,' she said. 'You have been disloyal.'

With a guilty recollection of unguarded remarks, Tess could not deny the charge. Instead she sank her pride to make an appeal.

'I don't want to inflict a sob story on you, but I really need this work. I came over here from Canada when my parents died and I have no friends in England. Jobs are so scarce at present. Will you give me a second chance? I promise you I'll do better in future.'

Miss Ratcliffe looked at her with cold impersonal eyes as she touched her bell.

'My decision is final,' she said.

As Miss James bustled into the office and opened the door pointedly, Tess had a sudden vision of the eagle beating his great wings over the mountain top. The memory flooded over her, filling her with a wave of power.

She realised that she too was free and able to meet Ratcliffe on equal ground.

'You are a cruel, petty woman,' she said. 'The most junior typist has more right in the Peninsular than you have. You've bought your power – not earned it. And instead of using it, you abuse it. When worthwhile people are dying every day, it is a crime for you to be alive.'

She was conscious of passers-by in the corridor who paused to look into the office before Miss James pushed her outside and shut the door.

On her way to the cashier's office, she met Don in the corridor – stooping like a defeated man.

'The Gestapo's got me too, Don. I'm sacked.'

'I'm deeply grieved,' he told her. 'But your conscience is clear, while I have something to regret … When I first had news of my – my resignation, I was so stunned that – in trying to save myself – I threw someone to the lions. That hurts most.' He added regretfully with a lapse of his grand manner, 'Besides, it did me no good.'

As the admission sank in, fitting the circumstances of her own dismissal, Tess felt that she had been struck by the hand of a friend.

'You,' she muttered as she turned away.

The second shock made her feel numbed to reality. After she was paid off, she went to the cloakroom and mechanically changed into white slacks and a rose-red pullover. Her hair was beginning to get bushy, as she drew her white cap over it, in an instinctive desire to look her best when she met Clement.

ited for Clement for a long time in the canteen, but he
ot appear. Presently she accepted the disappointment
w... dreary fatalism. Too overwrought to eat, she went out
of the Peninsular grounds. All she wanted was to escape
to the Steepes and climb the rough ascent to the Spike – to
stand on the mountain top and meet the healing friction of
the wind.

Owing to its precipitous quarried sides, the Steepes were
accessible from the town by a small funicular which carried
patrons up the face of the cliff. The girl at the turnstile who
collected the tickets was a local character. Abnormally sharp,
although she looked a child, her mop of red hair had gained
her the obvious title of 'Ginger'.

'Does it bring you luck?' she asked as her quick eyes
noticed the white heather brooch on Tess's cap.

'You may have the lot at bargain price,' Tess told her
bitterly.

On the summit of the Steepes stretched a wide level
expanse of threadbare turf where a cafeteria as well as chairs
and tables were provided for the community. The bulk of the
holidaymakers used to congregate there, eating, drinking,
reading and playing games; but it was deserted that afternoon owing to a circus performance in the town.

Tess struck off along a narrow path which wound, like a
pale green ribbon, amid clumps of whinberry and stems of
uncurled bracken. Farther off, on the left, the ground sloped
down to the rifle range.

She threw herself down on the heather. She wanted the
consolation of contact with primeval things. With a springy
cushion of twigs supporting her head, she gazed up into the

clear blue sky, when she noticed the flicker of wings.

Again the eagle was circling around the summit of the Spike, reminding her of her impulse to climb to the mountain top. It was a long, rough walk, for the steep track zigzagged continually across natural obstacles of bog and rock. Even the optimistic guidebook stated that two and a half hours were required for the ascent.

Swinging to her feet, she had a clear view of the path leading to the rifle range. Two figures – pressed closely together – stood upon the slope. Even at that distance, it was impossible to mistake the sunlit shimmer of the woman's silvery-blonde hair or the slack grace of her companion.

As she watched them, Dodd threw his arm around Miss Ratcliffe and bent his head, as though seeking her lips … At the sight, the blood rushed to Tess's head. Again she felt the blast of furnace heat while a wheel seemed to spin remorselessly inside her brain.

Recognising the terrifying symptoms which heralded a temporary extinction, she fought with all her strength to resist them, but while she was struggling, a rush of darkness swept over her like a black rocket. As she fell – face downward – on the heather in her last moment of consciousness, she noticed the watch on her outstretched wrist.

It was three o'clock.

It was four o'clock. Tess stared at her watch with frightened eyes. Only an instant before it was three o'clock. A whole hour had been rubbed out of her life …

She pressed her fingers to her eyes as the memory of Clem's treachery overwhelmed her. The knowledge made not only miserable, but cheap and ashamed, so that ᷄minant instinct was to hide. Soon the holidaymak- ᷄ould be spreading fanwise over the lower slopes of the Steepes.

Shrinking from the ordeal of meeting someone from the Peninsular Factory, she rose stiffly and looked around for her cap. To her annoyance, she could not see it and, after pulling apart the nearest clumps of heather, she had to give up the search. Stampeded by the sound of distant voices, she ran over the rough until she reached a slippery bank of turf which dropped sheer to a narrow ledge above a worked-out quarry.

A perilous climb along the rocky rim brought her to a shallow depression in the hillside which offered her sanctuary. When she leaned back in the hollow, she seemed perched upon a lip of some bottomless abyss. For a long time she lay there – watching the pageant of clouds which rolled past like a stormy sea.

When she forced herself to look at her watch, she grimaced.

'Gosh, it's late. Well – I've got to face people again.'

In spite of this resolution, she made a circle to avoid passing the crowd around the cafeteria. She could not understand the force of the instinct which warned her to remain hidden.

As she clicked through the 'OUT' turnstile, she noticed that Ginger was staring at her. The scrutiny alarmed her vaguely for it revived her dormant dread of her lost hour.

'Where did I go?' she questioned. 'What have I done? Do I show the marks of it in my face? Why does that girl stare at me? Oh, dear heart, I wish Ted was with me.'

Now that her infatuation for Clement had been shrivelled

by the knowledge of his treachery, her heart turned instinctively towards Lockwood. On the homeward journey, while she sat upon the hard wooden seats of the tram and watched long lines of mean houses slide past, the lines of Kipling's poem swam into her mind.

The Thousandth Man will stand by your side
To the gallows-foot — and after!

She lodged in a comfortable house which belonged to a florist. It welcomed her like a haven, that evening. The flowers had never looked so beautiful in the sunset glow when she walked through the garden. The shabby, dark-green sitting room was cool and a meal was spread on the table, so that she had only to make her tea from the electric kettle.

She was feeling refreshed and stimulated when her landlady entered the room to remove her tray.

'What news?' she clicked. 'Is it really true she's been murdered?'

'Who?' asked Tess, with a pang of foreboding.

'Your Miss Ratcliffe, of course. It's all over the town that she's been shot dead.'

As Tess stared blindly at her landlady, the scrape of the gate made the woman glance through the window.

'It's Mr Lockwood,' she announced. 'I'll go let him in.'

'I knew he'd come. I knew he'd come,' Tess told herself.

As he entered, she turned away and stood with clenched fists and locked jaws, fighting for self-control. She heard his step beside her but he did not speak until they were alone.

'Tess ... Darling.'

The new tenderness of his tone broke down her defences. Clinging to him, she pressed her face against his shoulder.

'We mustn't waste time,' he said. 'A copper will soon be here to question you. First of all, remember I'm with you, whatever you've done ... Did you kill her?'

Her face grew suddenly white as she repeated his question with stiff lips.

'Did I kill her? I don't know ... Tell me, has my cap been found?'

'Why?'

'Because it's gone. I had a blackout. I can't remember anything ... But my cap might tell me where I went.'

Lockwood's face grew grim as he heard her incoherent story.

'I know you are innocent,' he told her. 'But this is not exactly a water-tight yarn. Keep off it as much as you can. Don't lie, but let the police fish for themselves.'

'But why are they coming to me?'

In her turn, Tess listened to his account of the tragedy. A member of the rifle club had found Ratcliffe's body lying in the rough beyond the targets, about 4.30. She had been shot through the heart at close range. The doctor estimated the time of death as between 3 and 4 – but probably about 3.30. As Tess's rifle was found lying near, the police had made enquiries about her at the Peninsular Works, when they had learned about her dismissal and her subsequent threats.

He had just finished his story when the garden gate scraped again.

'It's the detective bloke,' Lockwood warned Tess. Don't forget I'm standing by.'

Inspector Pont reminded Tess of an uncle who grew prize dahlias. He was big and dark, with sleepy brown eyes which revealed nothing of his mental process.

Tess met him with the desperate courage of one mounting the scaffold.

'I am Tess Leigh. I am prepared to sign a statement.'

'Not so fast,' said the inspector. 'You'll be warned when I'm ready for that. I want to know if you remember making any of these remarks about the deceased?'

As Tess read the typewritten paper he handed her, her face flamed.

'Only one person could have told you these things,' she said. 'That's Clement Dodd ... Yes, I did say them. All of them – and more. They are true. She was a cowardly tyrant for she hit people who could not hit back. Cruelty or injustice always make me see red.'

'The turnstile girl at the Steepes has told me you were up there from between two and six,' Pont said. 'What were you doing during that time?'

'Walking,' replied Tess.

'Where?'

'I don't know ... It's no good asking me. I've been in an air crash which has affected my memory. I was terribly upset ... But I walked.'

'Did you lose your cap during your walk? The turnstile girl tells me you were wearing one when you clicked in, but that you were bare-headed when you returned.'

'That's right. But I don't know where I lost it. I tell you – I don't know.'

'I'd like a description of it.'

After the inspector had entered the particulars in his note-book he turned towards the door. Lockwood noticed the glint in his eyes when he spoke to Tess.

'That cap's got to be found. I'll have bills out tomorrow. Meantime, a notice goes up on the station board. I don't expect any results tonight, but hold yourself ready to come and identify it.'

Directly the door closed, Lockwood held Tess tightly in his arms.

'I'm standing by you,' he said. 'We'll wait together.'

She was not comforted because she knew that he too was feeling the same strain of suspense. She felt his start when the telephone bell began to ring in the hall.

'I'll take it,' he said quickly.

When he returned, his smile was unnaturally broad.

'We're going for a joyride,' he told her. 'My bus is parked outside.'

The journey to the police station had a nightmare quality. The lines of smoke-grimed houses seemed to flash by so that Tess – who was dreading the end of the ride – caught her lip when the car stopped under the blue lamp. Still in an evil dream, she stumbled into a tiled hall, when an open door gave her a clear view into a room.

Standing under the glare of an unshaded electric bulb, Clement Dodd was smoking a cigarette. He appeared entirely at his ease until he saw Tess. His face grew red and he turned his back to avoid meeting her eyes.

'This way,' said a constable.

Supported by the pressure of Lockwood's arm, Tess

followed the man into another office where Inspector Pont was seated before a table littered with official papers.

'Yours?' he asked, holding out a white Angora cap for her inspection. She glanced mechanically at her name printed inside the band and nodded assent, before she realised that he was smiling at her.

'My congratulations,' he said. 'This cap was brought in by two hikers – strangers to the district – who chanced to see the notice on the board. They say they picked it up among the rocks on the top of the Spike, soon after four this afternoon. As the official time for the ascent is two and a half hours and the deceased was alive at three, according to medical evidence, it stands to reason that you could not have committed the murder and afterwards climbed the mountain, all within an hour.'

As she listened, Tess's head reeled, for she realised that the story was full of holes. Before she could protest, Lockwood grabbed her arm.

'Miss Leigh's our champion athlete,' he told the inspector. 'Thanks very much. I'll run her home now.'

'I may ring you later,' remarked the inspector. 'I am going to chat with another party. If you're interested, you could take your time going out.'

Tess understood the reason for his wink when they reached the hall, for after the detective entered the room where Clement Dodd was waiting, he left the door slightly ajar.

'There's just one point I want cleared up, Dodd,' he said in a loud, cheerful voice. 'It's common knowledge that two articles were found on the scene of the crime. One – a rifle

— has been identified as the property of a stenographer — Tess Leigh. The other article has still to be identified.'

'But her name's inside the band.' Clement spoke quickly and confidently. 'Besides, everyone knows her white heather brooch.'

'I was referring to a pencil stamped with "PENINSU-LAR",' remarked the inspector. 'The cap you describe was picked up at the top of the Spike at four o'clock this afternoon.'

'That's a damned lie. I saw it—'

'You saw it?' prompted the inspector as Dodd broke off abruptly. 'Go on. Now that Miss Leigh has a perfect alibi, I must go further into your own movements.'

He shut the door and Lockwood dragged Tess outside to the car.

As they reached the front door of Tess's lodging, they heard the telephone bell ringing in the hall, when, once again, he rushed to receive the call.

When he rang off, his face was beaming.

'Dodd's confessed to the crime,' he said. 'The inspector said he was in such a state of nerves after he made that slip that he cracked directly they got to work on him. It appears that old Donovan — when he was ratting for Ratcliffe — found out that Dodd had been embezzling money from the accounts. He told Ratcliffe and she taxed Dodd.

'As usual, she pretended that she alone had been so clever as to discover the fraud, so he reasoned that if he bumped her off, no one would know. I am assuming old Don blew the gaff from something he said to me. Dodd admitted that he got Ratcliffe to come with him to the range, to talk it over, so it was a cold-blooded crime.'

As she listened. Tess felt almost light-headed with relief.

'Oh, it's wonderful to know I never killed her. And I'm glad Don didn't give me away. It was Clem he "threw to the lions" … I was feeling that I could trust no one. And then – you walked with me to the gallows-foot. And after—'

Lockwood began to laugh as he interrupted her.

'I've some good news for you. It didn't matter before. Nothing mattered then but you … But Eustace has asked Daddy to carry on until young John returns from America. Looks as if the good times are coming back to the Peninsular … But what's the girl frowning about now?'

'My cap,' replied Tess. 'If it had been found near the body, I should be convinced that I had killed her. I should have confessed to it – and Clem would not have been brought into it. I should have cleared him … But how did that cap get on the top of the Spike? I passed out between three and four. Besides, no one on earth could have made the climb in that time.'

'No one on earth,' said Lockwood. 'But what about someone in the air! There's a simple and natural explanation. My hunch is that Dodd saw you asleep after he shot Ratcliffe – in that white rig you'd be conspicuous on the heather – so he stole your cap and placed it beside the rifle, to frame you. That's why he crashed so badly. Nothing rattles a liar so much as to be disbelieved when he is telling the truth – and he knew it was inside the range. There was no wind, but probably it stirred a bit in the breeze.

'Enter Mr Eagle. He sees something white and fleecy moving on the heather. He swoops down on it, soars up again, realises he's been fooled and drops it again in disgust

… By the luck of the air currents, it fell on the top of the mountain instead of the lower slopes. You owe your perfect alibi to your friend – the eagle.'

Fourth of July Picnic

Rex Stout

1

Flora Korby swivelled her head, with no hat hiding any of her dark brown hair, to face me with her dark brown eyes. She spoke.

'I guess I should have brought my car and led the way.'

'I'm doing fine,' I assured her. 'I could shut one eye too.'

'Please don't,' she begged. 'I'm stupefied as it is. May I have your autograph – I mean when we stop?'

Since she was highly presentable I didn't mind her assuming that I was driving with one hand because my right arm wanted to stretch across her shoulders, though she was wrong. I had left the cradle long ago. But there was no point in explaining to her that Nero Wolfe, who was in the back seat, had a deep distrust of moving vehicles and hated to ride in one unless I drove it, and therefore I was glad to have an excuse to drive with one hand because that would make it more thrilling for him.

Anyway, she might have guessed it. The only outside interest that Wolfe permits to interfere with his personal routine of comfort, not to mention luxury, is Rusterman's restaurant. Its founder, Marko Vukcic, was Wolfe's oldest and closest friend; and when Vukcic died, leaving the restaurant to members of the staff and making Wolfe executor of his estate, he also left a letter asking Wolfe to see to it that the restaurant's standards and reputation were maintained; and Wolfe had done so, making unannounced visits there once or twice a week, and sometimes even oftener, without ever grumbling – well, hardly ever. But he sure did grumble when Felix, the maître d'hôtel, asked him to make a speech at the Independence Day picnic of the United Restaurant Workers of America. Hereafter I'll make it URWA.

He not only grumbled, he refused. But Felix kept after him, and Wolfe finally gave in when Felix came to the office one day with reinforcements: Paul Rago, the sauce chef at the Churchill; James Korby, the president of URWA; H. L. Griffin, a food and wine importer who supplied hard-to-get items not only for Rusterman's but also for Wolfe's own table; and Philip Holt, URWA's director of organisation. They also were to be on the programme at the picnic, and their main appeal was that they simply had to have the man who was responsible for keeping Rusterman's the best restaurant in New York after the death of Marko Vukcic. Since Wolfe is only as vain as three peacocks, and since he had loved Marko if he ever loved anyone, that got him. There had been another inducement: Philip Holt had agreed to lay off of Fritz, Wolfe's chef and housekeeper. For three years Fritz had been visiting the kitchen at Rusterman's off and on as a consultant, and Holt had been pestering him, insisting that he had to join URWA. You can guess how Wolfe liked that.

Since I do everything that has to be done in connection with Wolfe's business and his rare social activities, except that he thinks he does all the thinking, and we won't go into that now, it would be up to me to get him to the scene of the picnic, Culp's Meadows on Long Island, on the Fourth of July. Around the end of June James Korby phoned and introduced his daughter Flora. She told me that the directions to Culp's Meadows were very complicated, and I said that all directions on Long Island were very complicated, and she said she had better drive us out in her car.

I liked her voice, that is true, but also I have a lot of foresight, and it occurred to me immediately that it would be a new and exciting experience for my employer to watch me drive with one hand, so I told her that, while it must be Wolfe's car and I must drive, I would deeply appreciate it if she would come along and tell me the way. That was how it happened, and that was why, when we finally rolled through the gate at Culp's Meadows, after some thirty miles of Long Island parkways and another ten of grade intersections and trick turns, Wolfe's lips were pressed so tight he didn't have any. He had spoken only once, around the fourth or fifth mile, when I had swept around a slowpoke.

'Archie. You know quite well.'

'Yes, sir.' Of course I kept my eyes straight ahead. 'But it's an impulse, having my arm like this, and I'm afraid to take it away because if I fight an impulse it makes me nervous, and driving when you're nervous is bad.'

A glance in the mirror showed me his lips tightening, and they stayed tight.

Passing through the gate at Culp's Meadows, and winding around as directed by Flora Korby, I used both hands. It was a quarter to three, so we were on time, since the speeches were scheduled for three o'clock. Flora was sure a space would have been saved for us back of the tent, and after threading through a few acres of parked cars I found she was right, and rolled to a stop with the radiator only a couple of yards from the canvas. She hopped out and opened the rear door on her side, and I did likewise on mine. Wolfe's eyes went right to her, and then left to me. He was torn. He didn't want to favour a woman, even a young and pretty one, but he absolutely had to show me what he thought of one-handed driving. His eyes went right again, the whole seventh of a ton of him moved, and he climbed out on her side.

2

The tent, on a wooden platform raised three feet above the ground, not much bigger than Wolfe's office, was crowded with people, and I wormed through to the front entrance and on out, where the platform extended into the open air. There was plenty of air, with a breeze dancing in from the direction of the ocean, and plenty of sunshine. A fine day for the Fourth of July. The platform extension was crammed with chairs, most of them empty. I can't report on the condition of the meadow's grass because my view was obstructed by ten thousand restaurant workers and their guests, maybe more. A couple of thousand of them were in a solid mass facing the platform, presumably those who wanted to be up front for the speeches, and the rest were sprayed around all over, clear across to a fringe of trees and a row of sheds.

Flora's voice came from behind my shoulder. 'They're coming out, so if there's a chair you like, grab it. Except the six up front; they're for the speakers.'

Naturally I started to tell her I wanted the one next to hers, but didn't get it out because people came jostling out of the tent onto the extension. Thinking I had better warn Wolfe that the chair he was about to occupy for an hour or so was about half as wide as his fanny, to give him time to fight his impulses, I worked past to the edge of the entrance, and when the exodus had thinned out I entered the tent. Five men were standing grouped beside a cot which was touching the canvas of the far side, and a man was lying on the cot. To my left Nero Wolfe was bending over to peer at the contents of a metal box there on a table with its lid open. I stepped over for a look and saw a collection of bone-handled knives, eight of them, with blades varying in length from six inches up to twelve. They weren't shiny, but they looked sharp, worn narrow by a lot of use for a lot of years. I asked Wolfe whose throat he was going to cut.

'They are Dubois,' he said. 'Real old Dubois. The best. They belong to Mr Korby. He brought them to use in a carving contest, and he won, as he should. I would gladly steal them.' He turned. 'Why don't they let that man alone?'

I turned too, and through a gap in the group saw that the man on the cot was Philip Holt, URWA's director of organisation. 'What's the matter with him?' I asked.

'Something he ate. They think snails. Probably the wrong kind of snails. A doctor gave him something to help his bowels handle them. Why don't they leave him alone with his bowels?'

'I'll go ask,' I said, and moved.

As I approached the cot James Korby was speaking. 'I say he should be taken to a hospital, in spite of what that doctor said. Look at his colour!'

Korby, short, pudgy and bald, looked more like a restaurant customer than a restaurant worker, which may have been one reason he was president of URWA.

'I agree,' Dick Vetter said emphatically. I had never seen Dick Vetter in person, but I had seen him often enough on his TV show – in fact, a little too often. If I quit dialling his channel he wouldn't miss me, since twenty million Americans, mostly female, were convinced that he was the youngest and handsomest MC on the waves. Flora Korby had told me he would be there, and why. His father had been a busboy in a Broadway restaurant for thirty years, and still was because he wouldn't quit.

Paul Rago did not agree, and said so. 'It would be a pity,' he declared. He made it 'peety', his accent having tapered off enough not to make it 'peetee'. With his broad shoulders and six feet, his slick black hair going grey, and his moustache with pointed tips that was still all black, he looked more like an ambassador from below the border than a sauce chef. He was going on. 'He is the most important man in the union – except, of course, the president – and he should make an appearance on the platform. Perhaps he can before we are through.'

'I hope you will pardon me.' That was H. L. Griffin, the food and wine importer. He was a skinny little runt, with a long narrow chin and something wrong with one eye, but he spoke with the authority of a man whose firm occupied a whole floor in one of the midtown hives. 'I may have no right to an opinion, since I am not a member of your great organisation, but you have done me the honour of inviting me to take part in your celebration of our country's independence, and I do know of Phil Holt's high standing and wide popularity among your members. I would merely say that I feel that Mr Rago is right, that they will be disappointed not to see him on the platform. I hope I am not being presumptuous.'

From outside the tent, from the loudspeakers at the corners of the platform, a booming voice had been calling to the picnickers scattered over the meadow to close in and prepare to listen. As the group by the cot went on arguing, a state trooper in uniform, who had been standing politely aside, came over and joined them and took a look at Philip Holt, but offered no advice. Wolfe also approached for a look. Myself, I would have said that the place for him was a good bed with an attractive nurse smoothing his brow. I saw him shiver all over at least three times. He decided it himself, finally, by muttering at them to let him alone and turning on his side to face the canvas. Flora Korby had come in, and she put a blanket over him, and I noticed that Dick Vetter made a point of helping her. The breeze was sweeping through and one of them said he shouldn't be in a draught, and Wolfe told me to lower the flap of the rear entrance, and I did so. The flap didn't want to stay down, so I tied the plastic-tape fastening to hold it, in a single bowknot. Then they all marched out through the front entrance to the platform, including the state trooper, and I brought up the rear. As Korby passed the table he stopped to lower the lid on the box of knives, real old Dubois.

The speeches lasted an hour and eight minutes, and the ten thousand URWA members and guests took them standing like ladies and gentlemen. You are probably hoping I will report them word for word, but I didn't take them down and I didn't listen hard enough to engrave them on my memory. At that, the eagle didn't scream as much or as loud as I had expected. From my seat in the back row I could see most of the audience, and it was quite a sight.

The first speaker was a stranger, evidently the one who had been calling on them to gather around while we were in the tent, and after a few fitting remarks he introduced James Korby. While Korby was orating, Paul Rago left his seat, passed down the aisle in the centre, and entered the tent. Since he had plugged for an appearance by Philip Holt I thought his purpose might be to drag him out alive or dead, but it wasn't. In a minute he was back again, and just in time, for he had just sat down when Korby finished and Rago was introduced.

The faces out front had all been serious for Korby, but Rago's accent through the loudspeakers had most of them grinning by the time he warmed up. When Korby left his chair and started down the aisle I suspected him of walking out on Rago because Rago had walked out on him, but maybe not, since his visit in the tent was even shorter than Rago's had been. He came back out and returned to his chair, and listened attentively to the accent.

Next came H. L. Griffin, the importer, and the chairman had to lower the mike for him. His voice took the loudspeakers better than any of the others, and in fact he was darned good. It was only fair, I thought, to have the runt of the bunch take the cake, and I was all for the cheers from the throng that kept him on his feet a full minute after he finished. He really woke them up, and they were still yelling when he turned and went down the aisle to the tent, and it took the chairman a while to calm them down. Then, just as he started to introduce Dick Vetter, the TV star suddenly bounced up and started down the aisle with a determined look on his face, and it was easy to guess why. He thought Griffin was going to take advantage of the enthusiasm he had aroused by hauling Philip Holt out to the platform, and he was going to stop him. But he didn't have to. He was still two steps short of the tent entrance when Griffin emerged alone. Vetter moved aside to let him pass and then disappeared into the tent. As Griffin proceeded to his chair in the front row there were some scattered cheers from the crowd, and the chairman had to quiet them again before he could go on. Then he introduced Dick Vetter, who came out of the tent and along to the mike, which had to be raised again, at just the right moment.

As Vetter started to speak, Nero Wolfe arose and headed for the tent, and I raised my brows. Surely, I thought, he's not going to involve himself in the Holt problem; and then, seeing the look on his face, I caught on. The edges of the wooden chair seat had been cutting into his fanny for nearly an hour and he was in a tantrum, and he wanted to cool off a little before he was called to the mike. I grinned at him sympathetically as he passed and then gave my ear to Vetter. His soapy voice (I say soapy) came through the loudspeakers in a flow of lather, and after a couple of minutes of it I was thinking that it was only fair for Griffin, the runt, to sound like a man, and for Vetter, the handsome young idol of millions, to sound like whipped cream, when my attention was called. Wolfe was at the tent entrance, crooking a finger at me. As I got up and approached he backed into the tent, and I followed. He crossed to the rear entrance, lifted the flap, manoeuvred his bulk through the hole, and held the flap for me. When I had made it he descended the five steps to the ground, walked to the car, grabbed the handle of the rear door, and pulled. Nothing doing. He turned to me.

'Unlock it.'

I stood. 'Do you want something?'

'Unlock it and get in and get the thing started. We're going.'

'We are like hell. You've got a speech to make.'

He glared at me. He knows my tones of voice as well as I know his. 'Archie,' he said, 'I am not being eccentric. There is a sound and cogent reason and I'll explain on the way. Unlock this door.'

I shook my head. 'Not till I hear the reason. I admit it's your car.' I took the keys from my pocket and offered them. 'Here. I resign.'

'Very well.' He was grim. 'That man on the cot is dead. I lifted the blanket to adjust it. One of those knives is in his back, clear to the handle. He is dead. If we are still here when the discovery is made you know what will happen. We will be here all day, all night, a week, indefinitely. That is intolerable. We can answer questions at home as well as here. Confound it, unlock the door!'

'How dead is he?'

'I have told you he is dead.'

'Okay. You ought to know better. You do know better. We're stuck. They wouldn't ask us questions at home, they'd haul us back out here. They'd be waiting for us on the stoop and you wouldn't get inside the house.' I returned the keys to my pocket. 'Running out when you're next on the programme, that would be nice. The only question is do we report it now or do you make your speech and let someone else find it, and you can answer that.'

He had stopped glaring. He took in a long, deep breath, and when it was out again he said, 'I'll make my speech.'

'Fine. It'd be a shame to waste it. A question. Just now when you lifted the flap to come out I didn't see you untie the tape fastening. Was it already untied?'

'Yes.'

'That makes it nice.' I turned and went to the steps, mounted, raised the flap for him, and followed him into the tent. He crossed to the front and on out, and I stepped to the cot. Philip Holt lay facing the wall, with the blanket up to his neck, and I pulled it down far enough to see the handle of the knife, an inch to the right of the point of the shoulder blade. The knife blade was all buried. I lowered the blanket some more to get at a hand, pinched a fingertip hard for ten seconds, released it, and saw it stay white. I picked some fluff from the blanket and dangled it against his nostrils for half a minute. No movement. I put the blanket back as I had found it, went to the metal box on the table and lifted the lid, and saw that the shortest knife, the one with the six-inch blade, wasn't there.

As I went to the rear entrance and raised the flap, Dick Vetter's lather or whipped cream, whichever you prefer, came to an end through the loudspeakers, and as I descended the five steps the meadowful of picnickers was cheering.

Our sedan was the third car on the right from the foot of the steps. The second car to the left of the steps was a 1955 Plymouth, and I was pleased to see that it still had an occupant, having previously noticed her – a woman with careless grey hair topping a wide face and a square chin, in the front seat but not behind the wheel.

I circled around to her side and spoke through the open window. 'I beg your pardon. May I introduce myself?'

'You don't have to, young man. Your name's Archie Goodwin, and you work for Nero Wolfe, the detective.' She had tired grey eyes. 'You were just out here with him.'

'Right. I hope you won't mind if I ask you something. How long have you been sitting here?'

'Long enough. But it's all right, I can hear the speeches. Nero Wolfe is just starting to speak now.'

'Have you been here since the speeches started?'

'Yes, I have. I ate too much of the picnic stuff and I didn't feel like standing up in that crowd, so I came to sit in the car.'

'Then you've been here all the time since the speeches began?'

'That's what I said. Why do you want to know?'

'I'm just checking on something. If you don't mind. Has anyone gone into the tent or come out of it while you've been here?'

Her tired eyes woke up a little. 'Ha,' she said, 'so something's missing. I'm not surprised. What's missing?'

'Nothing, as far as I know. I'm just checking a certain fact. Of course you saw Mr Wolfe and me come out and go back in. Anyone else, either going or coming?'

'You're not fooling me, young man. Something's missing, and you're a detective.'

I grinned at her. 'All right, have it your way. But I do want to know, if you don't object.'

'I don't object. As I told you, I've been right here ever since the speeches started, I got here before that. And nobody has gone into the tent, nobody but you and Nero Wolfe, and I haven't either. I've been right here. If you want to know about me, my name is Anna Banau, Mrs Alexander Banau, and my husband is a captain at Zoller's—'

A scream came from inside the tent, an all-out scream from a good pair of lungs. I moved, to the steps, up, and past the flap into the tent. Flora Korby was standing near the cot with her back to it, her hand covering her mouth. I was disappointed in her. Granting that a woman has a right to scream when she finds a corpse, she might have kept it down until Wolfe had finished his speech.

3

It was a little after four o'clock when Flora Korby screamed. It was 4:34 when a glance outside through a crack past the flap of the tent's rear entrance, the third such glance I had managed to make, showed me that the Plymouth containing Mrs Alexander Banau was gone. It was 4:39 when the medical examiner arrived with his bag and found that Philip Holt was still dead. It was 4:48 when the scientists came, with cameras and fingerprint kits and other items of equipment, and Wolfe and I and the others were herded out to the extension, under guard. It was 5:16 when I counted a total of seventeen cops, state and county, in uniform and out, on the job. It was 5:30 when Wolfe muttered at me bitterly that it would certainly be all night. It was 5:52 when a chief of detectives named Baxter got so personal with me that I decided, finally and definitely, not to play. It was 6:21 when we all left Culp's Meadows for an official destination. There were four in our car: one in uniform with Wolfe in the back seat, and one in his own clothes with me in front. Again I had someone beside me to tell me the way, but I didn't put my arm across his shoulders.

There had been some conversing with us separately, but most of it had been a panel discussion, open air, out on the platform extension, so I knew pretty well how things stood. Nobody was accusing anybody. Three of them – Korby, Rago and Griffin – gave approximately the same reason for their visits to the tent during the speechmaking: that they were concerned about Philip Holt and wanted to see if he was all right. The fourth, Dick Vetter, gave the reason I had guessed, that he thought Griffin might bring Holt out to the platform, and he intended to stop him. Vetter, by the way, was the only one who raised a fuss about being detained. He said that it hadn't been easy to get away from his duties that afternoon, and he had a studio rehearsal scheduled for six o'clock, and he absolutely had to be there. At 6:21, when we all left for the official destination, he was fit to be tied.

None of them claimed to know for sure that Holt had been alive at the time he visited the tent; they all had supposed he had fallen asleep. All except Vetter said they had gone to the cot and looked at him, at his face, and had suspected nothing wrong. None of them had spoken to him. To the question, 'Who do you think did it and why?' they all gave the same answer: someone must have entered the tent by the rear entrance, stabbed him, and departed. The fact that the URWA director of organisation had got his stomach into trouble and had been attended by a doctor in the tent had been no secret, anything but.

I have been leaving Flora out, since I knew and you know she was clear, but the cops didn't. I overheard one of them tell another one it was probably her, because stabbing a sick man was more like something a woman would do than a man.

Of course the theory that someone had entered by the back door made the fastening of the tent flap an important item. I said I had tied the tape before we left the tent, and they all agreed that they had seen me do so except Dick Vetter, who said he hadn't noticed because he had been helping to arrange the blanket over Holt; and Wolfe and I both testified that the tape was hanging loose when we had entered the tent while Vetter was speaking. Under this theory the point wasn't who had untied it, since the murderer could have easily reached through the crack from the outside and jerked the knot loose; the question was when. On that none of them was any help. All four said they hadn't noticed whether the tape was tied or not when they went inside the tent.

That was how it stood, as far as I knew, when we left Culp's Meadows. The official destination turned out to be a building I had been in before a time or two, not as a murder suspect – a county courthouse back of a smooth green lawn with a couple of big trees. First we were collected in a room on the ground floor, and, after a long wait, were escorted up one flight and through a door that was inscribed DISTRICT ATTORNEY.

At least 91.2 percent of the district attorneys in the State of New York think they would make fine tenants of the governor's mansion at Albany, and that should be kept in mind in considering the conduct of DA James R. Delaney. To him at least four of that bunch, and possibly all five, were upright, important citizens in positions to influence segments of the electorate. His attitude as he attacked the problem implied that he was merely chairing a meeting of a community council called to deal with a grave and difficult emergency – except, I noticed, when he was looking at or speaking to Wolfe or me. Then his smile quit working, his tone sharpened, and his eyes had a different look.

With a stenographer at a side table taking it down, he spent an hour going over it with us, or rather with them, with scattered contributions from Chief of Detectives Baxter and others who had been at the scene, and then spoke his mind.

'It seems,' he said, 'to be the consensus that some person unknown entered the tent from the rear, stabbed him, and departed. There is the question, how could such a person have known the knife would be there at hand? but he need not have known. He might have decided to murder only when he saw the knives, or he might have had some other weapon with him, and, seeing the knives, thought one of them would better serve his purpose and used it instead. Either is plausible. It must be admitted that the whole theory is plausible, and none of the facts now known are in contradiction to it. You agree, Chief?'

'Right,' Baxter conceded. 'Up to now. As long as the known facts are facts.'

Delaney nodded. 'Certainly. They have to be checked.' His eyes took in the audience. 'You gentlemen, and you, Miss Korby, you understand that you are to remain in this jurisdiction, the State of New York, until further notice, and you are to be available. With that understood, it seems unnecessary at present to put you under bond as material witnesses. We have your addresses and know where to find you.'

He focused on Wolfe, and his tone changed. 'With you, Wolfe, the situation is somewhat different. You're a licensed private detective, and so is Goodwin, and the record of your high-handed performances does not inspire confidence in your – uh – candour. There may be some complicated and subtle reasons why the New York City authorities have stood for your tricks, but out here in the suburbs we're more simple-minded. We don't like tricks.'

He lowered his chin, which made his eyes slant up under his heavy brows. 'Let's see if I've got your story straight. You say that as Vetter started to speak you felt in your pocket for a paper on which you had made notes for your speech, found it wasn't there, thought you had left it in your car, went to get it, and when, after you had entered the tent, it occurred to you that the car was locked and Goodwin had the keys, you summoned him and you and he went out to the car. Then Goodwin remembered that the paper had been left on your desk at your office, and you and he returned to the tent, and you went out to the platform and resumed your seat. Another item: when you went to the rear entrance to leave the tent to go out to the car, the tape fastening of the flap was hanging loose, not tied. Is that your story?'

Wolfe cleared his throat. 'Mr Delaney. I suppose it is pointless to challenge your remark about my candour or to ask you to phrase your question less offensively.' His shoulders went up an eighth of an inch, and down. 'Yes, that's my story.'

'I merely asked you the question.'

'I answered it.'

'So you did.' The DA's eyes came to me. 'And of course, Goodwin, your story is the same. If it needed arranging, there was ample time for that during the hubbub that followed Miss Korby's scream. But with you there's more to it. You say that after you and Wolfe re-entered the tent, and he continued through the front entrance to the platform, it occurred to you that there was a possibility that he had taken the paper from his desk and put it in his pocket, and had consulted it during the ride, and had left it in the car, and you went out back again to look, and you were out there when Miss Korby screamed. Is that correct?'

As I had long since decided not to play, when Baxter had got too personal, I merely said, 'Check.'

Delaney returned to Wolfe. 'If you object to my being offensive, Wolfe, I'll put it this way: I find some of this hard to believe. Anyone as glib as you are needing notes for a little speech like that? And you thinking you had left the paper in the car, and Goodwin remembering it had been left at home on your desk and then thinking it might be in the car after all? Also there are certain facts. You and Goodwin were the last people inside the tent before Miss Korby entered and found the body. You admit it. The others all state that they don't know whether the tape was tied or not when they visited the tent; you and Goodwin can't very well say that, since you went out that way, so you say you found it untied.'

He cocked his head. 'You admit you had had words with Philip Holt during the past year. You admit he had become obnoxious to you – your word, obnoxious – by his insistence that your personal chef must join his union. The record of your past performances justifies me in saying that a man who renders himself obnoxious to you had better watch his step. I'll say this, if it weren't for the probability that some unknown person entered from the rear, and I concede that it's quite possible, you and Goodwin would be held in custody until a judge could be found to issue a warrant for your arrest as material witnesses. As it is, I'll make it easier for you.' He looked at his wristwatch. 'It's five minutes to eight. I'll send a man with you to a restaurant down the street, and we'll expect you back here at nine-thirty. I want to cover all the details with you, thoroughly.' His eyes moved. 'The rest of you may go for the present, but you are to be available.'

Wolfe stood up. 'Mr Goodwin and I are going home,' he announced. 'We will not be back this evening.'

Delaney's eyes narrowed. 'If that's the way you feel about it, you'll stay. You can send out for sandwiches.'

'Are we under arrest?'

The DA opened his mouth, closed it, and opened it again. 'No.'

'Then we're going.' Wolfe was assured but not belligerent. 'I understand your annoyance, sir, at this interference with your holiday, and I'm aware that you don't like me – or what you know, or think you know, of my record. But I will not surrender my convenience to your humour. You can detain me only if you charge me, and with what? Mr Goodwin and I have supplied all the information we have. Your intimation that I am capable of murdering a man, or of inciting Mr Goodwin to murder him, because he has made a nuisance of himself, is puerile. You concede that the murderer could have been anyone in that throng of thousands. You have no basis whatever for any supposition that Mr Goodwin and I are concealing any knowledge that would help you. Should such a basis appear, you know where to find us. Come, Archie.'

He turned and headed for the door, and I followed. I can't report the reaction because Delaney at his desk was behind me, and it would have been bad tactics to look back over my shoulder. All I knew was that Baxter took two steps and stopped, and none of the other cops moved. We made the hall, and the entrance, and down the path to the sidewalk, without a shot being fired; and half a block to where the car was parked. Wolfe told me to find a phone booth and call Fritz to tell him when we would arrive for dinner, and I steered for the centre of town.

As I had holiday traffic to cope with, it was half-past nine by the time we got home and washed and seated at the dinner table. A moving car is no place to give Wolfe bad news, or good news either for that matter, and there was no point in spoiling his dinner, so I waited until after we had finished with the poached and truffled broilers and broccoli and stuffed potatoes and herbs, and salad and cheese, and Fritz had brought coffee to us in the office, to open the bag. Wolfe was reaching for the remote-control television gadget, to turn it on so as to have the pleasure of turning it off again, when I said, 'Hold a minute. I have a report to make. I don't blame you for feeling self-satisfied, you got us away very neatly, but there's a catch. It wasn't somebody that came in the back way. It was one of them.'

'Indeed.' He was placid, after-dinner placid, in the comfortable, big made-to-order chair back of his desk. 'What is this, flummery?'

'No, sir. Nor am I trying to show that I'm smarter than you are for once. It's just that I know more. When you left the tent to go to the car your mind was on a quick getaway, so you may not have noticed that a woman was sitting there in a car to the left, but I did. When we returned to the tent and you went on out front, I had an idea and went out back again and had a talk with her. I'll give it to you verbatim, since it's important.'

I did so. That was simple, compared with the three-way and four-way conversations I have been called on to report word for word. When I finished he was scowling at me, as black as the coffee in his cup.

'Confound it,' he growled.

'Yes, sir. I was going to tell you, there when we were settling the details of why we went out to the car, the paper with your notes, but as you know we were interrupted, and after that there was no opportunity that I liked, and anyway I had seen that Mrs Banau and the car were gone, and that baboon named Baxter had hurt my feelings, and I had decided not to play. Of course the main thing was you, your wanting to go home. If they had known it was one of us six, or seven counting Flora, we would all have been held as material witnesses, and you couldn't have got bail on the Fourth of July, and God help you, I can manage in a cell, but you're too big. Also if I got you home you might feel like discussing a raise in pay. Do you?'

'Shut up.' He closed his eyes, and after a moment opened them again. 'We're in a pickle. They may find that woman any moment, or she may disclose herself. What about her? You have given me her words, but what about her?'

'She's good. They'll believe her. I did. You would. From where she sat the steps and tent entrance were in her minimum field of vision, no obstructions, less than ten yards away.'

'If she kept her eyes open.'

'She thinks she did, and that will do for the cops when they find her. Anyhow, I think she did too. When she said nobody had gone into the tent but you and me she meant it.'

'There's the possibility that she herself, or someone she knew and would protect— No, that's absurd, since she stayed there in the car for some time after the body was found. We're in a fix.'

'Yes, sir.' Meeting his eyes, I saw no sign of the gratitude I might reasonably have expected, so I went on. 'I would like to suggest, in considering the situation, don't bother about me. I can't be charged with withholding evidence because I didn't report my talk with her. I can just say I didn't believe her and saw no point in making it tougher for us by dragging it in. The fact that someone might have come in the back way didn't eliminate us. Of course I'll have to account for my questioning her, but that's easy. I can say I discovered that he was dead after you went back out to the platform to make your speech, and, having noticed her there in the car, I went out to question her before reporting the discovery, and was interrupted by the scream in the tent. So don't mind me. Anything you say. I can phone Delaney in the morning, or you can, and spill it, or we can just sit tight and wait for the fireworks.'

'Pfui,' he said.

'Amen,' I said.

He took in air, audibly, and let it out. 'That woman may be communicating with them at this moment, or they may be finding her. I don't complain of your performance; indeed, I commend it. If you had reported that conversation we would both be spending tonight in jail.' He made a face. 'Bah. As it is, at least we can try something. What time is it?'

I looked at my wristwatch. He would have had to turn his head almost to a right angle to glance at the wall clock, which was too much to expect. 'Eight after eleven.'

'Could you get them here tonight?'

'I doubt it. All five of them?'

'Yes.'

'Possibly by sunup. Bring them to your bedroom?'

He rubbed his nose with a fingertip. 'Very well. But you can call them now, as many as you can get. Make it eleven in the morning. Tell them I have a disclosure to make and must consult with them.'

'That should interest them,' I granted, and reached for the phone.

4

By the time Wolfe came down from the plant rooms to greet the guests, at two minutes past eleven the next morning, there hadn't been a peep out of the Long Island law. Which didn't mean there couldn't be one at three minutes past eleven. According to the morning paper, District Attorney Delaney and Chief of Detectives Baxter had both conceded that anyone could have entered the tent from the back and therefore it was wide open. If Anna Banau read newspapers, and she probably did, she might at any moment be going to the phone to make a call.

I had made several, both the night before and that morning, getting the guests lined up; and one special one. There was an address and phone number for an Alexander Banau in the Manhattan book, but I decided not to dial it. I also decided not to ring Zoller's restaurant on 52nd Street. I hadn't eaten at Zoller's more than a couple of times, but I knew a man who had been patronising it for years, and I called him. Yes, he said, there was a captain at Zoller's named Alex, and yes, his last name was Banau. He liked Alex and hoped that my asking about him didn't mean that he was headed for some kind of trouble. I said no trouble was contemplated, I just might want to check a little detail, and thanked him. Then I sat and looked at the slip on which I had scribbled the Banau home phone number, and with my finger itching to dial it, but to say what? No.

I mention that around ten-thirty I got the Marley .38 from the drawer, saw that it was loaded, and put it in my side pocket, not to prepare you for bloodshed, but just to show that I was sold on Mrs Banau. With a murderer for a guest, and an extremely nervy one, there was no telling.

H. L. Griffin, the importer, and Paul Rago, the sauce chef, came alone and separately, but Korby and Flora had Dick

Vetter with them. I had intended to let Flora have the red leather chair, but when I showed them to the office, Rago, the six-footer with the moustache and the accent, had copped it, and she took one of the yellow chairs in a row facing Wolfe's desk, with her father on her right and Vetter on her left. Griffin, the runt who had made the best speech, was at the end of the row nearest my desk. When Wolfe came down from the plant rooms, entered, greeted them, and headed for his desk, Vetter spoke up before he was seated.

'I hope this won't last long, Mr Wolfe. I asked Mr Goodwin if it couldn't be earlier, and he said it couldn't. Miss Korby and I must have an early lunch because I have a script conference at one-thirty.'

I raised a brow. I had been honoured. I had driven a car with my arm across the shoulders of a girl whom Dick Vetter himself thought worthy of a lunch.

Wolfe, adjusted in his chair, said mildly, 'I won't prolong it beyond necessity, sir. Are you and Miss Korby friends?'

'What's that got to do with it?'

'Possibly nothing. But now, nothing about any of you is beyond the bounds of my curiosity. It is a distressing thing to have to say, in view of the occasion of our meeting yesterday, the anniversary of the birth of this land of freedom, but I must. One of you is a miscreant. One of you people killed Philip Holt.'

The idea is to watch them and see who faints or jumps up and runs. But nobody did. They all stared.

'One of us?' Griffin demanded.

Wolfe nodded. 'I thought it best to begin with that bald statement, instead of leading up to it. I thought—'

Korby cut in. 'This is funny. This is a joke. After what you said yesterday to that district attorney. It's a *bad* joke.'

'It's no joke, Mr Korby. I wish it were. I thought yesterday I was on solid ground, but I wasn't. I now know that there is a witness, a credible and confident witness, to testify that no one entered the tent from the rear between the time that the speeches began and the discovery of the body. I also know that neither Mr Goodwin nor I killed him, so it was one of you. So I think we should discuss it.'

'You say a witness?' Rago made it 'weetnuss'.

'Who is he?' Korby wanted to know. 'Where is he?'

'It's a woman, and she is available. Mr Goodwin, who has spoken with her, is completely satisfied of her competence and bona fides, and he is hard to satisfy. It is highly unlikely that she can be impeached. That's all I—'

'I don't get it,' Vetter blurted. 'If they've got a witness like that why haven't they come for us?'

'Because they haven't got her. They know nothing about her. But they may find her at any moment, or she may go to them. If so you will soon be discussing the matter not with me but with officers of the law – and so will I. Unless you do discuss it with me, and unless the discussion is productive, I shall of course be constrained to tell Mr Delaney about her. I wouldn't like that and neither would you. After hearing her story his manner with you, and with me, would be quite different from yesterday. I want to ask you some questions.'

'Who is she?' Korby demanded. 'Where is she?'

Wolfe shook his head. 'I'm not going to identify her or place her for you. I note your expressions – especially yours, Mr Korby, and yours, Mr Griffin. You are sceptical. But what conceivable reason could there be for my getting you here to point this weapon at you except the coercion of events? Why would I invent or contrive such a dilemma? I, like you, would vastly prefer to have it as it was, that the murderer came from without, but that's no good now. I concede that you may suspect me too, and Mr Goodwin, and you may question us as I may question you. But one of us killed Philip Holt, and getting answers to questions is clearly in the interest of all the rest of us.'

They exchanged glances. But they were not the kind of glances they would have exchanged five minutes earlier. They were glances of doubt, suspicion and surmise, and they weren't friendly.

'I don't see,' Griffin objected, 'what good questions will do. We were all there together and we all know what happened. We all know what everybody said.'

Wolfe nodded. 'But we were all supporting the theory that excluded us. Now we're not. We can't. One of us has something in his background which, if known, would account for his determination to kill that man. I suggest beginning with autobiographical sketches from each of us, and here is mine. I was born in Montenegro and spent my early boyhood there. At the age of sixteen I decided to move around, and in fourteen years I became acquainted with most of Europe, a little of Africa, and much of Asia, in a variety of roles and activities. Corning to this country in nineteen-thirty, not penniless, I bought this house and entered into practice as a private detective. I am a naturalised American citizen. I first heard of Philip Holt about two years ago when Fritz Brenner, who works for me, came to me with a complaint about him.

My only reason for wishing him harm, but not the extremity of death, was removed, as you know, when he agreed to stop annoying Mr Brenner about joining your union if I would make a speech at your blasted picnic. Mr Goodwin?'

I turned my face to the audience. 'Born in Ohio. Public high school, pretty good at geometry and football, graduated with honour but no honours. Went to college two weeks, decided it was childish, came to New York and got a job guarding a pier, shot and killed two men and was fired, was recommended to Nero Wolfe for a chore he wanted done, did it, was offered a full-time job by Mr Wolfe, took it, still have it. Personally, was more entertained than bothered by Holt's trying to get union dues out of Fritz Brenner. Otherwise no connection with him or about him.'

'You may,' Wolfe told them, 'question us later if you wish. Miss Korby?'

'Well—' Flora said. She glanced at her father, and, when he nodded, she aimed at Wolfe and went on, 'My autobiography doesn't amount to much. I was born in New York and have always lived here. I'm twenty years old. I didn't kill Phil Holt and had no reason to kill him.' She turned her palms up. 'What else?'

'If I may suggest,' H. L. Griffin offered, 'if there's a witness as Wolfe says, if there *is* such a witness, they'll dig everything up. For instance, about you and Phil.'

She gave him an eye. 'What about us, Mr Griffin?'

'I don't know. I've only heard talk, that's all, and they'll dig up the talk.'

'To hell with the talk,' Dick Vetter blurted, the whipped cream sounding sour.

Flora looked at Wolfe. 'I can't help talk,' she said. 'It certainly is no secret that Phil Holt was – well, he liked women. And it's no secret that I'm a woman, and I guess it's not a secret that I didn't like Phil. For me he was what you called him, a nuisance. When he wanted something.'

Wolfe grunted. 'And he wanted you?'

'He thought he did. That's all there was to it. He was a pest, that's all there is to say about it.'

'You said you had no reason to kill him.'

'Good heavens, I didn't! A girl doesn't kill a man just because he won't believe her when she says no!'

'No to what? A marriage proposal?'

Her father cut in. 'Look here,' he told Wolfe, 'you're barking up the wrong tree. Everybody knows how Phil Holt was about women. He never asked one to marry him and probably he never would. My daughter is old enough and smart enough to take care of herself, and she does, but not by sticking a knife in a man's back.' He turned to Griffin. 'Much obliged, Harry.'

The importer wasn't fazed. 'It was bound to come out, Jim, and I thought it ought to be mentioned now.'

Wolfe was regarding Korby. 'Naturally it raises the question how far a father might go to relieve his daughter of a pest.'

Korby snorted. 'If you're asking it, the answer is no. My daughter can take care of herself. If you want a reason why I might have killed Phil Holt you'll have to do better than that.'

'Then I'll try, Mr Korby. You are the president of your union, and Mr Holt was an important figure in it, and at the moment the affairs of unions, especially their financial affairs, are front-page news. Have you any reason to fear an investigation, or had Mr Holt?'

'No. They can investigate as much as they damn please.'

'Have you been summoned?'

'No.'

'Had Mr Holt been summoned?'

'No.'

'Have any officials of your union been summoned?'

'No.' Korby's pudgy face and bald top were pinking up a little. 'You're barking up the wrong tree again.'

'But at least another tree. You realise, sir, that if Mr Delaney starts after us in earnest, the affairs of the United Restaurant Workers of America will be one of his major concerns. For the murder of Philip Holt we all had opportunity, and the means were there at hand; what he will seek is the motive. If there was a vulnerable spot in the operation of your union, financial or otherwise, I suggest that it would be wise for you to disclose it now for discussion.'

'There wasn't anything.' Korby was pinker. 'There's nothing wrong with my union except rumours. That's all it is, rumours, and where's a union that hasn't got rumours with all the stink they've raised? We're not vulnerable to anything or anybody.'

'What kind of rumours?'

'Any kind you want to name. I'm a crook. All the officers are crooks. We've raided the benefit fund. We've sold out to the big operators. We steal lead pencils and paper clips.'

'Can you be more specific? What was the most embarrassing rumour?'

Korby was suddenly not listening. He took a folded handkerchief from his pocket, opened it up, wiped his face and his baldness, refolded the handkerchief at the creases, and returned it to his pocket. Then his eyes went back to Wolfe.

'If you want something specific,' he said, 'it's not a rumour. It's a strictly internal union matter, but it's sure to leak now and it might as well leak here first. There have been some charges made, and they're being looked into, about kickbacks from dealers to union officers and members. Phil Holt had something to do with some of the charges, though that wasn't in his department. He got hot about it.'

'Were you the target of any of the charges?'

'I was not. I have the complete trust of my associates and my staff.'

'You said "dealers". Does that include importers?'

'Sure, importers are dealers.'

'Was Mr Griffin's name mentioned in any of the charges?'

'I'm not giving any names, not without authority from my board. Those things are confidential.'

'Much obliged, Jim,' H. L. Griffin said, sounding the opposite of obliged. 'Even exchange?'

'Excuse me.' It was Dick Vetter, on his feet. 'It's nearly twelve o'clock and Miss Korby and I have to go. We've got to get some lunch and I can't be late for that conference. Anyway, I think it's a lot of hooey. Come on, Flora.'

She hesitated a moment, then left her chair, and he moved. But when Wolfe snapped out his name he turned. 'Well?'

Wolfe swivelled his chair. 'My apologies. I should have remembered that you are pressed for time. If you can give us, say, five minutes?'

The TV star smiled indulgently. 'For my autobiography? You can look it up. It's in print – *TV Guide* a couple of months ago, or *Clock* magazine, I don't remember the date. I say this is hooey. If one of us is a murderer, okay, I wish you luck, but this isn't getting you anywhere. Couldn't I just tell you anything I felt like?'

'You could indeed, Mr Vetter. But if enquiry reveals that you have lied or have omitted something plainly relevant that will be of interest. The magazine articles you mentioned – do they tell of your interest in Miss Korby?'

'Nuts.' Many of his twenty million admirers wouldn't have liked either his tone or his diction.

Wolfe shook his head. 'If you insist, Mr Vetter, you may of course be disdainful about it with me, but not with the police once they get interested in you. I asked you before if you and Miss Korby are friends, and you asked what that had to do with it, and I said possibly nothing. I now say possibly something, since Philip Holt was hounding her – how savagely I don't know yet. Are you and Miss Korby friends?'

'Certainly we're friends. I'm taking her to lunch.'

'Are you devoted to her?'

His smile wasn't quite so indulgent, but it was still a smile. 'Now that's a delicate question,' he said. 'I'll tell you how it is. I'm a public figure and I have to watch my tongue. If I said yes, I'm devoted to Miss Korby, it would be in all the columns tomorrow and I'd get ten thousand telegrams and a million letters. If I said no, I'm not devoted to Miss Korby, that wouldn't be polite with her here at my elbow. So I'll just skip it. Come on, Flora.'

'One more question. I understand that your father works

in a New York restaurant. Do you know whether he is involved in any of the charges Mr Korby spoke of?'

'Oh, for God's sake. Talk about hooey.' He turned and headed for the door, taking Flora with him. I got up and went to the hall and on to the front door, opened it for them, closed it after them, put the chain-bolt on, and returned to the office. Wolfe was speaking.

'... and I assure you, Mr Rago, my interest runs with yours – with all of you except one. You don't want the police crawling over you and neither do I.'

The sauce chef had straightened up in the red leather chair, and the points of his moustache seemed to have straightened up too. 'Treeks,' he said.

'No, sir,' Wolfe said. 'I have no objection to tricks, if they work, but this is merely a forthright discussion of a lamentable situation. No trick. Do you object to telling us what dealings you had with Philip Holt?'

'I am deesappointed,' Rago declared. 'Of course I knew you made a living with detective work, everybody knows that, but to me your glory is your great contributions to cuisine – your *sauce printemps*, your oyster pie, your *artichauts drigants*, and others. I know what Pierre Mondor said of you. So it is a deesappointment when I am in your company that the only talk is of the ugliness of murder.'

'I don't like it any better than you do, Mr Rago. I am pleased to know that Pierre Mondor spoke well of me. Now about Philip Holt?'

'If you insist, certainly. But what can I say? Nothing.'

'Didn't you know him?'

Rago spread his hands and raised his shoulders and brows.

'I had met him. As one meets people. Did I know him? Whom does one know? Do I know you?'

'But you never saw me until two weeks ago. Surely you must have seen something of Mr Holt. He was an important official of your union, in which you were active.'

'I have not been active in the union.'

'You were a speaker at its picnic yesterday.' Rago nodded and smiled. 'Yes, that is so. But that was because of my activity in the kitchen, not in the union. It may be said, even by me, that in sauces I am supreme. It was for that distinction that it was thought desirable to have me.' His head turned. 'So, Mr Korby?'

The president of URWA nodded yes. 'That's right,' he told Wolfe. 'We thought the finest cooking should be represented, and we picked Rago for it. So far as I know, he has never come to a union meeting. We wish he would, and more like him.'

'I am a man of the kitchen,' Rago declared. 'I am an artist. The business I leave to others.'

Wolfe was on Korby. 'Did Mr Rago's name appear in any of the charges you spoke of?'

'No. I said I wouldn't give names, but I can say no. No, it didn't.'

'You didn't say no when I asked about Mr Griffin.' Wolfe turned to the importer. 'Do you wish to comment on that, sir?'

I still hadn't decided exactly what was wrong with Griffin's left eye. There was no sign of an injury, and it seemed to function okay, but it appeared to be a little off centre. From an angle, the slant I had from my desk, it looked normal.

He lifted his long narrow chin. 'What do you expect?' he demanded.

'My expectations are of no consequence. I merely invite comment.'

'On that, I have none. I know nothing about any charges. What I want, I want to see that witness.'

Wolfe shook his head. 'As I said, I will not produce the witness – for the present. Are you still sceptical?'

'I'm always sceptical.' Griffin's voice would have suited a man twice his size. 'I want to see that witness and hear what she has to say. I admit I can see no reason why you would invent her – if there is one it's too deep for me, since it puts you in the same boat with us – but I'm not going to believe her until I see her. Maybe I will then, and maybe I won't.'

'I think you will. Meanwhile, what about your relations with Philip Holt? How long and how well did you know him?'

'Oh, to hell with this jabber!' Griffin bounced up, not having far to bounce. 'If there was anything in my relations with him that made me kill him, would I be telling you?' He flattened his palms on Wolfe's desk. 'Are you going to produce that witness? No?' He wheeled. 'I've had enough of this! You, Jim? Rago?'

That ended the party. Wolfe could have held Korby and Rago for more jabber, but apparently he didn't think it worth the effort. They asked some questions, what was Wolfe going to do now, and what was the witness going to do, and why couldn't they see her, and why did Wolfe believe her, and was he going to see her and question her, and of course nobody got anything out of that. The atmosphere wasn't very cordial when they left. After letting them out I returned to the office and stood in front of Wolfe's desk. He was leaning back with his arms folded.

'Lunch in twenty minutes,' I said cheerfully.

'Not in peace,' he growled.

'No, sir. Any instructions?'

'Pfui. It would take an army, and I haven't got one. To go into all of them, to trace all their connections and dealings with the man one of them murdered ...' He unfolded his arms and put his fists on the desk. 'I can't even limit it by assuming that it was an act of urgency, resulting from something that had been said or done that day or in the immediate past. The need or desire to kill him might have dated from a week ago, or a month, or even a year, and it was satisfied yesterday in that tent only because circumstances offered the opportunity. No matter which one it was – Rago, who visited the tent first, or Korby or Griffin or Vetter, who visited it after him in that order – no matter which, the opportunity was tempting. The man was there, recumbent and disabled, and the weapon was there. He had a plausible excuse for entering the tent. To spread the cloud of suspicion to the multitude, all he had to do was untie the tape that held the flap. Even if the body was discovered soon after he left the tent, even seconds after, there would be no question he couldn't answer.'

He grunted. 'No. Confound it, no. The motive may be buried not only in a complexity of associations but also in history. It might take months. I will have to contrive something.'

'Yeah. Any time.'

'There may be none. That's the devil of it. Get Saul and

Fred and Orrie and have them on call. I have no idea for what, but no matter, get them. And let me alone.'

I went to my desk and pulled the phone over.

5

There have been only five occasions in my memory when Wolfe has cut short his afternoon session with the orchids in the plant rooms, from four o'clock to six, and that was the fifth.

If there had been any developments inside his skull I hadn't been informed. There had been none outside, unless you count my calling Saul and Fred and Orrie, our three best bets when we needed outside help, and telling them to stand by. Back at his desk after lunch, Wolfe fiddled around with papers on his desk, counted the week's collection of bottle caps in his drawer, rang for Fritz to bring beer and then didn't drink it, and picked up his current book, *The Fall* by Albert Camus, three or four times, and put it down again. In between he brushed specks of dust from his desk with his little finger. When I turned on the radio for the four o'clock newscast he waited until it was finished to leave for his elevator trip up to the roof.

Later, nearly an hour later, I caught myself brushing a speck of dust off my desk with my little finger, said something I needn't repeat here, and went to the kitchen for a glass of milk.

When the doorbell rang at a quarter past five I jumped up and shot for the hall, realised that was unmanly, and controlled my legs to a normal gait. Through the one-way glass panel of the front door I saw, out on the stoop, a tall lanky guy, narrow from top to bottom, in a brown suit that needed pressing and a brown straw hat. I took a breath, which I needed apparently, and went and opened the door the two inches allowed by the chain-bolt. His appearance was all against it, but there was no telling what kind of a specimen District Attorney Delaney or Chief of Detectives Baxter might have on his staff.

I spoke through the crack. 'Yes, sir?'

'I would like to see Mr Nero Wolfe. My name is Banau, Alexander Banau.'

'Yes, sir.' I took the bolt off and swung the door open, and he crossed the sill. 'Your hat, sir?' He gave it to me and I put it on the shelf. 'This way, sir.' I waited until I had him in the office and in the red leather chair to say, 'Mr Wolfe is engaged at the moment. I'll tell him you're here.'

I went to the hall and on to the kitchen, shutting doors on the way, buzzed the plant rooms on the house phone, and in three seconds, instead of the usual fifteen or twenty, had a growl in my ear. 'Yes?'

'Company. Captain Alexander Banau.'

Silence, then: 'Let him in.'

'He's already in. Have you any suggestions how I keep him occupied until six o'clock?'

'No.' A longer silence. 'I'll be down.'

As I said, that was the fifth time in all the years I have been with him. I went back to the office and asked the guest if he would like something to drink, and he said no, and in two minutes there was the sound of Wolfe's elevator descending and stopping, the door opening and shutting, and his tread. He entered, circled around the red leather chair, and offered a hand.

'Mr Banau? I'm Nero Wolfe. How do you do, sir?'

He was certainly spreading it on. He doesn't like to shake hands, and rarely does. When he was adjusted in his chair he gave Banau a look so sociable it was damn close to fawning, for him.

'Well, sir?'

'I fear,' Banau said, 'that I may have to make myself disagreeable. I don't like to be disagreeable. Is that gentleman' – he nodded at me – 'Mr Archie Goodwin?'

'He is, yes, sir.'

'Then it will be doubly disagreeable, but it can't be helped. It concerns the tragic event at Culp's Meadows yesterday. According to the newspaper accounts, the police are proceeding on the probability that the murderer entered the tent from the rear, and left that way after he had performed the deed. Just an hour ago I telephoned to Long Island to ask if they still regard that as probable, and was told that they do.'

He stopped to clear his throat. I would have liked to get my fingers around it to help. He resumed.

'It is also reported that you and Mr Goodwin were among those interviewed, and that compels me to conclude, reluctantly, that Mr Goodwin has failed to tell you of a conversation he had with my wife as she sat in our car outside the tent. I should explain that I was in the crowd in front, and when your speech was interrupted by the scream, and confusion resulted, I made my way around to the car, with some difficulty, and got in and drove away. I do not like tumult. My wife did not tell me of her conversation with Mr Goodwin until after we got home. She regards it as unwise to talk while I am driving. What she told me was that Mr

Goodwin approached the car and spoke to her through the open window. He asked her if anyone—'

'If you please.' Wolfe wiggled a finger. 'Your assumption that he hasn't reported the conversation to me is incorrect. He has.'

'What! He has?'

'Yes, sir. If you will—'

'Then you know that my wife is certain that no one entered the tent from the rear while the speeches were being made? No one but you and Mr Goodwin? Absolutely certain? You know she told him that?'

'I know what she told him, yes. But if you will—'

'And you haven't told the police?'

'No, not yet. I would like—'

'Then she has no choice.' Banau was on his feet. 'It is even more disagreeable than I feared. She must communicate with them at once. This is terrible, a man of your standing, and the others too. It is terrible, but it must be done. In a country of law the law must be served.'

He turned and headed for the door.

I left my chair. Stopping him and wrapping him up would have been no problem, but I was myself stopped by the expression on Wolfe's face. He looked relieved; he even looked pleased. I stared at him, and was still staring when the sound came of the front door closing. I stepped to the hall, saw that he was gone and hadn't forgotten his hat, and returned and stood at Wolfe's desk.

'Goody,' I said. 'Cream? Give me some.'

He took in air, all the way, and let it out. 'This is more like it,' he declared. 'I've had all the humiliation I can stand.

Jumping out of my skin every time the phone rang. Did you notice how quickly I answered your ring upstairs? Afraid, by heaven, afraid to go into the tropical room to look over the Renanthera imschootiana! Now we know where we are.'

'Yeah. Also where we soon will be. If it had been me I would have kept him at least long enough to tell him—'

'Shut up.'

I did so. There are certain times when it is understood that I am not to badger, and the most important is when he leans back in his chair and shuts his eyes and his lips start to work. He pushes them out, pulls them in, out and in, out and in … That means his brain has crashed the sound barrier. I have seen him, dealing with a tough one, go on with that lip action for up to an hour. I sat down at my desk, thinking I might as well be near the phone.

That time he didn't take an hour, not having one. More like eight minutes. He opened his eyes, straightened up, and spoke.

'Archie. Did he tell you where his wife was?'

'No. He told me nothing. He was saving it for you. She could have been in the drugstore at the corner, sitting in the phone booth.'

He grunted. 'Then we must clear out of here. I am going to find out which of them killed that man before we are all hauled in. The motive and the evidence will have to come later; the thing now is to identify him as a bone to toss to Mr Delaney. Where is Saul?'

'At home, waiting to hear. Fred and Orrie—'

'We need only Saul. Call him. Tell him we are coming

there at once. Where would Mr Vetter have his conference?'

'I suppose at the MXO studio.'

'Get him. And if Miss Korby is there, her also. And the others. You must get them all before they hear from Mr Delaney. They are all to be at Saul's place without delay. At the earliest possible moment. Tell them they are to meet and question the witness, and it is desperately urgent. If they balk I'll speak to them and—'

I had the phone, dialling.

6

After they were all there and Wolfe started in, it took him less than fifteen minutes to learn which one was it. I might have managed it in fifteen days, with luck. If you like games you might lean back now, close your eyes and start pushing your lips out and in, and see how long it takes you to decide how you would do it. Fair enough, since you know everything that Wolfe and I knew. But get it straight; don't try to name him or come up with evidence that would nail him; the idea is, how do you use what you now know to put the finger on him? That was what Wolfe did, and I wouldn't expect more of you than of him.

Saul Panzer, below average in size but miles above it in savvy, lived alone on the top floor – living room, bedroom, kitchenette and bath – of a remodelled house on 38th Street between Lexington and Third. The living room was big, lighted with two floor lamps and two table lamps, even at seven o'clock of a July evening, because the blinds were drawn. One wall had windows, another was solid with books, and the other two had pictures and shelves that were cluttered with everything from chunks of minerals to walrus tusks. In the far corner was a grand piano.

Wolfe sent his eyes around and said, 'This shouldn't take long.'

He was in the biggest chair Saul had, by a floor lamp, almost big enough for him. I was on a stool to his left and front, and Saul was off to his right, on the piano bench. The chairs of the five customers were in an arc facing him. Of course it would have been sensible and desirable to arrange the seating so that the murderer was next to either Saul or me, but that wasn't practical since we had no idea which one it was, and neither did Wolfe.

'Where's the witness?' Griffin demanded. 'Goodwin said she'd be here.'

Wolfe nodded. 'I know. Mr Goodwin is sometimes careless with his pronouns. The witness is present.' He aimed a thumb at the piano bench. 'There. Mr Saul Panzer, who is not only credible and confident but—'

'You said it was a woman!'

'There is another witness who is a woman; doubtless there will be others when one of you goes on trial. The urgency Mr Goodwin spoke of relates to what Mr Panzer will tell you. Before he does so, some explanation is required.'

'Let him talk first,' Dick Vetter said, 'and then explain. We've heard from you already.'

'I'll make it brief.' Wolfe was unruffled. 'It concerns the tape fastening on the flap of the rear entrance of the tent. As you know, Mr Goodwin tied it before we left to go to the platform, and when he and I entered the tent later and left by the rear entrance it had been untied. By whom? Not by someone entering from the outside, since there is a witness to testify that no one had—'

James Korby cut in. 'That's the witness we want to see. Goodwin said she'd be here.'

'You'll see her, Mr Korby, in good time. Please bear with me. Therefore the tape had been untied by someone who had entered from the front – by one of you four men. Why? The presumption is overwhelming that it was untied by the murderer, to create and support the probability that Philip Holt had been stabbed by someone who entered from the rear. It is more than a presumption; it approaches certainty. So it seemed to me that it was highly desirable, if possible, to learn who had untied the tape; and I enlisted the services of Mr Panzer.' His head turned. 'Saul, if you please?'

Saul had his hand on a black leather case beside him on the bench. 'Do you want it all, Mr Wolfe? How I got it?'

'Not at the moment, I think. Later, if they want to know. What you have is more important than how you got it.'

'Yes, sir.' He opened the lid of the case and took something from it. 'I'd rather not explain how I got it because it might make trouble for somebody.'

I horned in. 'What do you mean "might"? You know damn well it would make trouble for somebody.'

'Okay, Archie, okay.' His eyes went to the audience. 'What I've got is these photographs of fingerprints that were lifted from the tape on the flap of the rear entrance of the tent. There are some blurry ones, but there are four good ones. Two of the good ones are Mr Goodwin's, and that leaves two unidentified.' He turned to the case and took things out. He cocked his head to the audience. 'The idea is, I take your prints and—'

'Not so fast, Saul.' Wolfe's eyes went right, and left again. 'You see how it is, and you understand why Mr Goodwin said it was urgent. Surely those of you who did *not* untie the tape will not object to having your prints compared with the photographs. If anyone does object he cannot complain if an inference is made. Of course there is a possibility that none of your prints will match the two unidentified ones in the photographs, and in that case the results will be negative and not conclusive. Mr Panzer has the equipment to take your prints, and he is an expert. Will you let him?'

Glances were exchanged.

'What the hell,' Vetter said. 'Mine are on file anyway. Sure.'

'Mine also,' Griffin said. 'I have no objection.'

Paul Rago abruptly exploded. 'Treeks again!'

All eyes went to him. Wolfe spoke. 'No, Mr Rago, no tricks. Mr Panzer would prefer not to explain how he got the photographs, but he will if you insist. I assure you—'

'I don't mean treeks how he gets them.' The sauce chef uncrossed his legs. 'I mean what you said, it was the murderer who untied the tape. That is not necessary. I can say that was a lie! When I entered the tent and looked at him it seemed to me he did not breathe good, there was not enough air, and I went and untied the tape so the air could come through. So if you take my print and find it is like the photograph, what will that prove? Nothing at all. Nuh-theeng! So I say it is treeks again, and in this great land of freedom—'

I wasn't trying to panic him. I wasn't even going to touch him. And I had the Marley .38 in my pocket, and Saul had one too, so if he had tried to start something he would have got stopped quick. But using a gun, especially in a crowd, is always bad management unless you have to, and he was twelve feet away from me, and I got up and moved merely because I wanted to be closer.

Saul had the same notion at the same instant, and the sight of us two heading for him, with all that he knew that we didn't know yet, was too much for him. He was out of his chair and plunging toward the door as I took my second step.

Then, of course, we had to touch him. I reached him first, not because I'm faster than Saul but because he was farther off. And the damn fool put up a fight, although I had him wrapped. He kicked Saul where it hurt, and knocked a lamp over, and bumped my nose with his skull. When he sank his teeth in my arm I thought, That will do for you, mister, and jerked the Marley from my pocket and slapped him above the ear, and he went down.

Turning, I saw that Dick Vetter had also wrapped his arms around someone, and she was neither kicking nor biting. In moments of stress people usually show what is really on their minds, even important public figures like TV stars. There wasn't a word about it in the columns next day.

7

I have often wondered how Paul Rago felt when, at his trial a couple of months later, no evidence whatever was introduced about fingerprints. He knew then, of course, that it had been a treek and nothing but, that no prints had been lifted from the tape by Saul or anyone else, and that if he had kept his mouth shut and played along he might have been playing yet.

I once asked Wolfe what he would have done if that had happened.

He said, 'It didn't happen.'

I said, 'What if it had?'

He said, 'Pfui. The contingency was too remote to consider. It was as good as certain that the murderer had untied the tape. Confronted with the strong probability that it was about to be disclosed that his print was on the tape, he had to say something. He had to explain how it got there, and it was vastly preferable to do so voluntarily instead of waiting until evidence compelled it.'

I hung on. 'Okay, it was a good trick, but I still say what if?'

'And I still say it is pointless to consider remote contingencies. What if your mother had abandoned you in a tiger's cage at the age of three months? What would you have done?'

I told him I'd think it over and let him know.

As for motive, you can have three guesses if you want them, but you'll never get warm if you dig them out of what I have reported. In all the jabber in Wolfe's office that day, there wasn't one word that had the slightest bearing on why Philip Holt died, which goes to show why detectives get ulcers. No, I'm wrong; it was mentioned that Philip Holt liked women, and certainly that had a bearing. One of the women he had liked was Paul Rago's wife, an attractive blue-eyed number about half as old as her husband, and he was still liking her, and, unlike Flora Korby, she had liked him and proved it.

Paul Rago hadn't liked that.

Credits

'The Vindictive Story of the Footsteps that Ran' by Dorothy L. Sayers is reprinted by permission of David Higham Associates on behalf of the Dorothy L. Sayers estate

'The Silver Curtain' by Carter Dickson is reprinted by permission of David Higham Associates on behalf of the John Dickson Carr estate

'The Mouse Trap' by Michael Innes is reprinted by permission of Peters, Fraser and Dunlop (www. petersfraserdunlop.com) on behalf of Rights Limited

'The Border-Line Case' by Margery Allingham is reprinted by permission of Peters, Fraser and Dunlop (www.petersfraserdunlop.com) on behalf of Rights Limited

'A Good Hanging' by Ian Rankin is reprinted by permission of the Licensor through PLSclear